Teresa Solana has a degree in Philosophy from the University of Barcelona where she also studied Classics. She has worked as a literary translator and directed the Spanish National Translation Centre in Tarazona. She has published many essays and articles on translation and written several novels she preferred to keep in her drawer. Her first published novel, *A Not So Perfect Crime*, won the 2007 Brigada 21 Prize for the best crime novel written in Catalan and has been translated into French, German, Italian, Romanian and Spanish. In 2010 she won the Crims de Tinta Prize, Catalonia's main prize for noir fiction.

A SHORTCUT TO PARADISE

Teresa Solana

Translated by Peter Bush

BITTER LEMON PRESS
LONDON

BITTER LEMON PRESS

First published in the United Kingdom in 2011 by
Bitter Lemon Press, 37 Arundel Gardens, London W11 2LW

www.bitterlemonpress.com

First published in Catalan as *Drecera al paradis* by
Edicions 62, Barcelona, 2007

Bitter Lemon Press gratefully acknowledges
the financial assistance of the
Institut Ramon Llull and the Arts Council of England

A CIP record for this book is available
from the British Library

ISBN 978–1–904738–55–8

Typeset by Alma Books Ltd
Printed and bound by
Cox & Wyman Ltd. Reading, Berkshire

A Shortcut to Paradise

For Jaume and Pilar,
my parents

PART ONE

1

After his wife had left to take the children to school, Ernest Fabià sat down in his pyjamas at the formica kitchen table where they had eaten breakfast and decided to analyse the situation with a cool head. It came down to nine thousand euros. That was all. Nine thousand miserable euros. It didn't seem such a big deal.

But it was. It really was. While he weighed up the alternatives and the likely fall-out from their plight, he poured out another cup of coffee and tried not to wallow in one of those attacks of depression he'd been suffering for days. He wondered if it might not be a good idea to raid the medicine chest and knock back some of the tranquillizers his wife kept for emergencies, then had second thoughts. There was no point in putting himself to sleep. He needed to think straight, and that meant ensuring every single neuron was on active service. There must be something he could do. There just had to be.

About a week ago a complete stranger had called from his bank's arrears department to tell him he had two weeks to make up the deficit and pay the four months they owed on the mortgage. "Four months," this unknown quantity had emphasized in a most professional and unfriendly manner. On this occasion, the male voice had sounded aloof and had addressed him as "Mr Fabià", and that was a bad sign because, according to the latest telemarketing techniques dreamed up by some bright spark with an MBA, one should treat one's customer like a friend and be on first-name terms. Ernest immediately grasped that this ritual "sir" and pseudo-deference were extremely bad news.

And he was right. It was an ultimatum straight down the line. The man speaking on behalf of the bank had told him in no uncertain terms that apologies and promises were no longer enough. Another fortnight and they would be beyond the point of no return: if he and his wife didn't pay up, their flat would be repossessed. A mysteriously automatic procedure was activated in such situations, and mysteriously automatic procedures discounted the human factor. Their position was regrettable, that much the bank understood, but the computers dictating policy from some remote location only crunched numbers. And theirs, as he was only too well aware, couldn't get much deeper into the red.

He picked up yet again the Final Notice he still hadn't shown his wife that had arrived a few days after that exchange. Sipping the second cup of coffee he'd poured out in a fit of inertia, Ernest reread it several times, even though he knew the words by heart. Yesterday he'd heard the doorbell ring at half-past ten and assumed it was the postman who was the bearer of bad news. He was quite right, and that presentiment had now taken the palpable form of a cheap and threatening photocopy, the dreaded Notice. Those fucking bastards were telling him that if they didn't pay off the round sum of nine thousand euros they owed the bank, their mortgage would be cancelled, and that meant they would have to pay off every cent of the balance on their loan if they wanted to stop the bank snatching their flat from them. He and his wife had invested all their savings in those bricks and mortar and Ernest knew they would lose everything with the flat.

That Friday Ernest didn't even feel like switching on his CD player and listening to music. He usually preferred jazz in the mornings. Miles Davis, John Coltrane, Chet Baker. His galloping heartbeat echoed in the eerie, ominous silence. The neighbours must be all out at work or shopping, because he couldn't hear a soul in the inside yard. No one was washing up, hoovering or listening to the radio. He wasn't at all superstitious, but that silence didn't augur well.

Ernest crumpled the Final Notice in his fist, felt the bitter taste of cold coffee in his mouth and nostalgically recalled his youthful militancy on the far left, when he and his comrades-in-arms had ranted against capitalism, waved red flags and demanded that the banks be nationalized. Those distant, halcyon days seemed light years ago – twenty actually, though they could have been prehistoric for all the difference it made. True enough, Ernest was still ideologically in tune with the squatters in his neighbourhood (if not with their flea-ridden dogs whose turds dotted the pavements), but now neither he nor his friends were on the far left. On the left, at the most, if you were lucky. In fact, they were all happy simply to survive and for politicians and the tax inspectors to leave them in peace. As far as his generation was concerned, the time for utopias, like their youth, had gone for good.

He and his wife had bought that flat in Gràcia, near the Plaça del Diamant, a couple of years ago. Nothing luxurious. Ninety square metres built in the 1920s that needed lots of work, naturally. A flat they'd bought by making sacrifices galore and embracing all the illusions of the poor, just before Oriol (who was still the baby of the house) had come into the world. The purchase of that living space had been a big event at the time for the family, and Ernest and his wife gave a big party where Rioja and cava had flowed generously. The Fabiàs owned their home In Barcelona, where any flat was worth a mint! Ernest's parents, and his wife's, had had to make do with renting a tiny flat in the suburbs.

The fake economic prosperity that had trapped them in the property bubble was about to ruin their lives, although everyone had agreed their decision to buy a flat was eminently sensible given the astronomical levels reached by soaring Barcelona rents. That purchase had meant years of holidays eating chorizo sandwiches on the packed beaches in the Barceloneta, of doing without the little luxuries that ultimately gave life meaning, like eating out, going to the cinema or buying new clothes. Luckily ragged trousers and faded T-shirts were still the fashion, if only in their neighbourhood. Seven-year-old Jordi was the only one wearing new clothes in their household, and that was always thanks to the sales. A mere two-year-old, Oriol had to be satisfied with his brother's hand-me-downs and cast-offs from his female cousins, but luckily he was still a baby and hadn't noticed. Secretly, Ernest, who wasn't at all anti-gay, was rather worried his son might turn out to be a pansy after all those pink jerseys and trousers.

And all so they could buy a flat and have some security when the going got tough, which was more than likely when they both retired. If they ever reached that point, Ernest could only look forward to a pathetic pension, and Carmen, despite her degree in art history, was a humble temp on the minimum wage, who couldn't aspire to anything better.

Despite university studies they were both proud of – Ernest had a degree in anthropology as useful as any – their work was precarious and badly paid. And they could be thankful, because most of their friends were in an even more desperate state. In spite of all the facilities the banks advertised, they'd struggled to find one prepared to give them a mortgage. But they had been married for eight years, were paying a fortune in rent, so they dug their heels in until they finally managed to get a loan on a variable rate, after proving they had enough cash in hand to make a down payment and cope with the chunk taken out by the state, the famous ten per cent for costs that were euphemistically described as legal. Hence the need to save, scraping here and there and working more than all the hours God sent. The good news was that the value of their flat had increased by twenty per cent in two years, though nobody knew why exactly. In principle, they'd not done anything reckless. All the same, their foray into real estate had left Ernest and his wife flat broke.

Perhaps because he was young – a mere thirty-seven – and because he was generally in good health, Ernest hadn't foreseen that an illness, let alone an accident, would make him unable to translate a word for nigh on three months. He was a competent professional with a good reputation and wasn't short of work even though the rates were low. He translated from dawn to dusk, even longer sometimes, but he and his wife only just made ends meet. He usually worked for publishers and signed his translations, but occasionally he ghosted for other translators or translated boring reports for agencies that paid a little better.

The rot had set in with Ernest's car accident three months ago. It was the reason for their present financial problems, or at least the main reason. Oriol had been born shortly after they bought the flat, and from that day to this they'd not managed to save a single euro. When it wasn't one thing, it was another: Jordi's orthodontist, the unanticipated payments to repair guttering or plumbing, the refrigerator that went "pluff" one day and had to be replaced... Not to mention the monthly mortgage payments that impenetrable economic laws kept magically pushing up at the same time as they depressed their income. Ernest and his family lived from day to day, and faced ruin without the income he brought in, and the fact was he usually earned a lot more than his wife even if he wasn't on a salary.

And they were fortunate that it wasn't a particularly serious accident, though it looked dreadful and their car was reduced to scrap metal. No comas, paralysis or internal organs affected. In fact, only the bones of his hands, feet and ribs were fractured, and at his time in life bones mended sooner or later. However, he *had* broken something like a dozen bones, not to mention a couple of vertebrae that had been badly wrenched and were still playing him up. And as the driver of the four-by-four who crashed into him that night after jumping a red light had hit and run, there was no way he could have caught him. And the insurance company had procrastinated when it came to paying compensation because there'd been no witnesses. And he'd been unable to sit in front of his computer for three months because both his arms were in plaster. And he'd put his usual work to one side because he was about to sign a contract to translate a nine-hundred-page bestseller a publisher needed in a rush, which he'd then had to hand to someone else, into the bargain. And the flat they'd bought was to blame for the fact they had no money set aside... As far as banks and creditors were concerned, all such melodramatic explanations, albeit sincere, were simply poor excuses for their defaulting.

Consequently, over three long months of plaster casts, depression and painkillers, the bills had simply piled up in a drawer in the Fabià household. His wife's income was barely enough to put food on the table, pay for the older kid's nursery and buy nappies. The eight hundred and fifty euros net Carmen earned as a secretary in a legal practice that was reputed to be mafia-run (three hundred of which were paid in black money) didn't stretch any further.

Fortunately, family and friends had scrambled seven grand together, which was a real miracle because they were all stony-broke. They had their own problems when it came to paying their mortgages or rent for their matchboxes, or had lousy retirement pensions, or were out of work, or earned a ridiculous pittance for work they did in the vain hope of getting a steady job in the future. Nonetheless, friends and relatives, generously and in goodwill, had dug deep in their pockets and got together more than a million of the old pesetas. Ernest and his wife were still two grand short, to be sure, but he told himself that morning that finding two was a sight easier than finding nine. He wasn't going to allow them to steal a flat valued at more than three hundred and fifty-five grand on the open market. Right then, two fucking thousand euros marked the difference between a future worth living or destitution for Ernest and his family.

It was while he was rereading that threatening Final Notice for the nth time and imagining them all piling into the small flat his parents rented in Hospitalet that he reached a decision. He'd spent that week on bended knees before his bank manager and had rung all the financial institutions that advertised in the daily papers or on television, trying to get another loan, a puny loan of two grand you had to pay back fourfold in reasonably easy monthly instalments. To no avail. Ernest discovered the banks gave out money to pay for little luxuries, but not to clear debts. Banks didn't turn on the tap when you really needed it, when it was an emergency, or was, as Ernest kept telling everyone, the fault of that bastard, who'd been blind drunk, he was sure. It could be months, even years, before they received any insurance money, and to get that they'd certainly need to hire lawyers and pay out a pile of dough.

He knew what he was planning was pure madness and that he'd better not let on to anyone. Nonetheless, he was a man at the end of his tether and that threatening Final Notice didn't leave him any choice. He must act, and quickly. So rather than ducking out, drinking himself silly, mixing a cocktail of sleeping pills or walking out on a sinking ship, Ernest decided to put himself into the shoes of the heroes of the novels he translated and, for the first time in his life, he took the bull by the horns.

2

It was the third week into June and the heat was beginning to tell. Although it cooled off in the evening after the sun had set, everyone was expecting another long, oppressively hot summer. Their sea-side city was sentenced to endure muggy haze and urban sloth, and the lack of rain, championed only by the tourists lording it over the city centre in their bermudas, simply made things worse. It hadn't rained since April, and the lengthy drought meant everyone was beginning to feel rather frenzied. The weather prophets forecast ecological disasters to suit all tastes, but holidays were the main topic of conversation, particularly at work, where the air-conditioning was switched on and colds and allergies abounded. As on any Friday, the streets were a morass of cars, noise and fumes.

Ernest was determined to put his plan into action, before cold common sense could douse his enthusiasm, so he left home at ten thirty. He walked his aching bones to a toy shop he remembered seeing when driving by in his car. It wasn't a local corner-shop but a large store where he certainly wouldn't be the only customer. The shop assistants working there no doubt did so on a daily or weekly basis, employed by a firm that specialized in temporary contracts, and Ernest thought that was just what he needed given the circumstances. He walked in nervously and tried to find the boys' toy section. Although they had two sons, it was his wife who always bought their toys from an emporium run by a cheerful, enigmatic Chinese family. Consequently, Ernest had very little experience of toy shops and it took him a while to realize that the section he was looking for didn't exist. The shop had heeded the advice of educationalists and no longer discriminated along gender lines, as one of the assistants explained rather curtly, so pistols and machine guns were jumbled up with dolls and toy kitchens, Action Men were cheek by jowl with Barbies and racing cars, and footballs and Barça strips with cookers and hairdressing and make-up packs. Being a timid soul, Ernest realized that this unexpected cohabitation made life harder for him. While he searched the chaotic shelves in a state of shock, the long-lost residues from the Marxist politics still slumbering in a corner of his brain forced him to wonder if that post-feminist façade wasn't simply an excuse to justify a lack of staff and the consequent confusion, and, in addition, whether it wasn't behind the sudden interest girls now showed for uniforms and the colour khaki and the way boys had converted to the lucrative creed of metrosexuality.

After poking around and leisurely inspecting the broad range of toy pistols the market offered, Ernest selected a black and not very big item, which he thought could be mistaken for the real McCoy if he was fortunate enough not to bump into an expert. He paid in cash and had the forethought to ask them to wrap it up as a present, in case someone found it odd for a respectable-looking paterfamilias to be buying a pistol in a toy shop. A tense Ernest decided to catch a bus home straight away, with his innocent parcel tucked under one arm and evil machinations stirring in his mind.

He knew nobody would be in during the day. He wasn't expecting visitors and didn't intend to pick the phone up. His wife Carmen was out at work. There weren't good connections to her lawyers' practice, so she always got a bite to eat in one of the bars in the area. Oriol was at the nursery, where they gave him lunch and an afternoon snack, and Jordi would be at school until six. Back at their flat, Ernest locked the door and went into the dining room. He put the parcel on the table, carefully unwrapped it and put the box and the wrapping paper in a rubbish bag. He hid the toy pistol in a pocket in his jacket, which he hung up among the other jackets in their bedroom wardrobe. Then he went out, in his shirtsleeves, dropped the rubbish bag in the bin and hurried home. But then he stopped at the kiosk. He'd kicked the habit eighteen months ago, though he'd been having second thoughts for the past few days. The moment he'd purchased the pistol, he'd decided the seriousness of the situation fully justified a relapse. That first cigarette after such a lengthy abstinence made him feel slightly queasy, but it tasted wonderful.

He had to wait until the evening to implement his plan. He had twelve long hours ahead and felt uneasy. He switched on the television in search of distraction, but it didn't help. Nor could he get any shut-eye or concentrate on the novel he'd just begun. By midday he'd made himself a sandwich, more to while the time away than because he was really hungry, and ate while glancing at the newspaper. At half-past four, feeling rather sorry for himself, he went out again, this time to collect the boys from school.

It was a quarter to nine when his wife arrived home, weary and distraught. The Metro was down yet again due to construction work for the high-speed train. The boys were asleep and she didn't dare go in and give them a kiss in case they woke up, even though it was Saturday tomorrow and they didn't have to wake up early. Carmen wasn't hungry and her back was hurting. She felt guilty, particularly because of Oriol, who was still only small and missed her. Rather than playing with her son, as her mother had with her when she was young, Carmen was forced to spend eight hours a day trapped in a windowless office for a derisory wage, doing a job that brought her nil professional satisfaction or social life. But they needed her income, and that was why they'd parked Oriol at a nursery at the age of three and why she and Ernest could only devote what remained of the weekends to their sons once they'd done the shopping and cleaned the house while their kids gawped at those cartoon series they'd sworn they'd never let them watch. While Carmen thought about all that and wept her heart out in the shower, Ernest cooked an omelette and set the table.

He put on a cheerful front during supper and told her he'd arranged to have a drink with an old friend she didn't know. He'd bumped into him quite by chance in the street when he went to buy the paper, and they'd agreed to meet up that night. He sensed that his friend had money, so he was intending to see if he could extract a little cash from him that would ensure their life didn't go to the dogs.

"I haven't seen him for a hell of a long time," said Ernest apologetically. "What's more, he's divorced and childless, so it will probably spin out and I'll get back late..." he added, expecting his wife to react.

Carmen was usually quick to complain when he spent an evening out with his translator friends lamenting the sorry state of the profession, but she didn't moan and even told him not to worry. She simply asked him to wake her up when he came back and tell her how it had gone. She too was very worried by the disastrous state of their finances. Carmen realized their economic situation was bad, even though her man had generously spared her explanations of just how bad.

At around eleven, when Carmen was in bed, Ernest left home wearing old jeans, a white shirt and the brown jacket where he'd hidden the toy pistol. His cheap brand of sunglasses and beige cloth cap were also in one pocket. He stopped the first taxi that passed by the corner near their house, heart racing but mind made up, as there was everything to play for, and once inside he stammered: "To Up & Down, please."

There isn't a taxi driver in the whole of Barcelona who doesn't know where Up & Down is, particularly if they're on the night shift. North of the Diagonal, the disco had known better times, before other night spots, strategically placed in the Port Olímpic, usurped the top places in the glamour listings. Long gone were the days when it was *de rigueur* to wear a tie and sport shoes were banned; nevertheless, a selection process still existed that went from dress code to the size of one's wallet. Like most fashionable discos, Up & Down favoured an easygoing style that encompassed rough-cut designer jeans and top brands of sweatshirts, and the casual uniform of Conservative Party youth, sleek hair and boat shoes included. The eagle-eyed doormen would have been loath to allow someone as drab as Ernest to pass through the gates to that temple to bourgeois recreation, but he wasn't in fact intending to go in. He was going to stay outside and hover like a vulture waiting for an easy prey. Although he'd never crossed that threshold, it was common knowledge that Up & Down was one of the favourite haunts for the wealthy of Barcelona.

Ernest had finally decided on an easy enough solution to get hold of the two grand they desperately needed: he would steal it at pistol-point. Once he'd come to this decision, his ethical beliefs and strict scale of values forced him to limit his possible field to the rich. He didn't want to risk holding up someone as poverty-stricken as himself, although that wouldn't have been difficult. So after he'd chewed over his plan of action, he'd worked out that his best option was to travel to where the well-off lived and partied. On a Friday night, in a plush disco like that, he'd find the filthy rich thick on the ground. He was quite right. What's more, the place had the added bonus of being surrounded by badly lit boulevards with few passers-by.

The moral dilemma of the theft didn't bother him in the slightest at that point in time. It was one thing to steal in order to avoid work, he thought, and quite another to enter St Dismas's fraternity of thieves as a last resort. He wasn't out to steal to put food on their table, but worse still, to continue having a dining room to put a table where he could put their Spanish omelettes. Of course, he was a total novice and anguished about picking the right victim, and about ending up in the police station and becoming part of the problem rather than the solution.

When he reached the disco at around half-past eleven, Ernest realized it had only just opened its doors and that the restaurant next door was full of people dining out. The façade was a hundred per cent glass, as required by the canons of the ersatz modernity Barcelona now aped, which meant too many witnesses and casual onlookers. Three extremely young men, all in black, with small gadgets attached to their ears, were inspecting the people entering Up & Down, and allowing them in or turning them away. Ernest became rather anxious and kept his distance, trying to keep outside their line of vision. He was planning to accost someone who staggered out drunk and then lead him to a cash point, so he was probably in for a wait. It might be hours before he found the right victim for his toy pistol, so he decided to take it easy and go for a drink in an Irish pub on the other side of the road.

The pub was packed and filled with a smoky haze. The lights were dimmed and a Premier League match was being shown on the screen which some foreigners were enthusiastically watching. Fortunately, his presence went totally unnoticed. Ernest sat at the bar, pretended to watch the football and ordered a beer. He went to the lavatory a couple of times to pee, more a question of nerves than an ailing prostate, and at one thirty exited the pub, thinking he'd snoop discreetly around the disco. He made good use of the darkness and the dark-orange low-consumption streetlights installed courtesy of the mayor, as he lurked in the shadows trying not to attract attention while he made sure the place wasn't bristling with bodyguards or bouncers.

That beer and the couple of whiskies he'd downed while killing time had been a good idea, like the supply of nicotine in his pocket. It was just what he needed to bring on the Dutch courage required by that turning point in his life. He noted how every muscle in his neck was taut and how his heart had begun to race and thud. If he'd been a hunter, he'd have recognized that silent injection of adrenaline coursing through his veins, but as he wasn't, he had a panic attack, thinking it might be a heart attack in the making. He had to calm down, so he took several long, deep breaths as he'd been instructed in the hospital. That night Ernest Fabià, translator of English literature and specialist in the mating rituals of the Tupi-Guarani Indians, was about to become a thief. What he couldn't imagine, however, was that he was also about to become the alibi for a man who'd be accused of murder the morning after.

3

As she went up in the lift to her bedroom at the Ritz, Marina Dolç looked into the mirror and sighed. She was ageing. She was surely the only person who could see in that face, now the wrong side of fifty, the shy but determined little twenty-something hungry for new experiences and ready to take on the world she had once been. Though the image in the mirror became increasingly unpleasant by the day, she still believed she had a lifetime ahead of her, as if the now half-visible horizon of old age and death was a distant nightmare that didn't become either her or the array of projects still bubbling in her head. Marina usually tried to avoid thinking of such things, but mirrors didn't lie and the years passed relentlessly by, and even more so now. However reluctantly, she had to accept she was mature and menopausal, and that time was taking its toll. And tonight she was exhausted. It was what she most hated about the cruel process of growing old. Not the wrinkles, not the way the years slowly and implacably aged her body, but the exhaustion she'd suddenly feel that prevented her from reliving the razzamatazz twenties she still mentally inhabited. For some time she'd felt her body clock saying enough is enough and she'd tamely become resigned to taking herself early to bed.

She stepped out of the lift and rummaged in her bag until she found the key to no. 507, her room. Whenever she came to Barcelona, Marina stayed at the Ritz and in this bedroom. It wasn't particularly spacious, but it looked out on the Gran Via and Marina liked to gaze at the city's thoroughfares and terraces from that vantage point. The bath and its large mosaic surround of pink and white tiles was inspired by designs from ancient Rome and the whole ostentatious decor verged on the baroque. The friezes and mouldings on the ceiling and walls were painted a tawny gold and matched the tapestry of gilded flowers on the wall, the counterpane and curtains. It wasn't the most expensive suite she could have afforded, but she preferred it for sentimental reasons. Room 507 was the first one she stayed in when she could allow herself the luxury of residing at the Ritz, and over the years that room had become familiar territory and part of her life-story. She liked the feeling of returning, of knowing she was surrounded by objects and furniture she already knew, like the two bronze naked athletes locked in a struggle in front of the fireplace who always made her smile. They reminded her of the *palazzo* she owned in Tuscany, where she felt so much at home. Marina Dolç had turned Italy into her second birthplace and had spent long periods there for years. As everyone remarked, friends and enemies alike, she was an eccentric, wealthy Catalan sybarite who'd chosen to live between the landscape of pines and holm oaks of her modernist house in the Vallès and the vines and olive trees around her Renaissance palace in Tuscany. The novelist hoarded within its walls paintings and sculptures of a value and beauty that sent a shiver down the spine.

She switched the light on and took her shoes off. It was a coolish fourteen degrees inside and she decided a hot shower was in order before going to bed. She was worn out, even though it was only a few minutes past two. She'd drunk and smoked far too much and was dying to unzip her tight-fitting silk dress and feel the warm water massaging her back .

She'd not even begun to undress when there was a knock at the door. She glanced at the clock and heaved a second deep sigh of resignation as she stifled her annoyance at that untimely visit. She struggled to squeeze her swollen feet back into her high-heeled sandals, tucked her belly in and walked over to the door, ready to put a pleasant face on it. It was not the moment to display a fit of bad temper, she told herself, repressing a yawn. Perhaps she'd left something in the bar, or her mobile was switched off and it was something urgent related to the prize. She'd find out soon enough. Her first interview was at ten, and if she didn't go to bed now, she'd wake up with bags under her eyes and a face out of sorts. She always stocked her suitcase with up-market lotions when travelling, but was well aware make-up and creams couldn't work miracles, whatever the advertisements claimed. Tonight prudence counselled Marina to get between those sheets as soon as she could.

She breezily opened the door and was amazed to discover who was knocking at that late hour. Nonetheless she invited her visitor in, the last person she'd been expecting to see, and found herself unable to suppress a smile. Perhaps the idea was to apologize or attempt to ruin her big night. She'd soon know. Marina might be tired, but she felt strong enough to put on an affable, even accommodating front.

"Would you like a drink? I expect there's whisky?" she asked, stooping to inspect the little bottles in the mini-bar.

Those were her last words. A sharp stab of pain in the parietal area of her skull, total darkness she experienced for the briefest couple of moments, and it was all over. The other four, five or six blows didn't hurt. She had ceased to exist. Flecked with heavy, whitish brain matter, her dark, almost black blood began to seep onto the carpet, which absorbed it like blotting paper and framed her shattered head in a large purple halo. Within seconds, the rusty iron stench of blood began to meld with the other smells floating in the bedroom that had unexpectedly transmuted into a mortuary chamber. The chemical fragrance from the red roses her publishers had sent hours before. Her own expensive floral scent, a musk-based perfume. And the icy breath from the familiar face that had ended her life so unexpectedly.

She had been hit with the base of the heavy bronze statuette she'd only just received as the winner of the Sixth Edition of the Golden Apple Fiction Prize: a misshapen fruit with a bite taken out, clutched by a hand attached to a square of Thassos marble that served as a pedestal. A few strands of hair were stuck to the bloodstained edge.

The killer put the statuette down next to the body and, taking care not to step in the blood slowly spreading all around, fingered the writer's wrist, looking for her diamond-encrusted white-gold watch. The murderer moved the minute-hand twenty minutes on and picked up the statuette again and struck the watch-face, using enough force to break but not smash it, so as not to destroy the hands and the time they were recording. He then placed the statuette back beside the motionless body and bent over Marina Dolç. The writer was face down, eyes open, hair bloodied. She breathed no more.

The assassin spent a few seconds checking that everything was in order, walked towards the door, and left the room after making sure nobody was in the corridor; he silently closed the door, and took the lift to the bar in the basement under the entrance lobby. The killer entered the bar and mingled unobtrusively with the other guests while reclaiming a previously abandoned gin-and-tonic. Less than a quarter of an hour had passed, but the ice had melted. Heart beating normally and hands steady, the murderer asked the barman what the time was, and repeated his answer loudly, thanked him and ordered another gin-and-tonic. Everybody was chatting excitedly, louder than necessary, under the euphoric influence of alcohol. No one had noticed the absence of the killer, who had discreetly rejoined a little group that was now pontificating on the subject of the evils endemic to contemporary literature, and nobody noticed that the killer's eyes were decanting an icy cold that could have frozen the drinks the guests were still raising in toasts.

4

Amadeu Cabestany arrived at the Up & Down club at around half-past one. Bad-tempered and slightly tipsy, he'd left some time before the end of the big literary party being held at the Ritz, a traditional, luxury hotel on the right side of the Eixample in Barcelona that had changed owners and name and was now the Palace Hotel. But Amadeu Cabestany wasn't just irritated. He was also fed up. Everyone must have noticed the filthy mood he got into when he discovered he was runner-up for a prize that had been snatched from his grasp, as he'd put it. He felt humiliated, ridiculous and betrayed, and hadn't acted at all tactfully. However, nobody had batted an eyelid.

He stoically stood at the bar in the Ritz with the winner and the rest of those invited, until around one. Then he decided he'd had enough and it was time to leave. He bade goodbye, not entirely gracefully, to a few people, including Marina Dolç, and went up to his room, hovering between despondency and rage. He knew nobody would miss him, except perhaps his agent, Clàudia, with whom he occasionally shared a bed. However, that possibility was no consolation. Depressed and disappointed, Amadeu Cabestany simply felt like wallowing in self-pity, and who could deny he was a past master at that?

Back in his bedroom, he decided he hadn't the energy to talk to anyone, least of all his wife, and switched his mobile off. He also realized he'd never get to sleep, however hard he tried. And not because the din from the party reached his room in that five-star hotel, which it didn't, but because down in the bar a select band of literati who hadn't the slightest literary taste were euphorically celebrating with Marina Dolç the prize that had just been snatched from him. To rub salt into his wounds, Amadeu remembered that the undeserving winner was lodged in the room next to his, an absurd coincidence that meant his mood, stoked by envy and whisky, turned even darker.

He'd still not taken his jacket off when he had a sudden change of mind. Rather than trying to sleep or drink himself silly on the contents of the minibar, he decided to go out. The receptionist was the only person left in the lobby, but he could hear the racket the party-goers were creating in the bar downstairs. Unconsciously he scowled contemptuously in their direction, though nobody noticed, and muttered "bastards" under his breath, though nobody heard him. He thrust his hands into his pockets and strode out of the hotel, determined to salvage a scrap of pride, confront that fresh defeat and seek out a bar where he could lick his wounds in style with a proper dose of alcohol.

As he lived in Vic and was unfamiliar with the nightlife in Barcelona of more recent years, he'd no idea where to go. After meandering in the vicinity of the hotel, he decided to take a taxi and ask the driver to drop him somewhere peaceful where he could have a quiet drink.

The driver hesitated at first, but when he realized that the customer in the back seat wasn't from Barcelona and was elegantly dressed if slightly plastered and didn't look the type to go to strip clubs, he opted to take him to the Up & Down club via the longest route he could think of: along Gran Via to Plaça Tetuan, and then up and down the Passeig de Sant Joan to Diagonal before heading to Numància. It was almost one thirty when he dropped Amadeu outside one of the city's sassiest, most famous discos.

To tell the truth, both his age, on the cusp of thirty-seven, and his outfit would jar in that club, but the three doormen who were busy fending off the vulgar middle classes let him in without even making him pay. Perhaps the fact he was dressed all in black led them to think he was one of them, so they'd ignored him completely.

By now the place was in full swing, and most denizens were high on alcohol, hormones or pills. Amadeu sought out the area dedicated to smokers that was in the basement and jam-packed. He made his way gingerly to the bar through the crowd of youngsters and ordered a whisky. The average age was very early twenties and, unlike Amadeu, guys and girls were wearing jeans. Most of the guys had sleek, combed-back hair, immaculately ironed shirts tucked into their trousers and white or sea-blue jerseys buttoned to the neck. Others, the slightly more daring kind, sported two-day-old stubble and lurid sweatshirts. As for the girls, those brazen hussies wore torn jeans and high-heeled sandals and were baring breast. Nearly all flaunted fake tans and long hair dyed blonde.

That crowd, Amadeu quickly concluded, belonged to a generation and social class that were not his own. It struck him yet again that nobody recognized him or took the least interest in him, though that was hardly headline news. Amadeu Cabestany had the peculiar virtue of passing unnoticed wherever he went and his regrettable anonymity was only too familiar. However, possibly because his liver was working overtime that night while his neurons aimlessly sloshed in a sea of disappointment, Amadeu couldn't but wonder – surely relishing this self-inflicted torture – how on earth none of these young people had read a single one of his books or recognized his face. He had participated to no avail in three or four cultural programmes on Catalan television, and often wrote literary reviews in local newspapers and magazines. Amadeu had never understood why, but since his days at primary school he'd possessed that curious ability to pass unnoticed. On this occasion, his little black outfit made him almost invisible in the din and the darkness.

And that was despite the fact Amadeu had changed his style – his hairdresser and wife called it his "look" – a number of times in the hope he might gain more charisma. At the beginning of his career he'd let his hair grow long and tied it in a ponytail. Particularly when he was into poetry. Later, in his experimental novelist phase, he opted for a crew-cut and a little earring, but that risqué option only lasted till the night a complete stranger tried to stroke his bum, while whispering that his earring was a badge of gayness and that he shouldn't take it amiss if some hunk of muscle made rude suggestions in his ear-hole. Amadeu ditched his earring the next morning, and decided to let his hair grow again in attempt to reassert his own masculinity. Unfortunately, he now discovered he had bald patches and was forced to drop the idea.

Resigned to the indifference of his contemporaries in general and those enjoying themselves in that disco in particular, Amadeu Cabestany gulped down a second whisky and smoked half a packet of Camel Lights, realizing that, as his psychoanalyst would remind him in the emergency session he'd book as soon as he was back in Vic, his negative outlook and pose as a writer *manqué* only deepened a depression that he'd diagnosed as chronic years ago. Amadeu stood and observed the strutting, canoodling or gyrating couples around him and concluded that disco wasn't for him, but, rather than simply walking out (which is what his psychoanalyst would have advised), he vigorously ordered a third whisky, dead set on getting drunk. The strobe lights and thunderous din helped to numb him, which was what he was craving, although the music was hardly what he was used to and sounded dreadful. When a rumba blared out, boisterously sung by Rosario, the daughter of Lola Flores, Amadeu Cabestany tried to hear in his head the aria '*Sola, perduta, abandonata*' from *Manon Lescaut*, one of his favourites from his teenage years. Amadeu had always thought that Abbé Prévost's hapless character and himself had lots in common, although he couldn't pinpoint what exactly. In any case, he had to deal with this fresh failure in the great metropolis and right then whisky seemed the best antidote.

The critics in his native Vic, where he lived with his wife and two daughters, had dubbed him a difficult, precious writer. A pity nobody read him, but, as an older, more experienced writer had once told him, one couldn't expect to have talent *and* be read. Fortunately, a well-meaning policy of arts grants allowed him to publish despite his distinctly low sales and a post as a secondary school literature teacher gave him time enough to keep writing. He locked and bolted his office door when it was his tutorial time (it's ironic – he never gave tutorials!) and didn't have to teach. Now, as he savoured that third whisky, his fifth of the night, surrounded by the smoke, noise and flashing lights, Amadeu kept thinking how humiliating it was to have been defeated by that tear-jerking, if not pornographic novelist who wrote to entertain secretaries and housewives. He was profound and bold, a writer who dared publish enigmatic poems and experimental works: he was no literary mercenary. When Amadeu wrote, he did so for the critics and never for readers, who indeed he believed to be stupid, and he never stopped to think how other mortals might value his subtleties of style. He wrote in order to enter the annals of universal history, not any old history, as many of his colleagues did: his pen would earn him a passport to immortality. Willy-nilly – a word Amadeu adored mightily – his challenge was to write the new *Ulysses* and earn a place in the select republic of letters, not to enjoy ephemeral success with traditionally structured novelettes. No, he never touched on the trivial, and only broached the grandest themes, like the greatest of the great. And, as he told anyone who was prepared to listen – usually the pupils he happened to be teaching – he wasn't prepared to prostitute his art for a handful of silver or hordes of hysterical readers queuing up at the stalls in the Passeig de Gràcia on St George's day, not that he would really have minded a bit of that. He was difficult because he *was* profound, and if neither he nor his literature were what one could call cheerful, it was because the intensity of his despair led him to plumb the turbid waters of existential angst.

The world was a turbulent, tragic and terrible place – the three transcendental "ts" that constituted the key to his oeuvre – and existence was a perilous burden dominated by servitude to sex and lucidity in the face of death. Amadeu Cabestany had many virtues, but, as the director of studies once told him when they went for a beer after an evaluation session, light-hearted he wasn't.

Besides, that night he'd been robbed of a prestigious prize that had been earmarked for him. Well, earmarked as in really earmarked; well, hardly. Clàudia Agulló, his agent and occasional lover, had assured him that, if he entered a book this year, the Golden Apple was surely his for the taking. Amadeu had believed her, thinking it was all cut and dried, and had even written a little thirty-line speech that had kept him busy for a couple of weeks. After he'd been awarded that prize, Amadeu ruminated, the *crème de la crème* of the Catalan literary establishment would finally be forced to embrace his literary genius and welcome him into their ranks as an equal. He had followed Clàudia's advice and had said nothing, but everyone had noticed for days how Amadeu Cabestany seemed much more cheerful than usual. That Friday at the crack of dawn, he'd said goodbye to his wife and daughters in Vic, caught the train and reserved a room in the same hotel where the award was to be announced. He'd purchased a black summer suit, a black sweater, black socks and black lace-up shoes. That night Amadeu had even donned new underpants.

But he was runner-up to the prize and everyone knew that meant nothing. As usual, journalists had ignored him completely. His speech of thanks, primed and rehearsed, remained in his jacket pocket and was destined for the rubbish bin. No, being runner-up wasn't an option. Apart from the fact there was no cash reward, unlike the jackpot hit by the winner, there was the issue of public recognition. And it wasn't that he was hungry for such fame, not at all, he kept repeating, trying to convince himself in between whiskies, but it was a lethal blow to his already battered self-pride that the fly-by-night Marina Dolç was held to be a great writer and he was still a mere speck of dust, despite the eight audaciously avant-garde novels he had behind him. After all, Amadeu pondered, in metaphysical mode, as he propped up the bar at the Up & Down club, a little public recognition does no harm. It opens lots of doors, especially to pastures where the holy cows of Catalan literature roam, ones he aspired to share. The circles of those who don't write to earn fame and fortune, but enjoy them all the same, of those who dispose column inches and forums where they can pontificate. At his most euphoric, Amadeu had even dreamed of the Nobel Prize. Not now, naturally, he was too young, but perhaps in fifteen or twenty years... And who was this Marina Dolç, he asked himself, whose fingers at that very second must be reaching for the sky? A writer of third-rate novelettes, as smug as she was shallow and superficial. In fact, Amadeu had no need of literature to describe what he felt tonight. He simply hated Marina Dolç and everything she stood for from the bottom of his heart.

Depressed, misunderstood and disillusioned, as he had felt so often in his lifetime, Amadeu decided to abandon that disco, the haunt of beardless youngsters who reminded him too readily of his pupils. Too true, he was every inch a writer, but day in day out he had to devote part of his precious time to giving classes to a bunch of punky, apathetic teenagers in order to earn his shekels. If he'd won that prize, it would have meant a year's freedom in the form of a sabbatical and a new novel with which to harvest fresh successes. Amadeu had planned it all. Now, on the contrary, he'd be forced to go home, tail between legs, and go back to being a laughing stock for pupils and teachers alike. It was a cool, balmy night that invited one to go for a stroll, especially after the whiskies he'd added to the liquor he'd downed during the dinner. He needed to clear his head before going back to his hotel. He was in no hurry because he knew that in his condition he'd struggle to get to sleep. Although it was a dark and deserted area, the number of luxury cars parked in the street reassured him that it was safe.

When Amadeu began staggering along the streets around Up & Down, Ernest was still crouching in the shadows in an improvised lair between a white Mercedes and a black Audi. He'd been yawning for some time. When he saw the smartly dressed man tottering towards him, he thought here was the opportunity he'd been waiting for. Without giving it a second thought, he put on his hat and sunglasses and, imagining he was the hardest Clint Eastwood ever, he gripped the pistol and prayed his voice wouldn't waver.

"I'm very sorry, but this is a hold-up..." he found the strength to say.

At first Amadeu didn't hear and Ernesto had to repeat himself.

"This is a hold-up, I'm holding you up..." and he made sure his shocked victim could see the pistol. "In other words, I'd like your wallet please."

Amadeu was terrified. These things didn't happen in Vic. Imagine, attacking him like that, at pistol-point, in such a well-off part of the city... His thoughts were of his wife and two daughters, of what would become of them and his literary career if that individual who seemed quite peculiar and was no doubt on drugs had an attack of nerves and shot him there and then. He recalled that he hadn't a clue where he was and didn't know which direction he should run, so he decided to do as he was told and not play the hero. Besides, courage wasn't one of Amadeu's many virtues.

"By the way," added the would-be mugger, who was clearly nervous, "I only want cash, so we'd better find a cash point. How much are you carrying on you?"

Amadeu was carrying exactly two thousand euros in his wallet and a few coins in his pocket. Given the circumstances, thinking he'd won such a prestigious prize, he'd felt it better not to leave himself short. He always panicked that his credit card would let him down at the most inopportune moment and leave him looking a fool, something that had happened more than once. As he wasn't rich and they hardly paid their way at home, his Visa card had been over the limit for months, and when it wasn't the Visa people, it was the Town Hall embargoing their account because they hadn't paid their traffic fines in time, or some tax, or an unexpected charge levied by the flat-owners' committee that shot their account into the red. Just in case, he'd decided to go to the bank and travel to Barcelona in old-fashioned style, with a bundle of banknotes in his pocket. That evening, what with his disgust at not getting the prize and the whiskies he'd drunk, he'd not thought to leave the money at the hotel before going out.

"I beg you..." muttered Amadeu, handing his wallet over. "I have a wife and daughter..."

"So do I, that's my problem. Don't worry. I only want your money," said Ernest, who couldn't believe that the guy was carrying exactly what he needed to stop their flat being repossessed. "I know it's a real nuisance when you have to cancel your credit cards and renew your ID and driving licence, I know because I was mugged once..."

However, Ernest realized this wasn't the moment to fraternize, and shut up. His nerviness had made him forget to distort his voice slightly, something he was regretting now. Better finish this off fast. He had thought he might have to hold up two or three people before he got the two grand he needed, but tonight Lady Luck had sided with him, perhaps wanting to atone for all his misfortunes. He put the money in his pocket, and assumed the matter was closed.

"I am really sorry. In other circumstances... take this," he added, handing him a ten-euro note, "for the taxi."

And before the man he had just mugged could say a word, Ernest saw someone was approaching, and ran off, leaving his victim flabbergasted in the dark. The writer went off to track down a taxi and go back to his hotel, gripping the ten-euro note, not wanting to be mugged a second time. He stopped one on the Diagonal and asked the driver to drive straight to the Ritz, his voice shaking from the effects of fear and alcohol.

Things could definitely not get any worse, thought Amadeu, who was making an effort not to throw up. He hadn't won that generous prize that would have catapulted him to the heights of fame and fortune, but he had been mugged outside a disco and was rather tipsy into the bargain. But how wrong he was. A new surprise awaited him at the Ritz.

There was a huge commotion with people and police cars by the main entrance and Amadeu thought he saw an ambulance as well. However, his taxi driver decided to drive past and stop a street further on, on a deserted corner, far from all that hullabaloo. Oblivious to what all that might be about, Amadeu paid the amount on the meter and, feeling slightly queasy, walked the two hundred metres back to the hotel. Angry, and in a drunken haze, the writer wondered what the hell could have happened as he zigzagged along and contained his retching.

When he tried to go in the main entrance, three solemn-looking *mossos d'esquadra* strode over. They asked for his ID and, after scrutinizing it by the light from their torches, they asked him to wait, and started talking to someone over a kind of radio. Then, in front of everyone, the *mossos* stood him up against a wall, legs apart and hands in the air. More police came over and, when they'd finished frisking him, they put his hands behind him and handcuffed him.

"You are under arrest for possible involvement in a murder. You have the right not to make any statement that might possibly be incriminating..." he heard them drone as he fainted.

No, reflected Amadeu Cabestany, understanding fuck all as he recovered consciousness inside the patrol car, these things definitely didn't happen in Vic.

5

Ernest Fabià was back home by around four. He opened the door quietly, didn't switch on the light and took his shoes off in the hall so as not to make a noise. However, his wife still opened her eyes when he got into bed. Though physically and mentally exhausted, Carmen had programmed herself to wake up at whatever time he appeared. She wasn't intending to nag him, she was simply worried and wanted to find out how he'd got on with his friend.

"Couldn't have gone better. Ernest let me have all we needed," Ernest whispered, who'd decided on this name for his friend to avoid getting into a muddle. "I'm dead tired. I need to rest now."

"That's a relief! We'll go to the bank on Monday." Carmen hugged him tenderly and kissed him on the cheek. "You see, Ernest, we'll survive. You get some sleep now."

Ernest did just that and didn't put in an appearance on Saturday until well past midday. He was exhausted, and not only physically. He felt he'd crossed a frontier that had changed something in his life for ever, and not necessarily for the better. He'd threatened another human being with violence, a wealthy soul, to be sure, but a human when all's said and done. And sure, it was a toy pistol and he was incapable of hurting a fly, but he knew that the man he'd robbed in the early hours couldn't possibly have known he had a kind heart. He'd seen the panic on the wretched man's face through his sunglasses, and the sight had fazed him. That victim he'd selected at random had suffered a big shock that he might never get over, and Ernest was wracked by guilt and felt like a pathetic coward. He couldn't let on to his wife or his friends, and, as he wasn't a believer, he couldn't find relief from a distant deity or ask for absolution from the up above via priestly mediation. Ernest Fabià had always defended the anti-Machiavellian principle that the end didn't justify the means and, consequently, once he'd solved the problem that had driven him to commit a crime, he felt repelled by what he'd done.

His bones ached and he had a splitting headache. The first thing he did when he got up, against all his instincts, was to take a couple of aspirins and linger under the shower. His wife was alarmed by that sudden change in her husband's behaviour, because the first thing Ernest always did in the morning after going to the lavatory was to drink a cup of strong coffee in the kitchen. Carmen attributed his unlikely behaviour to an excess of alcohol and nicotine – it was impossible not to smell the stench of cigarettes given off by his clothes and hair – but she said nothing. She'd noticed how her husband had been tossing and turning all night, trying to get to sleep. Ernest had had one nightmare after another, and, once awake, the memory of those nightmares he couldn't disclose to anyone had generated another attack of stress. Unable to share his wife's bubbly optimism, Ernest breakfasted in silence while the kids watched a cartoon film on the TV.

Although he'd got the money together to deal with their debt, Ernest felt down for the whole weekend. He was afraid to read the newspapers in case they reported the mugging, and that Saturday only found the energy to flick through the pages of the literary supplements. He felt very tired, and gave a start whenever the phone rang. The aspirins he'd taken didn't seem to be having any effect and he was still hung over.

While they were having lunch, his wife heard a news item about the murder of Marina Dolç on the television and made some comment. Ernest paid no attention. He barely tasted the chickpeas with spinach and bacon Carmen had cooked, one of his favourite dishes, and spent Saturday afternoon in bed. He also got up late on Sunday, although that didn't mean he'd been able to rest, and his wife, who could read his moods, knew something was amiss and decided it was stress-related. She reckoned her husband needed a change of air, although she knew only too well that the last thing they could afford right then was a holiday. She couldn't drop her work, and he'd plunged top speed into a translation from English he'd been commissioned to do. All the same, Carmen's common sense told her they had to do something quickly before lethargy turned to chronic depression.

"Hey," she finally declared on Sunday evening, seeing that her husband wasn't cheering up, "why don't you accept the offer of that grant and go to Tarazona for a couple of weeks? You said you needed to shut yourself away and finish that translation…"

His friends had done him a favour, and Ernest had a four-hundred page novel to translate from English. True enough, it was no masterpiece, but four hundred pages meant at least three months' work. Ernest had applied for the grant his wife mentioned in February before he'd had his accident. He'd been translating a difficult novel before the crash and had applied to the Translators' House for a residency. He'd thought he could polish his prose there in peace and quiet, without his wife, his children or interruptions. Ernest had never visited the Translators' House, although many of his professional friends had told him about the place.

It was a small house with only room for five residents, and when Ernest applied in the middle of February, it was full. Places had been awarded and, he was told, his only hope was if someone fell ill. What with the accident, Ernest had completely forgotten Tarazona and had been concentrating on mending his bones. He and his wife hadn't spoken further about that option.

Finally, months later, someone dropped out and Ernest received an official letter from the centre offering him a residency. It wasn't for long and brought in no money, but the fare, accommodation and food were all provided for. When he received the letter, in the midst of their financial crisis, Ernest didn't have the heart to put everything aside and leave his wife alone in the breach struggling with children and creditors, so he'd turned down the offer. Ironically they were now so poor he couldn't even allow himself the luxury of accepting the award granted by that strange institution.

"I know you can't translate that novel in a fortnight, but the change of air will do you good," his wife insisted.

Carmen was hardly delighted by the idea of asking her mother for help with the children during the time Ernest was away, or by the prospect of a fortnight of lonely nights while her husband inhabited a world full of randy foreign women looking for love. Naturally, this was all in her head, because she'd always been the jealous type and still loved her husband as much as on the day their romance began. Nevertheless, Carmen knew Ernest tended to get depressed and needed to do something different from time to time in order to break out of his routine. Perhaps if he spent a few days surrounded by eccentric translators, talking about books and translation problems, it might improve his temper. Now that his body was cured, thought Carmen, her husband had to overcome the psychological fallout from the accident in order to get back to normal.

"But if I go, I'll take the train," declared Ernest, who suddenly felt it would be a good idea to put four hundred kilometres between himself and the scene of the crime he'd just committed.

Early on Monday morning, Ernest telephoned the Translators' House and told them he'd changed his mind. By the evening he was packing his bag.

6

The Herald, Monday 19 June 2006

Who killed Marina Dolç?

Amadeu Cabestany the writer, the main murder suspect, is being held in custody

Although the case remains open, the police consider it all but solved

The judge in Number 5 court in Barcelona yesterday announced that the proceedings would remain secret of a case that, according to police sources we have consulted, is considered to be all but solved. The death in tragic circumstances of the renowned writer Marina Dolç on the night she received the Golden Apple Fiction Award given by The Chameleon Press has made a deep impression on the Catalan literary world. The writer, who used to live in Sant Feliu de Codines though she was an Andorran national, had travelled to Barcelona for the prize ceremony and was staying at the renowned Palace Hotel (formerly the Ritz) in Barcelona. Josefina Peña, a friend of the writer, found Marina Dolç's lifeless body at 2.40 a.m. in her hotel room and informed the police.

According to the forensic report that this newspaper has seen, death was almost instantaneous. Marina Dolç received numerous blows to the head – between five and seven, according to the mentioned source – and all lethal. The weapon used was the very prize she had received, a heavy bronze statuette designed by the sculptor Eduard Subirachs that represents a hand holding an apple. According to various eyewitnesses, Amadeu Cabestany, who was the runner-up, made no secret of his disappointment when he heard the jury's verdict and threatened the writer publicly moments before leaving the party.

These reactions led the police to arrest Amadeu Cabestany that same Saturday morning and place him at the disposal of the magistrates. This newspaper has also learned that coincidentally the man under arrest was also staying at the Palace Hotel and that his room was next to the victim's. Various eyewitnesses have also declared that Amadeu Cabestany retired to his room in a drunken state some time before the deed was done. Up to the present time, the writer, who continues to protest his innocence and who insists he was being mugged outside the renowned Barcelona Up & Down club at the time of the murder, has still not been able to corroborate his alibi.

Thirty-seven-year-old Amadeu Cabestany resides in Vic, where he also teaches literature at the Josep Carner Secondary School. Although all the evidence that attests to the writer being the person who committed this crime remains circumstantial, the judiciary believe there is sufficient justification to support such a verdict. Police sources consulted are working on the presumption of unpremeditated homicide and regard revenge as the main motive for the crime.

The Nation, Monday 19 June 2006

Obituaries

Catalan writer Marina Dolç
passes away in tragic circumstances

The forty-nine year old author of enormously successful novels such as *The Rage of the Goddesses* and *Love Is Not For Me* was murdered in her hotel room a few hours after receiving the Golden Apple Prize for her novel *A Shortcut to Paradise.*

Marina Dolç was born in the Catalan locality of Sant Feliu de Codines in 1957. A prolific and controversial novelist, her novels have been translated into more than thirty languages. In the early hours of Saturday 17 June, the novelist died in tragic circumstances in the Palace Hotel in Barcelona, a city she had visited specifically to receive the Golden Apple Fiction Award promoted by the Chameleon Press.

RODRIGO JEREZ – The name of Marina Dolç (the literary pseudonym of Maria Campana Llopis) catapulted into the headlines in 1993 on the occasion of the publication of *The Rage of the Goddesses*, a novel set in Barcelona at the end of the Sixties, which chronicled the amorous feats of a group of rebellious, bourgeois girlfriends in the wake of the fall of the dictatorship and the explosion of the philosophy of "bare all". She followed this success three years later with *Milk Chocolate*, a torrid love story of a Catalan woman and a Senegalese immigrant translated into thirty-four languages, and *Love Is Not for Me*, which sold three million copies in record time. Although none of her later novels has rivalled the success of *Milk Chocolate* and *Love Is Not For Me*, Marina Dolç continues to be one of the female Catalan writers most widely read throughout the world.

The novels of Marina Dolç were always received with acclaim by readers but not so by the critics, who described her as clichéd, superficial and commercial. However, since 2002, the year the Generalitat of Catalonia awarded her the Cross of St George for her promotion of Catalan language and culture internationally, the critics have looked at her work with fresh eyes. Last Saturday, a few hours before being murdered in the hotel where she was staying, apparently by the hand of the author who was runner-up, the writer received the Golden Apple Prize – one hundred thousand euros from the chair of the jury.

Marina Dolç was a great patron of Catalan culture and devoted part of the profits from her novels to the support of cultural associations and publications. She was a tireless traveller and since 1999 had been switching between her main residence in the Principality of Andorra, and the magnificent mansions she owned in Tuscany, in Italy, and in her town of birth, Sant Feliu de Codines.

Today, Wednesday 21 June 2006

Obituaries

For Marina Dolç, in memoriam

Marina Dolç was born in Sant Feliu de Codines in 1957 and died in tragic circumstances in the early morning of 17 June. The writer had just won the VI Golden Apple Prize with her novel A Shortcut to Paradise.

Carles Clavé*– Marina, I discovered we would never again enjoy your gleeful, silver-toned laughter and stimulating, charming company when a handful of friends and I were celebrating at the Ritz of old the much deserved prize you had just been awarded. Horrendous destiny willed that we were but a few metres from the miserable place where a merciless soul wrenched your life away in its most glorious moment, the night your novel was deemed winner of the most generous prize that can honour a writer in this beloved country of ours. A few minutes before, while we were raising a toast – what irony! – to your good health, you had said you were tired and preferred to retire to your chambers. We protested in vain, we who desired to enjoy your delightful company a little longer. Like Cinderella, a queen for a night, you left the party in order to go to sleep.

The soirée had been a heady affair, full of moments of joy and gratitude you wanted to share with friends of long standing. I will always bitterly regret not insisting you stayed with us, thus avoiding the unexpected tragedy that today obliges me to pen these sad words of farewell. I could have spoken to you about my latest novel, *The Haven of the Wretched*, a modest reflection on the perverse nature of the human soul, which I know you would have liked because I had often discussed it with you. On that same evening you promised you would come to the launch of my book, which will take place next Thursday, at half-past seven, in the Rerefons Bookshop, on Carrer Valencia, and I thanked you from the bottom of my heart.

As I scribble these lines, I cannot but recall the dinner we enjoyed together last summer, when you were so kind as to invite me to your magnificent house in Sant Feliu de Codines. Whilst we savoured a Priorat that was a splendid twilight crimson, amid the scent from the jasmine and roses you so adored, we spoke of our books and our ancient craft as writers that so often goes unremarked. I recall from that summer repast your restless eyes so avid for life, bluer than the turbulent sky above, replete with elongated, silvery clouds that danced cheerfully over our heads blown by the summer breeze. I recall your nervous chatter, the way you liked to enthuse over the small things in life, the contagious optimism that suffused your bewitching laughter. You flattered me when you told me how much you had been moved when reading my novel, *The Stench from the Trench*, so acclaimed by reviewers, and, Marina, you will never know how our intimate midsummer conversation gave birth to *The Haven of the Wretched*, the novel I shall launch next Thursday, at half-past seven, in the Rerefons Bookshop on Carrer Valencia.

You had a conclusion that was true to style, Marina, a conclusion you penned yourself, not suspecting it would come to fruition on the night that was predestined to be one of the happiest in your life. Months before you submitted the work for the prize, you confided in me and granted me the honour of asking me to read the manuscript, something I was only too pleased to do, given that you had requested me to. Thereafter you allowed me to make a number of observations, which you gratefully accepted, and despite the dread despondency that has accompanied me ever since the night of your decease, I feel happy to think that my humble contribution perhaps helped to improve your writing of a few chapters, as you yourself so honestly and sincerely confessed to me in confidence.

We have been orphaned, Marina. May our wrath strike the wretched hand that clipped your wings so treacherously! At seven thirty, next Thursday evening, unfortunately you will not be there at the Rerefons Bookshop (on c/Valencia), and I and all the good friends accompanying me, with whom I shall then raise a glass of cava, will feel bereft. Nevertheless, I will be comforted by the thought that while I am presenting *The Haven of the Wretched* in the company of my friend the great poet Joan de Joan, you will be on the road to paradise, taking a short cut, between the stars. Speaking Catalan and charming the angels with your smile and your words that will now be for ever eternal.

* Carles Clavé is a writer

PART TWO

7

"Good morning, Eduard. Sorry I'm late," said my brother, gasping for air after opening our office door. "I had to collect a parcel, and there was a bottleneck on Muntaner..."

"Don't worry," I responded with a smile. "Take your time! It's a beautiful day!"

"I suppose you mean that it's hot..." he retorted as he took his jacket off. Apart from being flustered, he seemed downcast.

"So who got out of bed on the wrong side?" I replied gently.

"Let's just say I'm in no joking mood."

It was 19 June, and although it was a Monday and only three days to the start of the twins' and Arnau's holidays, I was in excellent spirits that morning. We'd spent the weekend in a rural retreat near Olot and the countryside is the best possible rest cure for my wife Montse. The sound of crickets and smell of cowpats have an aphrodisiac effect that oysters and chocolate can only dream of. I was walking on water and it must have showed on my face, because Borja looked me up and down as if he didn't recognize me. He was carrying a bulky parcel under his arm and, with a deep sigh, left it on top of what was supposed to be our secretary's desk.

"So what the hell's got into you today?" he asked, rather irritated, as if I had no right to be in good spirits.

"Nothing at all. I just feel happy."

"So I gather that *you* at least had a good weekend..."

Borja sat down on the sofa with a martyred expression all over his face. He did look tired.

"I've had a really terrible weekend!..." he muttered.

It was half-past ten and Borja had arrived half an hour late. That was unusual: he usually only arrived late to act big and impress our clients. Although we weren't currently engaged on a case, we'd agreed to meet at ten to see how we were going to handle the summer and, while we were at it, dust the four designer items in our office. We'd sweated blood for the last three weeks in pursuit of a Barça first-team player whose wife suspected he was giving her the runaround with a slip of a girl of indeterminate nationality. In the end it transpired she was the one deceiving him, a circumstance that enabled us to triple our fee and, in my case, allow myself the luxury of taking my family for a weekend away on full board.

"What do you mean? Women problems?" I asked, trying to loosen his tongue. "I suppose you've had another row with Lola..."

Lola is my sister-in-law, and she's got entangled with Borja, though she's not the only one. In fact, Merche is my brother's official girlfriend and she's a married woman who is well established and several years younger than Borja. The small, rather trendy attic flat on Muntaner where he's been living for the last couple of years belongs to Merche, as does the two-tone Smart that Borja drives around. Lola, on the other hand, is divorced and one of those lefty types who've recycled themselves into eastern mysticism, New Age philosophy and designer gear. For some reason I can't fathom, Lola is hooked on my brother, and he eggs her on.

"Don't you read the newspapers, or what?" he rapped, looking surprised. "Have you forgotten I was going to accompany Mariona to a literary do at the Ritz?"

"Not really, as we were out of town the whole weekend..." I replied by way of justification. "You know we left on Friday afternoon and didn't get back until very late last night..."

"I tried to ring you on your mobile, but you were out of range."

"Yes, we were slightly off the beaten track, and I'd left my charger at home. You know, these rural retreats are a great invention," I said, remembering the terrific impact wrought on Montse.

"You must be kidding! Give me a good five-star hotel, with room service, sauna, massage, Jacuzzi..."

"The countryside isn't like that. You just like your creature comforts."

"Haven't you read the newspapers? Or watched TV?" he came back at me.

"No, to tell you the truth, no papers or TV. The countryside, fresh air, first-class food, a good wine with dinner..."

"Well, we've got work to do," he added as he got up to fetch the parcel he'd left on the table, which he literally threw into my hands.

I took one glance. It contained around a hundred and fifty typed, double-spaced, unbound folios, held together by one of those brown elastic ribbons used to truss chickens. It looked like a novel, a door-stopper at that, and I didn't know what to say. Someone had underlined what must be the title, *A Shortcut to Paradise,* above what I imagined must be the writer's name on the front page. I hadn't read anything by her, but I was very familiar with the name Marina Dolç. She was one of those famous writers who were always appearing on the TV, and I tried to remember what she looked like. If my memory wasn't playing tricks on me, Marina Dolç was in her fifties, dark-haired, self-confident and attractive. She wasn't thin or tall, and I recalled her as being elegant, although always too made-up for my taste. I couldn't dredge up any other details, and I'm not at all convinced that the image in my head that day had any connection with reality.

"So what are we supposed to do with *this*?" I asked, rather taken aback. "I know we're not on a case at the moment, but is it so drastic that we've got to start reading novels?"

"Eduard," replied Borja, about to lose his patience, "Marina Dolç has been murdered."

Since my brother and I joined forces, some three years ago, we've only once been involved in a murder case. In fact we are consultants, not gumshoes, although the work that comes our way means we often almost are. We don't have a detective's licence and so don't spend time solving violent crime; that's what the police are for. True, we work for the upper classes, but usually the commissions we get have to do with the underhand buying or selling of properties, dealing with what we might call delicate matters and, from time to time, corroborating or refuting suspected infidelities. If on one occasion (that we might describe as exceptional) we did agree to investigate a murder case, it was only because of those coincidences that often happen to Borja and that meant my brother and I found ourselves in the middle of a great big mess really quite by chance. But at the time Borja solemnly promised me it would be the last time, and I believed him. What was the likelihood we would encounter a corpse again, given the select circles we move in? For the second time in three years, the word "murder" lit up the little red alarm light inside my head.

"Borja, I thought we'd agreed..."

"I know we did, but when I tell you about this one, you won't believe me."

My brother was quite wrong. If I've found out one thing since we've been partners, it is Borja's innate ability to get into tight corners. It's not that he doesn't know how to extricate himself, which is another of his specialities, but I'm always terrified that one day he'll be stuck for good.

"It's a rather strange case, but there's no need for you to worry," he began in that cocky manner he sometimes adopts and that really puts the wind up me. "On Friday night I accompanied Mariona to that literary party held at the Ritz."

"I know. You were dressed up to the nines. Lola told Montse."

"That's right. But what you don't know is that after dinner I had to spend six hours hiding under one of the dinner tables, surrounded by police. From three to eight a.m., and I kid you not. My back's still hurting."

I started to feel alarmed. Ever since we've been working in this phantom firm that doesn't exist for tax purposes and renting an office on Muntaner that's more like a theatre set, whenever I hear the word "police" my body goes into a cold sweat and I feel the need to put my head into a bag to breathe.

"Borja, you must be kidding? The police? What the hell have you done now?"

"Nothing whatsoever. When the *mossos d'esquadra* turned up, I just thought that they might ask for our ID cards, and obviously..."

"But what the fuck were the *mossos* doing there? Weren't you and Mariona going to some fucking prize-giving?" I was still confused.

As soon as he saw I was so angry, Borja realized it would be better to start at the beginning and give a strictly chronological account of the facts. He got up from the sofa and took the precaution of closing a window, which was open because our office was like a furnace. He sat down again, lit a cigarette and offered me one. I accepted it right away. Clearly my pledge to stop smoking after a weekend in the country was worth fuck all.

"Indeed we were," said Borja solemnly. "Mariona and I went to the Ritz, to the award ceremony for the Golden Apple Prize. You know, the one worth thousands."

"A hundred thousand, if I'm not mistaken."

"There were lots of people in attendance. Lots dressed for a party, lots of arse-lickers, a bunch of envious writers and the odd well-known politician... The chair of the jury announced the name of the winner around midnight, after a dinner that left much to be desired. A winner who was none other than Marina Dolç. Even *you* must have heard of her..."

"Course I have! She wrote a very famous novel, didn't she? *Love's Not My Thing* was the title, I think... I've seen it lying around the house."

"You mean *Love Is Not For Me.* I've not read it yet, but Lola gave it to me on St George's Day," he sighed. "I think it was a subtle hint."

"Very subtle."

"The fact is Marina Dolç is a famous writer, as well as being filthy rich. She's sold an amazing number of copies, particularly abroad."

"And this novel?" I asked, glancing at the manuscript Borja had just handed me.

"Obviously, it's the novel that won the prize," he said, as if it were self-evident.

"Really!..." I felt that things were beginning to get knotted. "Don't tell me you stole it?"

My brother looked at me as if he were deeply offended. I didn't think he was in the business of stealing the manuscripts of prize novels written by writers who get murdered in five-star hotels, but it was the only logical explanation that came to mind given the evidence before my eyes.

"Don't be such a fool! What on earth would be the point of stealing this manuscript? There must be loads of copies..."

I felt slightly guilty for harbouring evil thoughts, muttered an apology and asked him to go on unravelling what I assumed would be an entangled yarn. I promised not to interrupt him again.

"It turns out," he took a deep breath, "that after dinner and the usual thanksgiving speeches, the usual blather, people started to leave. However, as usually happens on these occasions, a small group headed by Marina went down to the bar in the basement of the Ritz to prolong the party. In fact, there were about forty of us at the start, including Mariona and me. She wanted to show off the Versace she'd bought in New York, naturally enough..."

Mariona Castany is a very wealthy friend of my brother, who treats her as if she were an auntie. As she's bored, she's decided to write her memoirs and hobnob in literary circles. She's around sixty-five, a widow and a wily old weasel. She lives alone, with her domestic staff, in one of the very few Modernist mansions still standing on Bonanova. From time to time, when her long-standing lover is otherwise engaged, Borja keeps her company.

"As you can imagine," he continued, "the plonk kept flowing and we were all rather the worse for wear. But, of course, Marina had lots of commitments the day after, press interviews and so on, and announced she would be going to bed just before two. She was staying at the Ritz. Apparently she always stayed there when she came down to Barcelona."

"Very sensible too."

"Lots of people had gone by that time and there were about twenty of us still at the bar: the publisher and his wife, a few friends, a few critics, a close friend of Marina's in a tight-fitting flowery dress that looked like a curtain..."

"Get to the point, Borja."

"So we said goodnight to Marina and Mariona insisted on ordering another round." Borja sighed yet again.

"Life's hard, right?"

"The fact is," he continued, ignoring my sarcasm. "I'd been introduced to a stinking-rich, rather dumb dentist and was trying to persuade him we could do good business together. You know the kind of thing, investments using black money... His wife wasn't so sure and I set about giving her the hard sell. Then, at about half-past two, the woman in the flowery dress noticed Marina had lost an earring. She'd found it on the floor, under a chair, and, as it was a diamond-and-pearl affair worth a fortune, she offered to take it up to her room."

"How very considerate of her. But it's odd Marina hadn't noticed."

"I suppose she didn't have time, maybe the murderer bumped her off the moment she got back to her room," he speculated. "Whatever. Two minutes later this woman, who went by the name of Josefina something or other, rushed back to the bar in a highly agitated state. She couldn't stop crying. She was so distraught she couldn't get a word out. We finally calmed her down slightly and she told us why she was so upset. Get this: she had just discovered her friend prostrate on the floor in her bedroom, in a pool of blood, her head all smashed up."

"Fucking hell! These writers don't do things by halves!"

"Too true. Just imagine. The party was suddenly over. Josefina couldn't stop shaking and crying... Nobody had a clue about what had happened. People were talking about robbery and revenge... Anyway, the police had been informed and Mariona wanted to stay. I suppose she'd decided to include the episode in her memoirs..." he paused and looked at me askance. "The minutes were ticking by and I was worried in case the police decided to question us and asked for my ID card."

"Quite," I commented sarcastically.

"It was no joke."

"I know," I said even more sarcastically.

"In the end," Borja went on, ignoring my grin, "I tried to excuse myself and scarper, but when I was in the lobby and about to exit, the place was suddenly awash with cops. I got cold feet and decided to hide in one of the rooms where we'd been wined and dined. That wasn't a good idea, because the police chose that exact place to use as a kind of operations centre, and it was soon packed with *mossos*."

"My God, what a mess!..." The mere idea cracked me up.

"I didn't know what to do, but I'd already found a hiding place when I saw them come marching in..." he sighed. "I'd slipped under one of the tables there, not suspecting I'd be there until eight on Saturday morning. Luckily the tablecloths reached almost to the floor, which was spotlessly clean..." he added, attempting to smile.

"Pep, don't try to soft-soap me. I've told you more than once that this Borja saga would land you in it one of these days," I rasped in his direction, upset rather than angry.

My brother's problem is that his name isn't Borja Masdéu Canals Sáez de Astorga, as he introduces himself and as it says on the elegant visiting cards he cheerfully hands out in Barcelona to his rich acquaintances, but Pep, or rather, Josep Martínez Estivill. It's not true either that he was born in Santander, as he often likes to claim grandiosely; in fact, he came into this world in the district of Gràcia, as I did; we are twins for a good reason. Obviously, nobody is aware of that little nugget, that we're twins as well as partners, absolutely nobody, not even my wife. By one of those strange quirks of nature, Borja and I don't look at all alike and that helps our subterfuge. Indeed, he's rather handsome, after our mother, and I turned out on the plain side.

"So how did you manage to leave without the police catching you?" I asked, intrigued. "Or did they?"

"No way! What with the racket made by guests coming down for breakfast, the waiters, journalists and police coming in and out, I was able to beat a discreet retreat!"

And he added, shrugging his shoulders, "What did you expect me to do? To risk the police revealing that I'm not Borja Masdéu in front of Mariona and all those people? If they found out I'm a common or garden Martínez, our business would be done for, Eduard. What would we do then?" he exclaimed, raising his eyebrows and snarling.

I swallowed. It's not that Trau Consultants – that is our company name – is the most prosperous business on the planet, but we can't complain. Being the trusted butler to the rich brings in more than you'd think. In my case, if we were forced to shut up shop for some reason I'd be hard put to find another line of work, and as for Borja... True, he has no family responsibilities, and between Merche, his rich girlfriend, Lola and that friend of his in the Barceloneta (who I'm positive deals in stolen goods), he'd no doubt get by. As for me, who's going to employ a forty-five-year-old ex-bank employee with no special talents? And in the improbable likelihood that I ever did find a job, how would we manage to survive at home on the minimum wage that is surely all I could aspire to with things as they are at the moment? Not that I've ever regretted the decision to leave my old position, but, unlike Borja, I find it difficult to keep cool and collected in moments of crisis.

"And what about this novel?" I asked, weighing it in my hand. "What are you intending to do with it? You haven't got sucked into the business of the murder of Marina Dolç..."

"Well, on that front... As I'd stood Mariona up in the middle of all that hassle, and as Mariona is a lady one cannot stand up... I naturally phoned her the following morning to apologize."

"How thoughtful."

"I logically needed a good excuse. So I told her..." – he paused, I expect in order to give me time to prepare psychologically for what I was about to hear – "that I had disappeared because the police had asked me to lend them a hand in the investigation. Unofficially, of course. As Mariona thinks you and I are proper detectives..."

I was speechless. While I was taking all this in, I was trying to imagine what the connection could be between the story my brother had spun Mariona in order to save face and the fact I was now holding the novel of a prize-winning, if murdered, author.

"In fact," he added rather nervously, seeing that I wasn't reacting at all, "as I was hiding so long, amid so many *mossos*, I found out lots. Time of death, murder weapon, suspects, eyewitness statements... I doubt there is anyone better informed."

"Borja, I still don't see what all that has to do with this novel," I said, waiting for him to give me a good reason why I should be holding that stack of paper.

"It's quite simple. Through Mariona's mediation, Clàudia Agulló, who is Amadeu Cabestany's agent, as well as Mariona's, we've been contracted to prove her protégé is innocent. He's in the clink at the moment."

"It's as clear as mud..."

As I'd still not read the newspapers, I hadn't the slightest idea who Amadeu Cabestany was or what Mariona Castany's literary agent's role was in all that mess. Nor could I see what the hell we were doing getting involved in what seemed to be a literary spat with a writer's corpse thrown in for good measure.

"Eduard, writers have literary agents" – Borja seemed unenthused about stating the obvious – "and Clàudia Agulló is the agent for the writer who was runner-up for the prize, this Amadeu Cabestany. According to Clàudia (who is really good-looking, by the way) he is one of these brilliant, misunderstood writers, who has surrendered himself to literature body and soul… All the same, the police believe he did in the Dolç woman out of resentment. And also because he'd had one too many. What's more, they were staying in adjacent rooms. What's more, Amadeu went up to his room a few minutes before she followed suit."

"That could be pure coincidence…"

"A bunch of eyewitnesses, including yours truly, saw the sour-grapes look on his face when the winner's name was announced. Not to mention the little speech he then delivered!… He was scathing about Marina, and, while he was at it, about the members of the jury. They're not so pretty, and he shat on them."

"People say these things when they're in a temper," I reasoned.

"True, but some guests heard him tell Dolç she'd live to regret the prize, and that can be read as quite a threat, in the light of what then happened."

"Yes, that *is* more damning," I allowed.

"In short, the police arrested him on the spot, after concluding that everything pointed to him as the main murder suspect."

"Yes, it certainly looks that way. And if he threatened her..."

"Yes, but Clàudia is convinced he is innocent. Obviously if Cabestany could back up his alibi, we'd be out of a job." The prospect seemed to dampen his spirits slightly. "He says he left the hotel five minutes after leaving the bar. He also says he took a taxi and went to the Up & Down club, and was held up at gunpoint when he left. The porter at the Ritz doesn't remember seeing him leave, but at that time of night lots of people were going in and out... For the moment none of the taxi drivers have been tracked down, and no eyewitnesses have appeared from the disco. And no news of the mugger either, who took all his cash but nothing else. Not his ID, credit cards or watch. And, according to Cabestany, he even gave him money for a taxi."

"That all sounds pretty implausible. Perhaps he is really guilty and made up the whole story. You did say he is a writer, didn't you? He can't be short of imagination..." I suggested.

"In any case, I have an envelope containing six thousand euros to encourage us to prove he is innocent. Courtesy of his agent." He took the envelope from his pocket and showed it to me. "What do you reckon?"

I let him see I was thinking hard, for appearance's sake. It was true that the case of the Barça player with the unfaithful wife had turned out to be more profitable than we'd expected, but in any case once solved it only sorted out our lives for a month and a half at most. Given the present state of our finances, with the prospect of a summer in Barcelona dying from the heat and Arnau and the twins on our backs day in day out, I thought that six thousand euros were six thousand good reasons to take the case on. There are five mouths to feed at home, and although the Alternative Centre for Holistic Well-being that Montse has set up in Gràcia works quite well, that cash cow's yield falls short.

"Very well, back to the grindstone!" I exclaimed, all resigned, as I lit up another cigarette. "But is this Cabestany really that good? I've never heard of him..."

"I don't know, my boy, I hadn't either. But I think Agulló is smitten and as she's a friend of Mariona and not short of the readies either..."

"Perhaps it was robbery," I suggested. "Have the police discounted that?"

"Yes, nothing was taken from the room. Jewels or money. Besides, there's the small matter of her skull being smashed open by the prize she'd just been given, a Subirachs statuette. And the murderer did a good job: her whole brain was in pieces. According to the police, it seemed..."

"That's enough!..." I cut him dead before the coffee and biscuits in my stomach decided to repeat on me. "You've still not told me what the hell this manuscript has to do with all this."

"From what I heard when I was under that table at the Ritz, the members of the jury told the police Marina Dolç was murdered in exactly the same way as the protagonist of her novel and in the same circumstances. In other words, the first thing we should do is read it carefully, don't you think?"

"Fat chance of finding anything. I mean, that was probably only a coincidence."

"Eduard, you know what I think on that front," he retaliated solemnly. "That God doesn't play dice."

8

We decided (or, more precisely, Borja decided) that I would devote a couple of days to reading *A Shortcut to Paradise* while he was busy negotiating something or other in the upper reaches of the city, which I think was related to a golf tournament in which Merche was competing. The novel was a five-hundred-page door-stopper I suggested we split between us. My idea didn't prosper.

"You were the one who studied Spanish literature," he countered.

"Yes, but I didn't finish my degree and that was years ago!"

"You might even enjoy it."

We now had real work, and rather than cleaning the office, I headed home, the manuscript under my arm, resigned to spending a good few hours of my life reading that unpublished novel. I usually like to read for a time in the evening, before going to sleep, and, unlike my brother, I don't only read thrillers. A novel normally lasts me at least a month – two if there are more than three hundred pages or if there are European Champions League matches – but now Borja wanted me to rattle through the novel and take notes into the bargain. According to the jury's unanimous verdict, *A Shortcut to Paradise* had deserved to win a prize that probably didn't have the prestige others enjoyed, but was certainly well-funded, and, as prize-winning novels automatically became best-sellers, I imagined it would at least be entertaining. I knew Montse liked Marina Dolç's novels and I thought I'd seen the odd one at home, although I must confess I'd never read any. My current bedside reading was a very entertaining book set in the Congo, which unfortunately would now have to wait.

Theoretically, Marina Dolç's latest novel might hold the key to finding out whoever had put its author out of circulation, though I thought it was extremely unlikely. Nonetheless my brother was right: a detective must be methodical and the novel might give us a lead. So I went home, knowing I'd have peace and quiet until six, when the kids got home from school. Montse was busy with her therapies at the Alternative Centre, and I knew she wouldn't be back for lunch. As the anti-smoking session is on Monday and there are always lots of relapses at the weekend, Montse spends the day bolstering her clients and battling with her own withdrawal symptoms. So I had a bite to eat while I leafed through the crime pages in the newspaper to put myself into the right frame of mind, and then picked up that pile of paper, ready to begin. I was curious but also felt somewhat respectful. It was the first time I'd read an original manuscript that very few people had previously read.

I'm no literary critic or expert, so I can't say whether *A Shortcut to Paradise* is or isn't a good novel. But the fact was that if Borja and I hadn't agreed to take on this case, I'd have put it back on the shelf at page thirty and gone for a stroll. It got off to a good start with a murder on page three and looked promising, but as my children would say, the rest was rubbish, a real brain-clogging hotchpotch of loves, betrayals and disillusion, to my mind without rhyme or reason. Perhaps it might be a very good novel, I can't deny that, but it was never-ending . Whenever I took another sip of coffee to help digest what I was reading, I'd remember Voltaire and his daily intake of twenty-eight cups, in order to calm my spirits, and, as far as I know, he never had a heart attack. When I did finally reach the end, my whole body was shaking and I had a stinking headache.

"You read it?" my brother asked impatiently over the phone on Tuesday evening.

"Not yet."

"You finished it?" he rasped on Wednesday.

"No, I haven't. It's rubbish!"

"Hurry up then."

It took me three days to swallow it all, though I think it remained undigested. It was Thursday by now, and as Borja had to take Lola out that night, we agreed to have a drink at Harry's. When I arrived, he was already there and on the phone, to Lola, I supposed. They seemed to be arguing. I acted as if I was oblivious and took out the notebook where I'd jotted down my reflections as I sped through the book. Borja ended the call straight away and asked me to start off. He appeared to be genuinely intrigued.

"First things first, the action takes place in Venice in the 1920s, in other words, it's a historical novel," I said, consulting my notes.

"Sounds good to me," interjected my brother, who felt rather guilty he'd landed me with reading that tome.

"The Twenties are a refined, very aristocratic period... Apart from all that shit in Russia, naturally."

"The main character is Countess Lucrècia Berluschina de Castelgandolfo," I continued, "a refined Italian aristocrat of Catalan provenance and a wealthy widow."

"You see? I told you..."

"Just wait. It turns out the Countess has written a novel and entered it under a pseudonym for a literary prize that's going to be awarded in a famous hotel in Venice."

"Of course, that must be the famous hotel in the Lido where Merche took me once. Did you know they shot a film there?"

"Then," I interrupted so as not to lose my thread, "the Countess, who lives in Rome, decides to go to Venice to collect the prize. Naturally, she stays at the hotel where the prize ceremony will be held and where coincidentally she bumps into a bunch of ex-lovers. The Countess is pretty, young, intelligent, cultured and so on and so forth, but is marginalized by the macho attitudes of male-dominated literary circles. She's very talented, but as she is a woman writer, everybody ignores her. What's more, she's envied by the other writers because she is so wealthy."

"Mmm... Like Marina Dolç," commented Borja.

"And there are even more coincidences. The novel the Countess enters for the prize under a pseudonym is called *A Shortcut to Paradise.*"

"You don't say it's the novel that won the prize," Borja deduced, beginning to get excited.

"Right first time! And that's not the end of it: that night after one of those parties you are so fond of, with champagne, oysters and caviar, the Countess is murdered in her bedroom. Someone smashes her head in."

"Just like Marina Dolç!"

"Not quite," I replied. "From what you told me, Marina Dolç opened the door to her murderer. I don't know if she had the time to realize what was happening before she died, but theoretically she saw who it was. The Countess, on the other hand, fell to the floor without setting eyes on her executioner. Although there is another coincidence…"

"Out with it."

"The murder weapon was the statue the Countess had just won: a to-scale reproduction of Michelangelo's *David*."

"Well, at least it's a notch up on the apple," added Borja. "Did you see the photos? That hand looked like the towers of the Sagrada Familia…"

"And all that happens in the first three pages and, surprise, surprise, the remaining four hundred and ninety-seven pages are the time the Countess takes to hit the ground. In that briefest of time spans (a few seconds, in fact) our good lady reviews her whole life in minute detail trying to deduce who the guilty party is." I took a swig of gin-and-tonic. "I can tell you that after two hundred pages I was ready to conclude that a quite different crime had well and truly been committed!"

"Well, she was a best-seller and was awarded the prize; the novel must have something going for it…" retorted Borja.

"Sure, every six or seven pages there's a steamy scene. The Dolç woman certainly knew her dirty language if nothing else… I was soon up to here with all that heaving flesh."

"All right. But who's the murderer at the end?" asked Borja impatiently. "A man? A woman? A lover? Another writer?"

"Well, it is true," I gave a heartfelt sigh, "after wading through all that trash, you're really desperate to know who killed her. If only to thank the person concerned..."

"But there must be some clue or other..."

"Well, no. According to my notes" – I consulted my notebook – "I've counted forty-three male and female lovers (with the requisite detailed description of forty-three corresponding fucks), two ex-husbands, four fathers-in-law, seven girlfriends, three gay friends, at least five envious writers, six maids and a couple of butlers. The list of motives and suspects is endless. In the eighties, at the low end."

"Fantastic," commented Borja, wrinkling his nose.

I was in need of another gin-and-tonic. Borja, on Cardhu as usual, ordered another round. It was a few minutes past eleven and Harry's was beginning to liven up and fill up with people and smoke. That cocktail bar in the Eixample was turning into our second office and I didn't regret that one bit: it was a sight more welcoming than the vaudeville set where we received our clients. Just as well there are still some of these establishments left in Barcelona, because I personally hate the snobby bars where Borja likes to hang out, where I feel ill at ease and always end up in a foul temper.

"Anyway, that would be too much of a coincidence, wouldn't it? I mean if Marina Dolç's murderer was a carbon copy of the fictional murderer of this Lucrècia," I added. "He'd have to be very stupid..."

"Or very clever."

"Obviously, on the other hand, if Amadeu Cabestany had glanced at the novel, however superficially, he had reason enough to see red when he saw she'd won the prize," I said, putting myself in his shoes. "I don't know what his novel is like, but..."

"Here you have it." Borja waved it at me. " I brought it along so you can take a look at it as well."

"You must be joking!" I refused point blank. "It's your turn now."

Amadeu Cabestany's novel was much shorter, barely two hundred pages, but its title wasn't at all appealing.

"*Squamous in the Tempest*," I read. "And what the hell is that supposed to mean?"

"Not a clue..." retorted Borja, now resigned to weathering the storm at the weekend. "But we can ask his agent. I've arranged an appointment at her office tomorrow."

A Shortcut to Paradise was a cul-de-sac. It was apparently no short cut at all to its author's murderer. We drank our second round and, as it was late, my brother offered to drive me home in the Smart. I immediately agreed. I wanted to get to bed and forget all about that wretched novel. If I hurried, Montse might still be awake. Perhaps I wasn't so fed up of flesh after all.

"You know we've a party on the roof terrace tomorrow," I said, remembering it was St John's Eve tomorrow. "Montse told me Lola has invited you."

"Yes, right, I'm not sure what I'm doing... Maybe I'll come for a while," he responded rather uneasily.

I imagined Merche, his official girlfriend, would be spending the night with her husband and their wealthy friends, so we'd have the pleasure of Borja eating cake on our terrace. I wasn't sure it was a good idea, particularly for Lola, whose hopes were raised by the day. She likes to vaunt her feminism and sexual liberation, but then wallows in self-pity. She may be a modern woman, but I'm sure she cries her heart out over Borja, and that's pain of her own making.

"I'll come for you at about ten thirty," Borja told me when we were in front of my place. "Don't be late."

"And I hope you enjoy the novel..." I replied with a smile, desperately praying it would be as dreadful as mine.

If my brother thought a couple of gin-and-tonics and a ride home would be enough for me to forgive him for making me swallow that door-stopper, he was wrong, wrong and wrong again.

9

Borja usually drives Merche's two-tone Smart she bought the moment they became the fashion among her wealthy girlfriends. Merche is a tax lawyer and also owns a stylish silvery Audi she usually uses when visiting Barcelona's upper reaches. However, that Friday the Audi was in the garage, and, as the Smart was hers, she'd driven it to work and left us carless. We had an appointment with Clàudia Agulló, Amadeu Cabestany's agent, at eleven, and my brother dropped by our flat well in advance to collect me. That was rather silly of Borja, because the agent's office was much closer to where he lived, but I'm sure he didn't trust me and wanted to run his eye over what I was wearing. To keep him happy and spare myself a sermon, I'd put on my Armani suit and the tie Mariona gave me for Christmas.

"It's really too hot, you know. Do I really need to wear a jacket?" I grumbled. I'd started to sweat and felt it would be ridiculous to wear a winter suit in the middle of June.

"No, you don't, but we'll have to sort something out..." And after giving me the once over, he added solemnly, "We'll go to Adolfo Domínguez's this afternoon. We'll find a decent outfit there."

Our professional expenses were basically the rent we paid on our office at the top of Muntaner and our clothes. My brother is always concerned to create a good impression, and, as we normally mix in the most select circles of Barcelona, he forces me to wear my Sunday best, whether it's hot or cold. Borja was wearing a Marengo grey summer suit, a sandy yellow shirt and a lurid tie, naturally all the exclusive brands. From what I remembered, he was never so self-conscious or worried about his image when he was young, but the second he returned to Barcelona as Borja, he began to spend most of his income on clothes. Luckily, the office rent is extremely low considering it's in such a high-class neighbourhood. That's a special dispensation from one of Borja's millionaire friends whom he rescued from a tight corner, although I'm none too sure there isn't an even shadier background to the deal. All in all, I'd rather not ask. As for Mariajo, the secretary we theoretically employ to answer calls and see to the paperwork, she's a virtual being invented by Borja and comes gratis. Her existence encompasses the little pot of red nail varnish sitting on what is supposed to be her desk and the Loewe headscarf draped over the back of her chair that Borja snaffled one day in a restaurant. When we're about to see a client, we spray around some *L'Air du Temps* we keep in a drawer and tell our client that the secretary is out running errands.

After he'd grumbled and given the *nihil obstat* to my appearance, we went to Major de Gràcia to get a taxi. There were very few about, and when we did finally track one down, Borja told the driver to leave us in Plaça Adrià. The vehicle reeked of cheap air freshener and I began to sneeze. The driver, who was on the phone, seemed to be in a rush. As there were no big hold-ups, we arrived in five minutes.

"My God, that guy was in a hurry!" I exclaimed, realizing I was still in a state of panic.

"He obviously had to get somewhere fast." Borja glanced at his watch and grimaced. "We'd better have a smoke. We're miles too early."

Clàudia Agulló's office was in a modern building, no doubt built in the Seventies, that was good quality if not the height of luxury. It looked over Plaça Adrià and had, naturally, a uniformed porter and a service lift. Borja smiled in anticipation.

"Good morning. We have an appointment with Mrs Clàudia Agulló," my brother announced when a young woman who must have been her secretary opened the door.

"I'll tell her right away," said the woman as she ushered us in and smiled at Borja.

We didn't have long to wait. A highly perfumed Clàudia Agulló was expecting us, and looked serious and on edge. Borja was right in one respect: she was attractive. Tall, thin but not skeletal, with a fine head of black hair and dark eyes, she wasn't exactly my type, but I can vouch that if that lady and I were the only survivors on the planet after a nuclear catastrophe, it wouldn't stay that way long, at least as far as I was concerned. Borja looked her languorously but politely up and down, and she didn't seem to object. It was obvious she was a woman accustomed to arousing passions and erections. Just in case, I thought it wouldn't be a bad idea to summon up the swim-suited image of my mother-in-law on the beach last summer: it never failed. Joana, Montse's mother, has many virtues, and *that* is one of them.

Clàudia Agulló invited us to sit down on her sparklingly new white leather sofa and told us they were waiting for the judge to decide whether to grant Amadeu Cabestany bail, though it seemed very unlikely, whatever the cost. The stink raised by the media over the crime had unleashed an incomprehensible panic in Catalan society and everybody was trying to cash in: the dailies boosting their sales, the police winning political points and the politicians, as usual, attacking each other. Given that state of affairs, it would be difficult for them to let him out. Clàudia seemed despondent and asked us about Marina Dolç's novel.

"I don't believe it will help us to identify her murderer," my brother had the gall to say, as if he'd read it. "You know, almost all the characters who appear in it are suspicious, and there's quite a crowd... Besides, I don't think Marina was expecting her head to be smashed in. She opened the door to her murderer and turned her back on him while she poured out drinks. At least that's what the police think."

"I know Amadeu is innocent," said Clàudia with real conviction. "But how come there are no witnesses? Somebody must have seen him at the Up & Down..."

"Perhaps the person we want is a husband who told his wife he was at a business supper. Or a young thing who in theory had gone to a friend's house to study," retorted Borja. "Besides, at that time of night everyone is either plastered or out of their mind. Who can say? People don't want hassle. End of story."

As murders are not exactly our speciality, we do have a problem and a big one at that. The fact that neither Borja nor I have an official status means we have no contacts with the police, so we had no way to inveigle ourselves into a position to find out how their investigation was going. As for the autopsy report, the time of death, DNA analyses and all the forensic palaver that was supposed to be so useful, Borja and I were in the dark. We read the papers and knew what Borja himself had heard first hand while under a table at the Ritz, but the police always like to keep an ace up their sleeves just in case, so we couldn't rely on that.

In a moment of candour or desperation, Borja told Clàudia of our difficulties in these areas. Despite her enthusiasm and the confidence she had shown in our skills, Borja must have been aware it's one thing to take advantage of the frailties of the rich and quite another for the life of an innocent man to be in our hands. Nonetheless, Amadeu's agent seemed to have blind faith in us and didn't see that as an obstacle. Mariona had clearly given us a good press and told Clàudia about our status as atypical, if not illegal, detectives.

"I think I have the solution," said Clàudia after listening to us. "I know a retired policeman who I am sure still has good contacts in the force. Lluís Arquer lives in the Raval. My mother and he were friends..." she added, as if she needed to justify herself. "He's rather prickly, but I bet he could do with some extra cash. Here's his number" – Clàudia wrote it on a piece of paper and gave it to Borja – "Give him a ring, but don't say I sent you. Act as if you'd found your own way to him. Don't worry, I'll look after the expenses."

Borja thanked her and put the scrap of paper in his pocket. I felt relieved to think that finally a true professional would intervene and give us the benefit of the experience and objectivity we both lacked. In any case, I couldn't fathom why Clàudia hadn't entrusted this task to a proper detective in the first place. Was Mariona Castany so persuasive? Was Borja so trusted by the wealthy? I sprang up from the sofa, convinced our meeting was at an end, but I was wrong. Borja had yet more questions for Clàudia, and was about to open a Pandora's box.

"Very well, Clàudia, now tell us a little bit about this writer Cabestany. Is he any *good?*" he enquired while I sank discreetly back into the sofa.

"I would say he is a difficult and little-understood..."

"Fine. But is he any *good?*" he repeated his question.

"You know, 'good' as in... Writers who write like Amadeu are always good..." I expect Clàudia wasn't expecting this kind of question. "I mean he is very deep... It's beside the point that his books don't sell," she responded uneasily.

"Or, in other words, as you see it, it is a great injustice that Marina Dolç was famous and sold mountains of books and he doesn't," continued Borja, trying not to sound rude. "If Amadeu Cabestany hardly sells any books, it hardly makes sense for you to be his agent, does it now?"

Clàudia turned red as a tomato and took a few seconds to come up with a reply.

"The truth is you never know in this business... Literature and talent are one thing, and reviews and sales quite another... There are the occasional surprises. Readers..."

"Clàudia, if you want us to help your protégé, please be straight with us." Ever since he'd been resurrected as the ruined heir of a family with aristocratic monikers, Borja had stopped believing in such a thing as disinterested altruism. "Are you two having an affair?"

Clàudia gave a start in her chair and turned an even darker shade of red. She took a packet of cigarettes from the drawer and lit up. She too was obviously trying to knock the habit. We decided on an act of solidarity and a smoky haze soon filled her office.

"I don't see how that might be relevant," she responded nervously, standing up. "He is a client of mine. I have to look after his interests... Besides," she reflected for a moment, before coming out with it, "he's married."

Bull's-eye. My brother had hit the target this time.

"Look, Clàudia, this is all in confidence: we couldn't care less if you and this Cabestany are seeing each other, could we, Eduard? But we need to know the lie of the land. A murder is like a jigsaw puzzle" – Borja had adopted a very professional tone – "and we need all the pieces if we are going to put it together. At the moment the pieces are saying he was the one who dispatched the Dolç woman to the other side."

"I'm sure he didn't kill her," Clàudia retorted, her eyes glinting.

"Well then," my brother insisted.

Clàudia stared out of the window and took her time to respond. She was weighing up what she should say. The uneasy silence justified Borja's suspicions: say nothing and admit to your guilt. After thirty seconds, in slightly better spirits, she sat slowly down, almost ready to launch into *La Traviata.* Ironically the fact that Borja had discovered her little secret had just upped our rating as detectives.

"We're not exactly lovers," she said finally, "we simply meet up when he comes to Barcelona, which is not very often. He has a family, a wife and two daughters, and I don't think he's the kind of man to leave everything for an *amour fou*," and she added rather soulfully, "though I suppose I am in love with him. I can't speak for him, however."

"Sufficiently in love to bump off Marina Dolç? You must have been really upset when you heard she was going to win the prize..." Borja hinted gently.

"I already knew she would win," her tone was icy. "I found out a week before. I knew I'd got it wrong and given him false hopes, but Amadeu seemed so depressed... I don't know why I didn't forewarn him, I suppose because he'd not been to Barcelona for two months and I really wanted to see him. I didn't think he would take being runner-up so badly. It was a struggle. If he'd known..."

"The truth," my brother said, turning to me, "is that Clàudia didn't leave the bar at any moment. I mean there's no way she could have bumped off Marina."

"I didn't even have time to look at myself in the mirror!" she said, shocked. "I was gossiping with everyone."

"You could have contracted someone to do it," I suggested.

Clàudia finally lost her temper. She didn't need to say that she thought I was a miserable little worm. She simply stared daggers at me and I thought she was going to slap me.

"How wonderful, so I'm one of your suspects, am I? Hell! If I had to kill off all the rival authors who sell more than mine..."

"No, not at all," said Borja, trying to pacify her. "That's simply a working hypothesis..."

"I sincerely hope so."

"You know, I don't understand why you didn't go up to his room if you wanted to spend the night with him," my brother added for good measure.

"I didn't know he'd reserved a room at the Ritz. I thought we'd go to my place, as we'd done previously, and that was a real surprise. Besides, if you remember, when Amadeu left the bar, he was furious. I thought it better to leave him alone for a while to calm down. I knew he was angry with me too. I had other writers to talk to. It's my job. I thought I'd go up later when everyone had left."

And she added remorsefully, "Perhaps I should have told him that Marina was going to win the prize. He'd at least have had time to digest the bad news, the poor man…"

"But you don't think that in a hot-headed moment he could have…"

"Of course not! Amadeu is the type that sinks into depression, not one to act… You don't know him: he's a congenital worrier. If he'd ever contemplated doing such a thing, he'd have acted like Hamlet in Vic for a month and then would have dropped the idea," she sighed. "No, Amadeu may be eccentric but he's no murderer."

"All right, let us know if they let him out," Borja concluded, getting up from his chair, presuming our meeting was over. "We need to speak to him. In any case, we should place an ad in the dailies to see if a witness comes forward to support his alibi. If, as he says, he did go to the Up & Down club, sooner or later someone has to recognize him."

"I'll make sure an ad is placed in two or three of the big-circulation dailies," said Clàudia, who still seemed rather upset.

"Best put my mobile as the contact number and say something like 'in absolute confidence'…" Borja suggested. "In case the person who recognizes him doesn't want to get involved with the police... If an eyewitness does turn up, we have our ways to make him talk."

I didn't know what my brother had in mind, though I imagine it's the kind of thing real detectives do. I couldn't imagine him dealing out blows and covering his Armani in blood.

"It's odd no taxi driver has shown signs of life," I mused aloud. "If things were as he says, and the entrance to the Ritz was jammed with police cars... I mean it's not a destination a taxi driver could forget just like that. I suppose the police must have contacted the association."

"I suppose so, but so far no news on that front. Amadeu doesn't know the make of car or the licence number. He has very hazy memories and you can see he was drunk. He only remembers that both taxis smelled of pine air freshener... As if that was much help!" she sighed.

"Memory plays that kind of trick..."

"Do whatever you have to, but you must find an eyewitness or the person who killed Marina Dolç. Her murderer..."

"Or murderess," I pointed out.

"OK, or murderess, but the fact is that while Amadeu is in prison, he or she wanders about free."

"We'll find the culprit, don't you worry," my brother assured her after giving her a peck on the cheek in the doorway. "By the way," he asked as he consulted the notebook with black covers he always carried with him, "what the hell does *Squamous in the Tempest* mean? That's not Catalan, is it?"

Clàudia looked blank and glanced at her watch, as if she were in a hurry and couldn't waste more time on us.

"Frankly I don't know. Amadeu's style is a bit cryptic at times. I've still not had time to get to the end of the book..." she confessed apologetically.

"No, it's not a quick read," my brother agreed, empathizing. "Well, I'll give it a look this weekend. It's not such a long novel..."

When we left the building, the hot noonday air blasted our cheeks. We felt we would melt there and then. Clàudia's air-conditioning had kept us cool in her office, but back in the street physical effort was the last thing the sultry Mediterranean climate encouraged, what with the heat from cars and the warm air blasting out from all the air-conditioning systems. I started to sweat and decided to take my jacket off and loosen my tie. My brother looked at me askance but said nothing. As it was still early, we went for a coffee and rang the number Clàudia had given us in order to arrange a meeting with one Lluís Arquer.

A grave, slightly hoarse voice answered, and it was evident from the start that the man was very irritable. Nonetheless, he seemed eager to see us, particularly when Borja hinted there would be an economic reward for his trouble. Then he backtracked, alleging he was very busy and not keen on time-wasters, but he gave us an appointment that morning in a bar on the Plaça Reial. Although we would go by taxi, it was a good way from where we were. Borja and I drank our coffees and set off.

For the moment, we hadn't decided whether the fact Clàudia and Amadeu were having an affair made our life easier or more complicated. We couldn't discount the fact that Clàudia's feelings towards Amadeu Cabestany might have clouded her judgement or, as Montse would say, sent her into a spin. Love and lucidity aren't good bedfellows, and perhaps Clàudia had a veil over her eyes that stopped her from seeing what the *mossos* could see so clearly: that Amadeu couldn't stomach the blow of not winning the prize and had killed Marina Dolç in an onset of rage. One hundred thousand euros are no joking matter, no, *senyor*. People kill for much less.

Luckily we didn't have to decide whether Amadeu was guilty or innocent, although if he was really innocent, it was our job to prove it. In a way, the life of a man we didn't know was in our hands because a rich lady like Mariona Castany had persuaded another rich lady that she could trust us, which, we should be under no illusions, was rather rash of her. When we left the bar, I expressed my concerns to Borja, who didn't seem at all put out.

"Stop agonizing and let's get to work. Your problem is you think too much."

"Pep, this fellow's life is at stake. Perhaps we should advise Clàudia to contract a proper detective."

"We solved the Lídia Font case, didn't we?" My brother was so happy back playing Sherlock Holmes again. "Besides," he added, puffing his chest out, "I have realized I possess the main quality a good detective needs."

"An absolute lack of common sense?" I suggested hesitantly.

But right then, before my brother could reduce me to a pulp, we managed to stop one of the very few unoccupied taxis driving down Muntaner and I was left still wanting to find out what exceptional virtue Borja possessed that gave him the wherewithal to triumph where the police were apparently failing.

10

Bad traffic meant it took us an hour to reach the Plaça Reial, where Lluís Arquer was drinking a beer and waiting for us in the Ambos Mundos. As he'd told Borja over the phone, he wore a straw hat and a crumpled, natural-coloured linen jacket. He was stumpy, though not exactly fat, and the way he sat and moved suggested he might have arthritis, something that was confirmed by the silver-topped stick he'd propped on the chair next to him.

"Mr Arquer? Lluís Arquer?" enquired Borja.

"Who else might I be?" he replied sourly, as if we were annoying him.

"I spoke to you on the phone a while ago. Someone told us you might be able to help," Borja went on, unsure what tone to adopt.

We sat down without waiting for his invitation. The square was full of tourists queuing outside restaurants and tramps and druggies sitting on the ground and occupying all the public benches. The fountain in the middle was surrounded by Arabs, Moroccans I expect. One came over to greet Lluís Arquer and thanked him effusively for some favour or other in halting Spanish. Arquer brushed him off rather paternally and told him he was busy at the moment. Compliments seemed to unsettle him, as if they were conflicting with the hard-man image he was trying to project.

He must have been around sixty-five and looked like a man to reckon with. His manner was prickly, as Clàudia had warned, but he seemed keen to know what we were after. He scrutinized us disapprovingly and lit a cigarette. Our yuppie dress-style jarred with the touristy-cum-ragamuffin atmosphere in the square, and I instinctively lifted my hand to my pocket to check my wallet was still in place. He grimaced loftily as he watched me. Then he took off his hat and ran his hand through his grey, rather wavy hair. He still had a good head of hair. I noticed his eyes were like Clàudia Agulló's, albeit sunk behind wrinkles that stuck out like scars.

"Mr Arquer…" Borja began.

"Arquer, drop the rest, no need to stand on ceremony."

"Arquer, then. I'm Borja Masdéu," continued my brother as he handed him one of his elegant visiting cards, "and this is my partner, Eduard Martínez. We aren't really detectives, but as a result of circumstances we don't need to dwell on, we've been asked to investigate (unofficially, of course) a matter that's related to a murder. We've been told you are retired but still have good contacts in the force."

"Maybe I do, and maybe I don't," he answered guardedly.

"We need certain information. A copy of the forensic report, of the fingerprints, a list of the clues the police found at the scene of the crime… All that sort of thing, you must know what I mean," my brother went on a little nervously.

Lluís Arquer listened and looked at him, not saying a word, as if Borja were a Martian who'd just landed from another planet. He must be thinking his sleek, greasy hair and flashy tie hardly squared with the job of tracking down murderers. We were like two sparrows in front of an old cat that was ready to show his claws.

"Drugs? Mafia? What the hell's all this about?" the detective blurted out, knitting his eyebrows.

"No, it's not like that. It involves writers. The victim's name is Marina Dolç."

"Mmm... Yes, I read about that in the newspapers. They smashed her head in at the Ritz, right? But I thought they'd jailed the fellow who did it."

"The police have got it wrong. That's why we..."

"And you say you're not detectives. What the hell are you then? Judging by your mugs, I'd say you're legal beagles..." he rasped as scornfully as he could.

"Not exactly," I answered. "We're consultants, we run a company..."

"So you aren't lawyers, then?"

"No, as I was saying..."

"Are you armed? You carrying a bazooka?"

"No, we smoke Camel Lights," replied Borja, taking a packet from his pocket.

"That's right... My partner is a real joker... Ha, ha, ha.... No, we're not carrying guns," I said after he noticed how red I'd gone. "Times have changed, what with computers and all that..." I continued apologetically. "As my partner said, we're not detectives, but in exceptional circumstances..."

"No need to tell me your life story," he cut me off in full flow. "I could make a couple of calls. I still have friends in the force who owe me a few favours. What's in it for me?"

"Say five hundred euros?" my brother suggested timidly.

"Make it a grand. Three hundred in advance," he went on, giving us no chance to bargain. "Come here on Tuesday, same time. I'll be here. And if you need to hire a man with a bazooka..." he concluded, tapping his jacket pocket.

"Thanks. We hope it won't come to that," I responded, hoping he didn't decide to show us his pistol. Just then a couple of *mossos* on their beat were briskly wandering our way.

We dug deep into our pockets and came up with two hundred and eighty euros between us. When we left home that morning, we'd never imagined we'd end up doing a deal with a low-life Barcelona detective and weren't carrying any more cash. Lluís Arquer carefully pocketed the notes and coins while giving us a withering look. It was clear that neither our dress sense nor my brother's courteous manners cut any ice with him. He gulped down what was left of his beer and stood up.

"I have to hit the road. This is on you." And he was gone.

Lluís Arquer had pulled a good trick: he'd cleaned us out completely at the Ambos Mundos and left us with a bill on the table of seven euros ninety. That was the cost of the three glasses of draught beer we'd drunk, although Borja, who was on a diet because according to him (and him alone) he was developing a paunch, hadn't even sipped his. We'd been forced to give the detective all the money we were carrying, and now needed to get money from a cash point. My brother had mislaid his wallet, which was par for the course (particularly when he's dining with Merche), but luckily I had mine. Relatively lucky, that's to say, because on the short walk between the terrace of the Ambos Mundos, where Borja was waiting under the steely gaze of the waiters, and the cash point on the Ramblas where I was heading to extract money, my wallet mysteriously disappeared from my pocket.

I won't deny that it was my fault, because I had been daydreaming for a few seconds, hypnotized by the perfectly synchronized movement of a pair of round, tanned breasts coming my way braless under a low-cut, tight-fitting tank top. There wasn't a cent in my wallet, but unfortunately it did contain my credit card as well as my ID, and that was a real nuisance. Luckily, as it was a few minutes to two, the bank was still open. I went in and explained my problem, but it was a complete waste of time. However hard I worked at telling them my wallet had just been stolen, I couldn't budge a single bank clerk, let alone get to see the manager. They were very sorry, they said, but they couldn't give me a single euro if I didn't have my ID. I persisted but finally had to give up. I knew the bank employees had their hands tied and could do nothing: I'd spent twenty years of my life behind a bank counter and knew how those places functioned. I did manage to block my card, but then had to return to the Ambos Mundos more skint than before and with my self-image shattered.

Borja, who was waiting impatiently for me, couldn't believe it when, shame-faced and feeling pathetic, I confessed my wallet had been stolen. We were stymied, because we were suddenly completely stuck in the Plaça Reial on a Friday lunchtime, without a cent in our pockets and a bill for three beers. Quite naturally, the waiters at the Ambos Mundos were beginning to seethe. They wouldn't swallow the story of the stolen wallet, or perhaps they did, but couldn't care less. I suppose it wasn't the first time somebody had tried this excuse to avoid paying the bill and they weren't impressed. A swarm of tourists were trying to take our table and hinting we should get up and go. Borja and I decided to sit this one out and stay calm.

I could always call Montse and ask her for help, but I knew my wife was very busy that day at her Alternative Centre. One of her partners was ill and she'd had to take responsibility for the yoga classes. If I forced her to stand up a dozen pre- and post-menopausal women with hot flushes and sugar- and nicotine-abstinence syndrome, my wife would be angry and quite rightly so. It's OK if pickpockets snaffle the wallets of flabby tourists idly strolling down the Ramblas, but I'm from Barcelona and I know you have to watch it on the Ramblas. Dodging the artful dodgers is one of the attractions of the territory, I suppose, and I'd acted the fool and been caught out. On the other hand, I imagine Borja was embarrassed about ringing Merche to ask for small change, and Lola's mobile was switched off or she'd left it at home. And we couldn't have recourse to Lluís Arquer, although we knew he lived nearby. We had no desire to confirm his suspicions that Borja and I were a couple of well-dressed dolts. The waiters at the Ambos Mundos didn't seem inclined to let us slip off, and, besides, there was the minor detail that we'd have to walk back to my house, which meant a good hour sweating under a blistering sun. I didn't want to be the one to renege on our agreement about keeping calm, but things were starting to look bleak. Finally, as usual, my brother had one of his brainwaves.

"Listen, Eduard," he sounded me out, "you could go to the Ramblas and act like a statue for a while. I bet you'd get the money in under an hour. I reckon twelve euros would do to pay for the beers and our metro tickets."

"What? Are you mad?" I roared. "Do you think I'm going to act like a statue in front of everyone! Forget it!" I wasn't going to let him bamboozle me into that one.

"All right! All right! So I'll have to come to the rescue, as usual," he said angrily. And he picked up the brown plastic saucer where they'd left the bill and headed for the Ramblas.

Human statues had been the fashion on the Ramblas for years. They stood still and when someone threw them a coin, they changed position or performed. Some were trite and some were sophisticated, from characters smeared with coppery make-up to look like GIs from the Second World War to a girl spectacularly bedecked in flowers and foliage trying to be an allegory of spring. Some were amusing and some were scary, like the guy doing a bloody, decapitated head routine served up on a silver platter on a white tablecoth. I can't think why tourists like being photographed next to that. There were so many statues that it had to be a good way to earn one's living, even if the competition was tough. For that very reason I wasn't at all clear that the sudden appearance from nowhere of an amateur dressed up like a yuppie would be welcomed by the mime professionals who suffered under thick face-packs from the early morning. I hoped my brother wouldn't return from his artistic debut with a black eye or his elegant Armani suit in tatters.

Nothing of the sort. Borja was back after half an hour, sweating and out of breath, but apparently safe and sound. He'd collected twelve euros and thirty cents and that meant we had enough to pay for the drinks and our metro tickets and spare ourselves a long walk which I really didn't fancy. We paid for the beers, left a forty-cent tip and headed for the Liceu station. It was almost three o'clock and my stomach was rumbling.

"You won't believe this, but I bumped into a golfing acquaintance while I was playing the fool," an amused Borja told me.

"Heavens, I'm so sorry!..." I replied sincerely. "You don't say you played the fool dressed up like that? Maybe you didn't need to go that far..."

"No, of course not, I simply acted myself. As I was the only one not wearing a disguise and not doing anything silly, the tourists were really fascinated by my character. But, even so, standing still is exhausting! At least I found a shady corner!..."

"So what did you do when they threw you a coin?" I asked, intrigued. "Because I suppose that's the fun bit, perform and..."

"Well, I bent down, picked it up and pocketed it, naturally. What did you expect me to do? A couple of fat cows in miniskirts had their photos taken with me and gave me two euros. And an American woman pinched my bum. A moustachioed guy in a tank top also tried it on, but I stopped him in his tracks."

"God, Borja, how desperate! And you met someone you know as well!... What did you tell him? Did you ask him for money?"

"You must be joking! We've not sunk that low!" he erupted in disbelief. "You know, when I ask for cash, it's always for five hundred euros or more… I made light of the situation and told him it was a bet and that I had to stay a statue until I'd collected twelve euros. He thought it was a hoot and gave me two euros. He said he wouldn't give me more or I wouldn't be playing straight. The bastard!…"

"And did he swallow the bet business?"

"Naturally. It was the most reasonable explanation, given the circumstances…" he smiled. "Besides, I told him that the blonde who'd laid the bet was out of this world and was waiting for me with a bottle of Moët and Chandon behind the curtains of a bedroom at the Oriente," he added, pleased by his little joke.

Yet again I was amazed by the sang-froid with which my brother faced up to the most ridiculous situations. You had to take your hat off to him. If I'd been in his shoes, I think I'd have died of embarrassment. Obviously, in the first place, I'd never have had the nous to do what he'd just done. Our sense of the ridiculous is really so very personal.

"You know, with that imagination of yours, you could get by writing novels," I said in admiration as we went down to the platform in the metro. "Perhaps it might be worth your while…"

"Well, I don't deny that if I tried my…" he responded, puckering his eyebrows, jutting out his chin and half-closing his eyes.

"Hey, hurry up, it's late and I'm hungry," I shouted, tugging on his sleeve when I heard a train approaching. "Watch out you don't knock into someone!"

My brother can decipher the complicated names that appear on menus in the most expensive restaurants and choose the right wine for each course, but he's totally bewildered by the Barcelona metro grid.

"Wow, there's even air-conditioning! Do you know how long it is since I travelled by metro?" he asked as we pushed our way into one of the compartments. "Though… what can I say! This may be quicker and cheaper, but frankly, I think taxis are much more comfortable, traffic jams and all. This is quite dreadful… What a stink in here! I'll have to take my suit to the dry-cleaners in the morning!"

I didn't bother to respond. A middle-aged woman, modestly dressed, her hair dyed aubergine, stood opposite us staring icily at Borja. You couldn't blame her. It was written on that good lady's face that she sweated out four lengthy trips on the metro every day in the rush hour, and I'd been a daily user of this mode of public transport for twenty years and perfectly understood how she felt. Fortunately, we soon reached Fontana and left the metro. The escalator wasn't working and we had to walk up. Outside the sun was still burning down but luckily we were only two minutes from home.

Our plan was to go and have a bite to eat and rest for a while. Montse wasn't around, Arnau was with his grandparents and the twins were on the rampage with friends. I'd promised Montse I would help her that evening to prepare for the party by taking chairs up to the terrace and going to buy the fireworks and cava. However, before complying with my domestic duties, I had to accompany Borja to buy a summer suit in the centre. My brother chose a beige item and bought me a couple of short-sleeved shirts – one dark, the other lightish – a belt, three pairs of black socks, one pair of brown shoes and a tie that went well with the suit and shirts. The sales were on, but even so, I had a shock when I saw the receipt I had to sign.

"Don't grumble!" remarked Borja, hearing me muttering as we left the shop. "If you'd gone for an Armani or Hermès, it would have been a good deal more expensive."

"Then perhaps we'd both have had to stand like statues in the Ramblas, for what's left of the summer!" I retorted angrily. "Frankly, Borja, I am quite unable to see the difference. There's a little shop round the corner from home..."

"Maybe you can't," he cut me off, "but I assure you other people can." I suppose he was referring to our rich, sophisticated clients. "And that's the whole point."

"What it is to be in the know..." I thought to myself while deciding not to contradict him. Borja's philosophy had worked wonders today and I wouldn't be the one to question it. The fact I personally believe it is scandalous that people take more notice of our appearance than of our CV makes not a jot of difference. On the other hand, we don't have much of a CV, appearance is the only card we can play, and Borja is right there. It's also true we're not the only ones to do these things, although we may do them more consciously. Montse's radical customers also like the fact that the woman helping them to give up smoking and enjoy the secrets of karma and the virtues of yoga wears that half-hippy half-ethnic look she's worn lately. If our rich customers are dazzled by the make of the clothes we wear, that's their problem, not ours, as my brother liked to say.

After giving him money for a taxi to the Passeig de Gràcia, I took a bus home, six hundred euros the poorer and loaded down with bags. Montse, who was back, wrinkled her nose when she saw them, but said nothing. She must assume it was Borja's doing, because she knows I hate shopping and that I prefer old jeans and the feel of cotton shirts when it comes to clothes, and preferably on the worn side. Luckily, my brother has yet to insist I spray myself with one of those eau-de-Cologne fragrances he likes so much. No guarantees though.

"The demands of work, love," I commented resignedly, as I put my purchases in the wardrobe, rather shame-faced after telling her about the theft on the Ramblas.

"Well, get changed, because you've got to help me to take things up to the terrace for tonight's party," she instructed me as she undid her plait and combed her hair. "We'll have a good crowd and as the neighbours have given us permission to hold it on the roof terrace, I've been forced to invite them too. But not to worry, they won't all come."

"I hope the Rottweiler doesn't show up," I said anxiously.

The Rottweiler is the chair of the flat-owners' association. No one can stand her, Montse in particular, who's had several rows with her.

"Don't worry, I don't think she'll stick her nose in," Montse smiled. "In fact, she's dying to put in a complaint and says she'll ring the police if we play music or make too much noise. It seems she's bought one of those little gadgets that measure decibels."

"She just has to be a witch!"

"I'm sure Carmen will come, the one on the first floor, with her two children. Her husband is away."

"They seem like nice people," I added as I changed my shirt. "He's a translator, isn't he?"

"Something of the sort. Hey, hurry up. And try not to knock the lift about when you're taking the chairs up."

"*Yes, sir!*" I answered, acting as if I was giving a military salute, and resigned to carrying out her orders without protesting in the slightest.

Those who wear the trousers are in charge, and that's Montse *chez nous*. Luckily, no one talks about hen-pecked husbands any more.

PART THREE

11

Josefina Peña was sad and distraught. She couldn't rid herself of the image of her friend sprawled out on the floor in her room at the Ritz with her head smashed open, and since she'd found Marina's corpse, the police had questioned her several times, as if they were still none the wiser. She had held on to the pearl-and-diamond earring she'd found quite by chance under a chair at the hotel, and didn't know what to do with it. Give it to the police? Keep it as a souvenir? It wasn't the piece's value that led her not to declare it, but the feeling that, by preserving the earring as a kind of relic, she would be preserving her friend whom she'd never see again. Josefina was a widow, her only son lived in London and she'd found in Marina the friend she'd never had. With no Marina at the other end of the line, she'd be alone again and would relapse into depression.

Unlike Marina, Josefina was a wealthy woman who came from a good family. And, also unlike Marina, her life had followed the hackneyed, random pattern of many young people of her generation and economic and social status: a difficult, well-heeled adolescence, an initiatory trip to India at eighteen and, on her return, nine years in Ibiza living in a commune, practising free love between one joint and the next. Josefina had spent ten years searching for her soul, bedding whomever, making and selling plastic necklaces she reckoned were arty and tripping on LSD. Unfortunately, the only thing she'd discovered in her hippy years were a number of sexually transmitted diseases and the growing feeling she was occasionally beginning to lose her memory. She was thirty when she returned to Barcelona, alone, pregnant and slightly unhinged. Her parents quickly found her a husband and opened a boutique for her in Sarrià. Josefina met Marina in that shop, which was called *The Oracle*, where she sold radical chic clothes from Ibiza. The novelist soon became one of her best customers and, in the process, her best and only friend.

However, Marina was a secret person. She never talked about her past. Josefina only knew that she was from Sant Feliu de Codines, where she owned a house, and had an ex she never saw and an Italian lover who never came to Barcelona. When Marina travelled down to the city, they'd both meet up for dinner or to go to the theatre or the Liceo. Josefina didn't really like opera but ever since her last boyfriend jilted her after helping himself to her current account, she found her eccentric friend's cheerful, disinterested company even more appealing. Marina was an optimist by nature, and her conversation worked better for Josefina than any anti-depressant.

That Friday her son and daughter-in-law were arriving from London and she'd bought cake and cava to celebrate St John's Eve at home with them. She wasn't at all keen on her daughter-in-law, a starchy Young Conservative who looked down on her ex-hippy mother-in-law. Her son was only twenty-five but he was a financial whizz-kid and earned a fortune in the City, where he'd met that young lawyer on the road to success whom he'd finally bedded and wedded. Josefina knew they'd both try yet again to persuade her to close her boutique and do something more respectable, like being a lady of leisure or looking after her grandchildren, if she could put her mind to it. Four years had gone by since her husband had died – her son didn't know he wasn't his biological father – and her child was intent on taking her to live with them to salve his conscience and, in the process, ensure his mother didn't fritter away the family inheritance. He knew nothing about her past or present boyfriends, and Josefina always played the role of the resigned widow to avoid disappointing him.

As her son and daughter-in-law were about to arrive, she decided to go to the laundry room to smoke the joint she'd just rolled so the house didn't smell of weed. They wouldn't understand, and if they got a sniff were sure to force her into a detox centre and might even find a judge to declare her incapacitated so they could close her shop. While she got high on the grass she'd bought from an acquaintance who cultivated a plantation of marijuana in her house, the tears welled up in Josefina's eyes. Deprived of her long, exhilarating conversations with Marina, she'd been driven back to dependence on anti-depressants, tranquillizers and joints, in that order.

On Saturday morning, after celebrating St John's Eve at home watching *Gertrud* and getting to bed relatively early, Oriol Sureda went out to buy some breakfast and returned home with a baguette, a butter croissant and a sheaf of papers under his arm, set up to spend the rest of the morning reading cultural supplements and literary reviews. He made coffee, put on Beethoven's Sonata Number 5 for piano and violin, and sat down at his dining table with his breakfast and a pile of magazines and newspapers. By that stage in June, classes at the university had wound down and Oriol felt he could spend Saturday afternoon, even the whole of Sunday if necessary, revising the paper on the death of the novel he'd agreed to read in the middle of July at a Congress in the Canary Islands. In fact, he'd be giving that lecture he'd written some ten years before for the fifth time. He would have to touch it up slightly, in case someone in the audience remembered it, or in case the organizers had garnered financial support and insisted on publication: he needed to change the order of the paragraphs, the title too, perhaps a couple of the quotations, incorporate different examples... An afternoon's labour or an afternoon and morning at most. He'd already published the same paper in three university journals under three different titles – 'The Slow Death of the Novel' (1998), 'European Narrative from Flaubert to Agustí Capdevánol' (2001) and '*Easy-reads* and the Degeneration of the Novel as a Genre' (2004) – although Oriol doubted any of his colleagues had bothered to read it, or if they had, that they'd paid sufficient attention to notice that it was the same text. In any case, it was common knowledge that it was what everybody did at the university and he had no need to feel embarrassed. In terms of lecturers' cloned publications in the area of philosophy and literature, there was a kind of tacit agreement, of academic *omertà*, that was scrupulously respected at every institutional level, from rectors and deans to the lowliest porter and teaching assistant hoping for a promotion. Oriol Sureda felt enormously proud to be a cornerstone of this mediocre, self-perpetuating system.

It was hot, and after skimming a few literary critical articles that revealed nothing to anyone but did some good for their authors' CVs, Oriol went into his kitchen in search of a Coke. He decided to put his cultural supplements to one side for a while and watch the news. The world continued to be in a mess, and he saw that the papers were still raking over the murder of Marina Dolç. He'd been one of the guests at the literary party at the Ritz the night she won the prize, even though he was one of her detractors. Apart from teaching literature classes at the university, Oriol doubled as a literary critic. Writers, especially young ones, feared him like some raging oracle and tried to ingratiate themselves with him. From the Olympus of his erudition, Oriol could consecrate or sink a writer, and childishly enjoyed wielding the burning tip of his pen in the weekly column he wrote for one of the nation's most prestigious dailies.

He was now nearing sixty, but was forty-four when he was asked to review the first novel by the then unknown author, Marina Dolç. At the time, Oriol was bottom of the pile in a university department where he languished attempting to build a reputation by dint of his second-hand theories on the dismal future of literature. Unfortunately he wasn't related to any of the pillars of the patriotic bourgeoisie that ruled that particular roost, and was no brain-box either, so he had to earn it by graft alone. He'd been warned it was a rubbish novel, though an impartial review was expected of him, if possible with a little blood and gore in bilious mode. Oriol Sureda, fretting for fame, didn't disappoint.

The Rage of the Goddesses was cliché-ridden, written in a rather puerile lyrical style that its author had tried to offset with a series of steamy sex scenes. The characters were limp, the plot contrived and the prose facile and transparent. Even so, Oriol Sureda was hooked on that ramshackle fictional world of intrigue and couldn't put it down. Oriol only read stodgy tomes that were unfathomable, which once you'd fathomed them, made you feel like committing suicide, so he felt quite bewildered when he enjoyed reading a novel for the first time in years. It took him three days to read it and thirty to write the review: nonetheless he trashed it.

He wrote a perceptive, cruelly sardonic review that was praised to the skies by the great patricians of culture in their respective eyries. Doors began to open to Oriol Sureda, including ones to a chair within ten years and others to a couple of lavatories he preferred not to step inside. Rather reluctantly he continued reviewing the novels Marina published, but from now on there were two Oriol Suredas sharing one body, one bald patch, one bank account and one brain.

He'd been suffering from terrible migraines recently and sometimes felt he was going to have a complete blackout. Perhaps he was ageing. When he finished reading the supplements, it was time for lunch. As happened every week, his housekeeping lady had left a supply of precooked dishes in the freezer. He took out the Tupperware container full of meatballs, which he heated in the microwave. He poured out a glass of red wine and ate the meatballs and a peach while he flicked on the TV. Then he made coffee, zapped through the different channels some more and decided he didn't really need to introduce big changes in the lecture he'd already written. In any case, he would dedicate Sunday afternoon to that. He switched off the television, went to his library and gingerly, as if it was a bibliophile's dream, took down the unbound copy of *A Shortcut to Paradise* that he'd received clandestinely from a member of the jury a day before the prize was announced. He drew his curtains slightly, sat in the armchair by the window and, with a *frisson* of ineffable pleasure, plunged for a third time into that novel which fascinated him, like all the fiction written by Marina Dolç.

Nothing was going right for Amàlia Vidal and she was livid. Her Colombian maid had rung early in the day to say she was ill and wouldn't be coming in. "The lazy bitch!" Amalia had thought when she'd hung up. She and her husband had guests that night and the flat looked like a pigsty, or so she felt. They'd celebrated St John's Eve the night before with friends, and dirty plates, glasses and empty bottles were piled up in the kitchen. In a filthy temper, cursing her maid, Amàlia tried to fit everything into the dishwasher and, wearing pink plastic gloves that were too big for her, she hurriedly cleaned the disaster area, wondering how she would cope. Her husband had gone to play tennis with one of his clients, and Amàlia was alone with the catastrophe. Moreover, she was suffering from a slight hangover and in no mood to start cooking. The final straw was when she looked in the mirror and saw that the wart that had appeared on her nose a few months ago was growing.

While cleaning the stove, she decided not to renew the girl's contract. She'd be the third maid in the house in two years, but Amàlia was very demanding and difficult to get on with. Andalusian girls were preferable, she thought, remembering her parents' maid. She'd come into their service at the age of sixteen and, as Mr Right never came her way, she went on living with them and still got their lunch ready now in her eighties. Nevertheless, it was absurd to have to pay a local girl four or five times what you had to pay a foreigner. On Monday, she decided, she'd speak to the agency again and they'd hear her complaints on Tibidabo.

Amàlia and her husband led an intense social life, particularly since their children married and they had finally managed to get them out of the house. She taught history at the university and wrote literary critical articles from time to time for the press. Her forte was women and the discriminations they suffered, and that explained why she was part of a committee set up by the Generalitat to evaluate the sexist nature of advertisements, and of a commission that kept itself busy ridding the language of oppressive, chauvinistic words. Amàlia was a militant feminist, admired by women and hated by men in equal parts. Her husband was the director of a powerful cosmetics company and he was proud to have a wife who published books and was invited on to TV chat shows. As he'd been seeing a retired model for years, Amàlia Vidal's husband had succeeded in striking a balance in terms of attitude and testosterone that made him the ideal lover and the perfect husband. His life was as calm as a millpond and the envy of his friends, even though they couldn't imagine what it was like to be married to a stalwart of new-wave feminism in the academy and civil life.

She would definitely not cook. She still had to clean the dining room and tidy the lounge, and her head was splitting. To avoid soiling the kitchen, she and her husband would grab a sandwich for lunch and she'd order take-away hot food for ten. As she was working on securing a professorial chair, and it was no easy move, she couldn't allow herself the luxury of cancelling dinner with her closest colleagues in the department. She knew the fact she'd been at the Ritz the night Marina Dolç was murdered had made her popularity rocket: everybody wanted to know who, how and why. Personally she'd never liked Marina Dolç, but, since she was a woman who'd triumphed in a male-dominated world, Amàlia had been forced to grit her teeth and pander to her. Now she could milk her death for what it was worth, if she played her cards right. For the moment, she'd been invited to participate in a debate on literature and discrimination – the subject of her thesis – on a peak-viewing-time programme, and a foundation had commissioned her to write a report on the chauvinism latent in the novels of Amadeu Cabestany, the man presumed to be the murderer. Yes, Marina might still prove useful, she thought, as she searched the city guide for a catering company she could order supper from. And best of all, now she'd passed on to a better life, Amàlia didn't have to put up with her in person.

12

Sebastià Rovira had a vice, a habit or a virtue, depending on how you looked at it: he liked to go whoring. It wasn't that he didn't love his wife, whom he'd been married to for the past twenty-three years, or didn't desire her, quite the contrary, but his weekly visit to a brothel was a ritual he'd practised from his nineteenth birthday and he couldn't survive without it. He had been a taxi driver from the age of twenty-six and was now fifty-one and the father of three daughters who lived at home and dreamed of becoming models. His only other vices were black tobacco, a coffee and cognac to put fire in his belly after lunch and the weekly work out at a knocking shop. Otherwise, Sebastià was a hard-working man, a good father and a loving, considerate husband. When he was driving in the morning he listened to the Cope, the Pope's station, and in the afternoon Ràdio Taxi, but he was polite and tried to avoid talking politics with his customers.

Sebastià usually dropped by a club of a Friday after dinner. There were three or four where they'd known him for years and he alternated them as he did the girls. He didn't feel guilty about being unfaithful to his wife and tried not to bed the same girl twice in a row to avoid experiencing remorse. He took precautions so as not to catch an infection, treated well the women, who depended on the oldest trade in the world, and never created problems. He told his wife that the Friday nightshift was lucrative and that had been true for the last few months. In the past he had simply parked his car near one of the clip joints where he relieved his excess testosterone on a weekly basis and pretended the money came from what he put aside during the week, but ever since his brother-in-law had got out of prison they'd done a deal: Jacinto drove his brother-in-law's taxi on the Friday nightshift and, before going home, returned the taxi to him and they shared the takings.

Jacinto was out of work. He'd spent a couple of years incarcerated in the Model accused of robbery with grievous bodily harm and three years more at Can Brians on a drugs rap. In fact, he was a small-time pusher who got badly duped, and, as far as the theft went, was unlucky that his victim decided to give chase and smashed his face in when he ran into one of those iron posts the council erects on pavements to stop illegal parking. Jacinto was no angel, but he wasn't violent either. Indeed, he was reputed to be considerate towards women and loyal to his friends. Nevertheless, his record meant no one wanted to risk taking him on, so he did little jobs for taxi drivers, like taking their cars to be washed or repaired and driving his brother-in-law's taxi when the latter went whoring.

On Friday morning, while he was eating breakfast in the O Pulpo Gallego bar and waiting for one of the taxi drivers who were around to give him an errand to run, Jacinto glanced at one of the free newspapers distributed in the city. He was really interested in the sports pages, but when he took the daily from the pile on the bar, the photograph on the front page caught his eye. The face of that terrified man immediately rang a bell and Jacinto's heart started to thud.

Jacinto had two assets: he didn't need to look at the clock to know the exact time within two or three minutes and he had a photographic memory. No doubt, if he'd been born into a different family, someone would have noticed his powers of recall and turned him into a valuable academic asset, but the only university in his neighbourhood was on the Carrer Entença. As soon as he saw the photo, Jacinto felt on edge because he recognized the guy at once: it was the man he'd taken to the Up & Down club the previous week when he was driving Sebastià's taxi, and the same man who, in an amazing coincidence, hailed him a couple of hours later on the Diagonal and asked to be dropped off at the Ritz.

Jacinto had realized it was the same customer, but as he was driving Sebastià's taxi illegally and tried to pass unnoticed by his customers, he said nothing. He also remembered how, when they were approaching the Ritz, he had been slightly alarmed to see half a dozen police cars and an ambulance parked in front of the entrance, and how, as a precautionary measure, he'd decided to drop his customer two hundred metres further on and make himself scarce as fast as traffic regulations allowed. Jacinto didn't possess a driving licence, only a shoddy fake based on his brother-in-law's, and if they caught him, the judge would more than likely put him inside for another stretch. After doing five years, he wasn't too sure he could stand it or that his family would continue to support him.

Although he didn't usually drink in the morning, he ordered a cognac and started to read the news story. That fellow, apparently a writer by the name of Amadeu, was being held in custody, accused of murdering a famous woman writer. The police were looking for an eyewitness to confirm his alibi, but didn't seem very hopeful. Jacinto looked at the photo again and swallowed. He knew from experience that customers rarely looked their taxi drivers in the face, but he couldn't be absolutely sure. Besides, this guy, who looked freaked out, must be having a really bad time in the Model, a place he knew only too well. He understood the responsibility that had now fallen on his shoulders and felt weighed down. Without more ado, he decided to order another cognac and ring his brother-in-law.

"Sebas, I must see you. It's important. Where are you?"

"Taking customers to Plaça Adrià. I'll be with you in five minutes."

"When you're done, switch the 'vacant' sign off and come to Cisco's bar. This is an emergency," he said gloomily.

"Yes, sir. I'll be with you in twenty minutes."

Sebastià was slightly uneasy. What had his brother-in-law done now? He hoped the emergency didn't mean he needed cash, or that he'd got into a tangle and expected him to come to the rescue. If it weren't for his sister and their two children... Basically, thought Sebastià, his brother-in-law wasn't a bad character, but he *was* good at landing himself in trouble. And, as everyone agreed, he was unlucky.

It took less than fifteen minutes to get to Cisco's bar. While Sebastià gulped down a beer and waited for his pork-and-pepper roll, Jacinto told him what was stressing him out, whispering so the other customers, mostly taxi drivers, in the bar couldn't hear. Sebastià listened carefully and felt relieved.

"The guy couldn't have killed her," Jacinto explained nervously. "I picked him up on the Gran Via and later on the Diagonal. The second time he was really in a bad way and he told me he'd been mugged. He was also slightly drunk."

"That's OK then. Someone else will remember him and tell the police," responded Sebastià, rather disconcerted.

"I thought I should..." Jacinto hesitated.

"That you should go to the police and tell them you were driving my taxi that night? Forget it. You'll do no such thing. If they find out you sometimes drive my taxi on the side... I'd lose my licence and you'd go straight back in the clink." And he added, "Cinto, you can't do that to us, either to me or to your wife. Do you really want to go back to the Model?"

"Of course I don't. I just wanted to know what you thought..."

"Keep quiet" was the message. Jacinto decided he'd change Cisco's bar for Antonio's for a few days, where they only had *Sport* and *The Sporting World*. As his brother-in-law had advised, he should forget that business and avoid the daily papers for a while. He had enough worries, apart from a criminal record, and the last thing he needed was an encounter with a shirty magistrate. So a rich woman writer had been murdered in a luxury hotel? Well, that didn't affect him or his struggle to keep afloat. His brother-in-law was right: sooner or later they'd find someone else to confirm the fellow's alibi and he'd be let out of the slammer. There must be a bunch of eyewitnesses. No need to worry.

But Jacinto suspected it wouldn't be so easy for him to forget the fear-filled eyes he'd seen in the newspaper that he now knew belonged to a man called Amadeu Cabestany. In the evening when he and Sebastià met up again at the family's St John's Eve party, they looked askance at each other but didn't mention the issue again. There was nothing more to say. However, that year Jacinto let off fewer crackers than usual, drank more cava than he could handle and was less interested in the generous bosoms being displayed by his sisters-in-law. The next morning, after getting up with a slight hangover and washing his face with cold water, he looked in the mirror and acknowledged that that man's features were as sharply defined as ever in his head, as if someone had super-glued them to each and every one of his neurones.

13

The first St John's Eve that Amadeu Cabestany spent in prison hardly warranted a firework display. He'd been shut up in the Model for six days, in a cell in the fifth gallery, and he was frightened to death. They'd accused him of a murder he hadn't committed and, for the first time in his life, this great fan of Kafka found himself in a Kafkaesque situation and wasn't at all amused. Amadeu had devoted many, many pages of his novels to cheerful themes like death, solitude and sorrow, and courageously explored in his labyrinthine prose the anguished tragedy of the human condition. Nevertheless, he now knew that nothing he'd written remotely resembled the nausea he'd been feeling from Sunday morning as a result of his imprisonment. In the Model, no less, a place that no longer harboured Republicans and Romantic anti-Franco fighters, but thieves, junkies and renowned killers belonging to merciless mafias. For the moment, none of Amadeu's sombre reflections made captivity more tolerable or helped him confront that nightmare with a brave heart, quite the contrary. Lucid appreciation of the world as a perverse place dominated by evil – and, in the specific case of the Model, thought Amadeu, by delinquents who probably hid a sharp knife under their blankets – prevented him from grasping at any fragile straws of hope.

With the exception of Clàudia his agent, everybody seemed convinced he was guilty, from his colleagues at the school where he taught to his wife who was threatening him with divorce. Amadeu was facing the real possibility that he might be tried for murder and sentenced to years and years in the slammer, and it was no foregone conclusion in his case that a long stay in jail would inspire a new *Death of Virgil*. Existence was surely an onerous burden driven by egotism and perversity, as he himself had written so often, but in the few days he'd been in prison, Amadeu had discovered it was easier to bear that particular burden in his little flat in Vic than in a filthy, grey cell that stank of disinfectant. And true enough, free will was an illusion and life was basically a swamp of misery, as he had affirmed so often, following Schopenhauer, but now, after five days of being shut up on the Carrer Entença, surrounded by delinquents towering at least half a metre above him, Amadeu was in no doubt at all it was infinitely preferable to savour the angst of existence with the help of a plate of local sausages and suffer the traumas of life with the aid of a bottle of wine from the Priorat.

He was surrounded by gross, unhinged men, their tattooed hides toughened by experience, who regarded him with a mixture of envy and contempt. Most were foreigners, but there were a lot of locals too and they were the ones who scared the novelist the most, perhaps because, if he tried hard, he could understand a little of what they said. With that white skin of his, his smart haircut and the build of a gentleman who'd never got a hernia shifting bricks or acting criminally, Amadeu was soon the object of the mockery and insults of the other prisoners. He spent the first few days on the point of collapse, like a sleepwalker, shaking like a leaf as he waited for the moment when one of those hulks – or perhaps more than one – raped him, beat him or stuck a knife between his ribs. In fact things weren't like that any more in the Model, but Amadeu had seen too many repeats of *Midnight Express* on the TV and was terrified.

By the third day, although still in a state of shock, Amadeu realized that a change was taking place in the attitude of the other inmates, particularly among those who shared a cell with him. They'd simply stopped scorning and insulting him, and seemed clearly to be avoiding him and even looked at him with loathing. But Amadeu remained silent, shit-scared, and though his state of acute panic prevented him from thinking clearly (that wasn't a strong point of his, by the way) he concluded that that gang of barbarians were plotting something. He felt alone and defenceless, a white explorer in the hands of a savage tribe in the middle of the jungle, unable to decipher its language or make himself understood; they'd soon do a boil-up and he'd be the prime ingredient. Yes, he reflected as he curled up in a corner of his cell, he'd ended up in the heart of darkness, except that in that prison there wasn't one Kurtz but hundreds. On the other hand, his cellmates eyed him suspiciously and reckoned they were the ones sentenced to live cheek by jowl with a monster. Amadeu didn't know this, but a rumour had begun to spread around the fifth gallery and the inmates had nicknamed him Hannibal.

The rumour soon reached the ears of the prison administrators. Educated on progressive ideas about rehabilitation and faith in occupational therapies, many of them members of various NGOs in their spare time, the prison warders had initially felt sympathetic towards him and his appearance as a disoriented, radical member of the provincial bourgeoisie. However, they soon began to change their tune. It was obvious their superiors were hiding something and that the rumour circulating within the prison walls wasn't simply the product of the devious imaginations of the inmates. The latter couldn't fathom the presence of a person like Amadeu, the perpetrator of a particularly brutal murder, in the Model, and they unconsciously began to apply the laws of Gestalt psychology and elaborate their own explanation in order to fit the facts together and endow them with a minimal logic. First of all, after one of the inmates had made the effort to read the news item in the paper and pass it on to his friends, the story did the rounds that Amadeu had killed the woman by smashing her head in with an apple. Shortly after, maybe as the result of underachievement at school, the prisoner who read the story didn't understand it properly and a fresh version began to circulate according to which Amadeu had taken a bite from the bloody apple after committing the crime. The day after, the story that spread throughout the Model was that the cannibal had eaten apple and scraps of raw brain.

On Thursday morning, during their yard-break, the jail-birds argued heatedly, as if possessed by the spirit of the *Lord of the Flies*. Some said Amadeu had used a Golden Delicious, because one of them, an expert jewel thief, recalled that "golden" meant " in Catalan, which is the colour of those apples. Some maintained it was Royal Gala, and others were adamant, with considerably more insight, that it was a Fuji, because it was common knowledge that Fuji apples are bigger and harder. On the other hand, they very quickly put his lack of appetite (Amadeu hardly tasted prison fodder, and when he did so, soon threw it up) to the fact that the balanced diet served in jail couldn't satisfy his depraved culinary tastes. Amadeu didn't know it, but Doctor Hannibal Lecter, from within the world of fiction, was saving his arse, if not his life.

The inmates couldn't wrap their heads around the fact that Amadeu Cabestany looked like a well-educated, well-off, cultured man, and so might be a computer hacker or corrupt politician but not a brutal murderer. The Model was home to men sent down for theft, rape, drug-trafficking and blood-curdling crimes, but none were writers and none passed through the prison gates elegantly dressed in black from head to toe. Besides, Amadeu didn't speak Spanish, Arab, Russian or Albanian, or any of the languages one could hear in that Babel of a jail. To be sure, he hardly ever spoke, but when he did, he did so in Catalan, and that disconcerted them even more. No doubt, he was the most eccentric prisoner they'd ever seen, as, so they thought, he seemed like a normal person. And as, by chance, they'd seen *The Silence of the Lambs* on television in their leisure time, the figure of that revenge-seeking cannibal persuaded some of their untutored minds to add one and one together and come up with two. Amadeu Cabestany the writer was in fact a refined criminal, endowed with an intellect as exceptional and perverse as Dr Lecter's, and consequently a cannibal, as they confused the prize trophy and the apple. And as cannibalism is an activity that is almost universally believed to be repulsive, capable of making the most hardened murderers vomit, everyone began to avoid him like the plague. What's more, his rather frail physique supported the hypothesis that he had a twisted, evil mind, capable of tremendous deviousness. Naturally, after reaching these conclusions that everybody thought extremely reasonable, no one at the Model wanted to have any dealings with him. No one, that is, except for Knocksie, who tried to befriend him.

Knocksie was in the same gallery as Amadeu but not in the same cell. That meant they had the same mealtimes and yard-time. He was a straightforward psychopath, but neither the health authorities nor the conservative judge that sentenced him were at all sure that he was mad enough to rate being shut up in the psychiatric ward in Can Brians. He'd been given thirty years for raping, murdering and carving up two old dears who were over eighty, and was waiting for the judiciary to pronounce their verdict on three similar crimes. Knocksie was thirty-three and had spent sixteen years in reformatory, the Model and other penitentiary establishments. Apart from the times when the psychologist was dealing with him, he spent his nights and most of his days alone, morbidly relishing his past butchery and dreaming of repeating his feats as soon as he got out. The judge had insisted, against the advice of some psychiatrists, that Knocksie perfectly recognized the difference between good and evil, and he'd ended up in the Model. The fact his junkie parents had abandoned him as a baby and that as a kid he'd been raped and mistreated by his own grandparents seemed irrelevant to the judge, although that's where he'd got his nickname from: from childhood he'd always been knocked to bits.

Those beatings had made him an incurable psychopath, deprived him of a number of teeth, and given him a coronary condition that his fondness for drugs only exacerbated.

Knocksie had no friends in the prison, and Amadeu's alleged cannibalism didn't scare him, rather it intrigued him. Maybe the next time he'd try the liver or heart of the next old lady who came by, he pondered while he listened warmly to the atrocities they accused Amadeu of, who seemed to have tasted more of his victims' organs by the hour. When they were in the yard on Friday morning, while Amadeu was silently lamenting that he'd have no cake or crackers that year, and that, on the contrary, someone might land him with Aids or lethal hepatitis, Knocksie attempted to strike up a conversation. Amadeu didn't seem in the least bit communicative, but, when he wanted, Knocksie could be polite and pleasant, and Amadeu felt infinitely lonely. After a kind of exchange in the form of a monologue on the part of Knocksie and monosyllables on the part of Amadeu, Knocksie offered him a cigarette that he accepted with alacrity.

The rest of the inmates weren't at all surprised that the two basket cases had linked up in that strange way, and the warders took note of the new and dangerous friendship. Naturally, Amadeu had no idea who Knocksie was and swallowed whole the story the latter told him: he was a third-rate thief who'd unluckily harmed, quite unawares, one of his victims while burgling a chalet under the influence of drugs in order to feed his family.

But something happened on Saturday that shocked everyone stiff and convinced inmates and administrators alike that the rumour circulating inside about Amadeu, now referred to by everyone as Hannibal, was the tip of the iceberg of the atrocities being attributed to him. When they went into the yard at about eleven that morning, Knocksie went over to Amadeu again and they started to chat. The psychopath was desperate to hear the most blood-curdling details of Marina Dolç's death agony, but, as the writer insisted he was innocent and as Knocksie didn't want to arouse the suspicions of his new friend, he thought it better to backtrack. Amadeu was beginning to like Knocksie, and gradually confided in him more. He told him he was married, lived in Vic and had two lovely daughters, and confirmed that he was a famous writer. Knocksie was intrigued and asked what kind of things he wrote, and Amadeu, comforted by the sight of someone taking a genuine interest in his work, told him he wrote novels and poetry. Death, grief and the slavery to sex were the main themes in his work, which unfortunately few readers knew how to appreciate. Mentally, Knocksie rubbed his hands and licked his lips. His friend was better than he'd ever imagined and a present straight from hell to satisfy his own lusts. The other inmates, who kept well away, were astounded by the pair's animated conversation and the warders were thinking that nothing good could come from it.

Knocksie crossed his legs and tried to hide the vigorous erection that had suddenly hit him and made an effort to ensure his nervous smile didn't betray him. He asked his friend to tell him more about his books. Surprised and flattered, Amadeu offered to recite a poem and Knocksie was delighted. The rest of the prisoners, standing a prudent distance away, couldn't hear what they were saying, but saw Amadeu move his lips rhythmically while Knocksie listened in a trance. Five minutes later, Knocksie collapsed to the ground, the victim of a heart attack.

Everybody realized what had happened. Just as in the film they'd seen a few days before, their Hannibal had related something that was so scary that Knocksie hadn't committed suicide but had had a cardiac arrest. The prison medical services could do nothing to revive him, despite trying mouth-to-mouth resuscitation and rushing to inject him straight in the heart. Knocksie was as dead as a doornail and everybody was staring at Amadeu.

It was futile for the writer from Vic to try to explain he had simply recited his long poem, 'The Exposed Entrails of the Night', which he was particularly proud of, or for the doctor to allude to contributing factors to the inmate's coronary condition such as his addiction to cigarettes and drugs. The incident reached the ears of the Director, who hurriedly got in touch with the judge in charge of the case and told her there was something extremely odd about that prisoner. He'd found out that the other inmates were sure – he supposed with some reason – that Amadeu Cabestany possessed cannibal instincts, and, as the warders had seen with the incident of Knocksie's death, he was a manipulator who possessed lethally seductive powers. The judge was livid, because it was a holiday and she was on duty; she had the request for bail for Amadeu on the table in front of her and took note. She pondered for fifteen seconds, wrinkled her nose as if that case stank to high heaven and finally threw out the defence's request. She would cover her back. Amadeu Cabestany would remain in custody in the Model until that grisly incident was cleared up.

Fortunately, the incident of Knocksie's death didn't reach the press. However, given that, apart from its saints, Vic is famous for its sausages and slaughterhouses, the judge thought the case through and asked the prosecutor to send some of his officers to the capital, and, covering all possible leads, to open a new line of investigation. It wouldn't be the first time a new crime had served to resolve cases that were on file, and if it turned out that Amadeu Cabestany was a psychotic writer who travelled the world murdering other writers and masticating Catalans, the judge, an able, right-wing, methodical woman, wanted to ensure none of that shit rubbed off on her and that any scandal forthcoming wouldn't catch *her* with her knickers down.

14

Deputy-Inspector Maria del Mar Alsina-Graells, of the *Mossos d'Esquadra* of the Generalitat, was twenty-nine and had been assigned twenty-five-year-old Marc Serra to accompany her on this mission. It was Tuesday, and as one thing always leads to another, Maria del Mar's period had started the moment she went to get the patrol car to drive to Vic. She and Marc were the *mossos* charged with starting "that second line of investigations just in case", as her boss had described it the day before while putting Maria del Mar in the picture and telling her what she was expected to do. Visibly in a foul temper at having to go to Vic and suffering that untimely onset from her female metabolism, she went to the lavatory to insert a Tampax and take an Espidifen while she was about it, which would make her slightly hazy but would at least curb the stabbing pain in her nether regions. She asked her colleague to drive, without telling him why, and spent the whole journey smouldering in a sulky silence. She found Serra intolerable, perhaps because he was a good lad but rather slow on the uptake, or perhaps because he always seemed to accompany her the day her period started and she was beginning to think the two things were related. Maria del Mar and her husband, who also a *mosso*, wanted to have a child, and it wasn't going to plan. If Maria del Mar was usually in a bad mood when menstruating, for the last year she'd been extremely irritable, worryingly so, on such occasions.

"Anything wrong, Maria del Mar? Don't you feel well?" Serra asked, genuinely concerned to see his colleague looking so sour.

"Concentrate on the road and don't give me hassle. I just want us to do a good job, so don't land us in it and don't speak to me," she cut him dead.

Serra had landed them in it a couple of times, which was perfectly understandable if you considered how he'd only just joined the force and was still in his probationary period. Thanks to his well-exercised athletic physique – over one metre ninety with impressive pecs – he'd passed the physical tests with flying colours. He'd struggled, however, with the intelligence and psychometric tests. But the boy was from Badalona, from a well-connected family, and as there wasn't much to choose from among the candidates, the examiners decided to turn a blind eye, let him pass and see what happened. The truth was he wasn't performing so badly, except when he had to work with Deputy-Inspector Maria del Mar, because then he became stressed and did and said foolish things. Serra had no idea about the Deputy-Inspector's maternal frustrations, and, although he knew she was married to an inspector and he himself had a steady girlfriend, he looked at her as any young heterosexual man looks at a pretty woman who deliberately mistreats him: with desire and deep admiration.

"You look on the pale side, Maria del Mar," her colleague insisted.

"Deputy-Inspector Alsina-Graells, if you don't mind, Serra. And stop getting on my nerves."

"Hell, I'm really sorry. It's just that everyone calls you Maria del Mar..."

The aspiring *mosso* Marc Serra decided it would be better to shut up and concentrate on his driving. The Deputy-Inspector was clearly not having a good day. Better not harass her. If she wanted him quiet, he'd keep quiet, but for heaven's sake it wouldn't do any harm if she told him what the hell they were going to investigate in Vic when they had Marina Dolç's murderer locked up in the Model.

"Mrs... I mean, Deputy-Inspector, at least you could tell me why we're going to Vic," he asked just as they were almost there.

"Serra, I'm sorry, I've got a very bad headache today." That seemed like an apology. "You're right, I should tell you what it's all about."

She paused, wondering how to angle her explanation. She didn't want to frighten her colleague, but sooner or later he would have to know the kind of monster they were after in Vic. She knew that Serra had been assigned to her for two reasons: first, because he'd studied Catalan literature, since both victim and suspect were writers; second (and this was her assumption), because he was as tall as a lamp post with a useful physique if anyone tried to mix it.

"Don't get into a state," the Deputy-Inspector began, "but there are rumours going around that this isn't the first murder committed by the suspect. Moreover, the rumours point to him having rather strange eating habits."

"You mean he's vegetarian? That he prefers a macrobiotic menu?" suggested Serra, for whom a jamón serrano roll or Majorcan spicy meat were pure ambrosia.

"No, Serra, by strange, I mean strange. Cannibalistic, to be precise."

"Fuck!… I mean, heavens!"

"It's important not to alarm anyone, right? We've got to approach the matter with the utmost tact. Imagine the panic that might spread through Vic if this news got out."

"Count on me," Serra assured her. "I give you my word."

Suddenly, as if the news the Deputy-Inspector had given him had hit home, Serra gave a start.

"But we won't find anything nasty in Vic, will we? I did what the psychologist told me and went to see lots of films full of blood and guts, but I still can't get used to…" he said anxiously, beginning to sweat.

"Serra, if you faint like last time, I swear I'll put in a complaint and get you expelled from the force. Who's ever heard of a *mosso* who's afraid of a drop of blood?"

"*Doña,* if it's a small wound… But I really can't stand mutilated bodies or corpses that have been opened up down the middle. I told the shrink that."

"Psychologist, Serra, psychologist!"

"Sorry, Deputy-Inspector. Do you want me to park here?"

Deputy-Inspector Alsina-Graells had decided they would first visit Amadeu Cabestany's home to talk to his wife. It was half-past ten and she knew Mrs Cabestany didn't go out to work. She hoped she'd not gone shopping or taken her daughters for a walk.

"Don't you think it would be better to ring first?" asked Serra, who wasn't as dim-witted as the Deputy-Inspector thought.

"I'd rather catch her by surprise and not give her time to think... Serra, not a word about the cannibalism business, right?"

"Don't you worry, boss."

After checking it was the right address, the Deputy-Inspector knocked at the door. Mrs Cabestany – Clara to her friends – opened it immediately, and as soon as she saw a couple of *mossos* in uniform, she looked even more stressed. She was wearing no make-up, had bags under her eyes and looked tired. She seemed to have lost several kilos in a few days, because the clothes she was wearing – jeans and a crumpled, short-sleeved blouse – looked big on her. Her hair was dyed brown but a closer look revealed a number of grey roots. She'd obviously not been to the hairdresser's or bothered to see to her hair herself, so she looked both down and dowdy. The Deputy-Inspector, who'd attended a course on the subject, realized she was thoroughly depressed and made a mental note of *her* state of mind. After introducing herself and showing her badge, she politely enquired whether she could ask a few questions, but didn't seem to leave her any option.

"Come in, if you wish, I don't know what else I can tell you..." she said nervously as she ushered them into her living room. "Are there any developments? Have they let him go?"

The Deputy-Inspector shook her head. The Cabestanys lived in a smallish, very central flat that was modestly but tastefully decorated. In the living room there were a couple of ashtrays full of butts and a number of strategically scattered boxes of tissues. The walls were lined with bookshelves, mostly poetry written or translated into Catalan, while the smell of stew from the kitchen made Serra feel peckish.

"The girls are on a school trip. They'll be back this evening..." she explained as she invited them to sit down and made every effort not to burst into tears. "Well, if there are no developments, you must tell me what you want to know."

"This is a routine check," began the Deputy-Inspector, trying to use a light touch. "I know your husband is currently the main suspect, but that doesn't mean we can't find new evidence that could lead us to rethink our investigation," she declared as if she were quite convinced of that.

"But do you think he did it?" piped up Clara as she dried her eyes with a tissue.

"Do *you* think he is capable of doing such a thing, Mrs Cabestany?" asked the Deputy-Inspector, intelligently firing her question back at her.

Tears streamed down Clara's cheeks again, but she tried to stay strong. Her world had collapsed on her eleven days ago, and she'd been trying to answer that question ever since. Could her husband, who was so sensitive and vulnerable, smash a woman's head in? She should have said: "Of course not! My Amadeu couldn't kill a fly! You're crazy!" But she didn't. In fact, Clara was absolutely beside herself.

"I... would never have imagined he could do such a thing," she mumbled, "but if the police are so certain... he'd set so much store by that prize!..."

"So you did know about it."

"Not exactly. I knew he'd been acting strange for days, but he'd not said anything to me about entering for a prize. He told me just before going to Barcelona." She seemed slightly resentful. "When he did so, he told me he knew for sure that he'd won and made me promise not to tell anyone. Poor fellow! He seemed so sure he'd get it!..."

"And had you noticed anything strange recently? I mean, were you having any problems, was he spending lots of time away from home or did he seem unusually hungry?..." she asked tactfully.

"'Did he seem unusually hungry?...' What do you mean?" The question not only sounded stupid, it *was* stupid.

"Mrs Cabestany." The effect of the painkiller the Deputy-Inspector had taken was beginning to wear off and she was on the verge of showing her foul temper. "We are the ones asking the questions, if you don't mind. Now, does your husband like cooking?"

"Does he like cooking? How the hell is that relevant?"

"Just please give me your answer," said Deputy-Inspector Maria del Mar, getting increasingly agitated. "Any small detail can be vital."

"Well, he sometimes cooks, when his friends or the family come for lunch..." she admitted, rather put out. "He always cooks the paella. And his pasta dishes are always very good. But why do you need to know?"

"And is he a hearty eater? Does he like gutting chickens or chopping up rabbits?" the Deputy-Inspector persisted, unable to think of any better way of broaching the suspect's culinary preferences.

"Look, miss, I don't know what all this is leading up to, but —" Clara was beginning to think, quite reasonably, that these *mossos* were making fun of her.

"Deputy-Inspector. I am a Deputy-Inspector. Please answer the question or —"

"I know these questions may seem strange, Mrs Cabestany," intervened Serra diplomatically, "but we are trying to assess your husband's personality using the latest test from the United States to determine whether he's the kind of person who is capable of committing a crime."

On this occasion, the Deputy-Inspector gave her colleague a look of gratitude. She was conscious her foul mood had been about to divert the conversation down a cul-de-sac. All in all, that boy wasn't perhaps as simple as she'd thought.

"All right then… If it's a test from the US… Amadeu never cleans anything, chicken, rabbit or whatever. He likes to cook, but he's one of those men who needs helpers, if you know what I mean…" she added, trying to smile through her tears.

"And has your husband been coming home later than usual or behaving strangely?" continued the Deputy-Inspector, making an effort to soften her tone of voice.

"You mean is he having an affair?" The Deputy-Inspector hadn't in fact been thinking of that possibility, but rather whether he disappeared now and then to go down to the woods or elsewhere to prepare a *carpaccio* of human flesh. "Well, I'm not entirely sure there isn't something going on with Clàudia what's-her-name, the woman who acts as his agent." She paused to smile her long-suffering smile. "You know what it's like being married to a writer… The fact is, I prefer not to know. We have two daughters, and I'm not… I wasn't prepared to break up my marriage if I found out he was carrying on with someone. If it was just an affair…" she shrugged her shoulders and wiped her eyes again.

Most conveniently, the telephone rang at that moment. Clara Cabestany whispered, "Excuse me," and went to pick the phone up. From the one side of the conversation she could hear, the Deputy-Inspector deduced it was a relative or friend who wanted to know how she was or if she had any news. Clara ended the conversation with the excuse that someone was knocking at the door. She didn't want to have to embark on explanations about the fact that two *mossos* were interrogating her about her husband's culinary preferences or his little bit on the side.

"That's a really nice smell coming from the kitchen," said the Deputy-Inspector. "Have you by any chance got one of those freezers that are the size of a wardrobe?" she asked, trying to make her question sound innocent enough, but it didn't work.

"A freezer the size of a wardrobe? You must be joking!... I don't know how we'd fit one into this flat." Mrs Cabestany was beginning to think Deputy-Inspector Alsina-Graells wasn't right in the head. "Why on earth do you ask such a question?"

"The Deputy-Inspector is thinking of buying one and can't make her mind up about which make..." lied Serra.

They all went silent, not knowing what to say next. As Deputy-Inspector Alsina-Graells couldn't ask Amadeu Cabestany's wife to her face whether her husband was in the habit of keeping human organs in their refrigerator or had any favourite cut for a *Sapiens sapiens* steak, she was at a loss about how to proceed. She was livid, and to a point it was justified. It was absurd what she had been asked to do! Her superiors had sent her to Vic to investigate whether there was any truth in the rumour relating to the suspect in the Marina Dolç case and cannibalistic practices, but what the hell did they expect her to do? The Deputy-Inspector knew there was someone behind that order who simply wanted to cover their backs in case they came under fire in the future. Someone who could put on record that he'd sent a couple of *mossos* to Vic to investigate and spare himself any responsibility if the shit hit the fan.

"We'll leave you in peace now." The Deputy-Inspector began to head for the door. "By the way, how old are your daughters?" she asked, looking tenderly at the photo of the two girls in the entrance hall.

"Eulàlia will be eight next month and Lara five in October," Clara said, bursting into tears again. "I do hope this turns out to be one big mistake. Just imagine, having to live in this place, with their father on murder charges..."

Deputy-Inspector Maria del Mar, who was from Cardedeu, preferred not to imagine what that would be like. She knew from experience how quickly towns and small cities could become hellish. If she'd not been in uniform, she'd have advised her to change city, to go to Barcelona, as she had, or to any city where no one knew her and where people had better things to do than interfere in other people's lives. But she didn't say a word. Vic was a small city, a wealthy, conservative city, and the honest locals wouldn't forget a homicidal neighbour overnight. What's more, if the rumours about Amadeu Cabestany's cannibalistic tendencies were confirmed, those girls and their distraught mother they had just questioned would soon need good psychological support and a place where they could start afresh. The Deputy-Inspector sympathized mentally with Clara Cabestany, while she wondered, wracked by doubt, if bringing children into the world was really worthwhile: a world packed with violent murderers, pederasts, rapists and now even... cannibals. Not to mention drugs and prostitutes. What was the statistical probability her son or daughter, if she finally did manage to procreate, would bump into one such felon before his or her eighth birthday. One in a thousand? In two thousand? In a hundred thousand? Deputy-Inspector Maria del Mar decided she'd consult the statistics as soon as she was back at the station.

"Where are we heading now?" asked Serra when they were back in the car.

"To the suspect's school. They're expecting us at twelve thirty," she said, looking at her watch and seeing they only had fifteen minutes.

They were there in five. They were met by a tall, thin, fair-haired man with a beard, who introduced himself as the Director of Studies. Joan Tamariu was forty-two and a maths teacher. He was wearing old jeans, a faded sky-blue T-shirt imprinted with an image from a comic and red Old Star shoes. From behind his spectacles, his deep blue eyes made the Deputy-Inspector flip. It had been a long time since anyone had looked at her like that and she felt weak at the knees.

By that stage in June, classes and exams were over and hardly anyone was at the school. The headmaster was on a training course in Barcelona and there were only two porters about. Not a single pupil was to be seen. The Director of Studies explained he was getting next year's timetables ready, took them to his office and asked them to sit down.

"Reconciling timetables is a sight more difficult than solving a murder case, I can tell you..." he smiled as he moved aside the rocky piles of paper heaped on his desk.

"You're the Director of Studies, so I assume you must be well acquainted with Amadeu Cabestany?" began the Deputy-Inspector.

"The fact is that I'm in Social Sciences and don't really have much contact with Cabestany," he said, still staring deep into her eyes. "I'm really sorry, but I've not been able to track down a single one of his colleagues from the literature department now classes have finished..."

"I'm fucked if I'm going to the school on Tuesday to talk to the police about that shit Cabestany" and "I don't care a fuck about that stuck-up sod Cabestany and besides I've got an appointment with my depilator tomorrow" had more or less been the responses he'd got from teachers in the department when he rang to ask them to drop by the school on Tuesday.

"What we'd really like to know is what kind of person Amadeu Cabestany is," said the Deputy-Inspector, taking the initiative. "If he's liked by his colleagues, if he's peculiar in any way..."

"Well, he's quite withdrawn. We call him 'The Marquis' in private."

"Marquis de Sade... sadism," reflected the Deputy-Inspector. "I suppose," added the Director of Studies, shrugging his shoulders, "that he thinks he's a literary genius, condemned to earn his bread teaching a collection of ignoramuses. But I wouldn't say he's any more peculiar than the others. This school has its fair share of eccentrics."

"What do you mean exactly?"

"Well, the philosophy teacher talks to himself in the corridors… The Latin master washes his hands in the lavatories at least thirty times a day… The English teacher sometimes turns up dressed as a drag queen…"

"In other words, you're the only normal guy around here?" commented the Deputy-Inspector, ironically returning his look.

"I teach maths. That automatically makes me a baddie," he smiled. Serra got the impression the Director of Studies liked Deputy-Inspector Maria del Mar a lot.

"What about Amadeu Cabestany? Does he do strange things too?" continued the Deputy-Inspector.

"Well, Amadeu avoids his pupils like the plague and locks his office door as soon as he can. But he's a man who doesn't want any problems. He always passes everyone, even those who don't turn up for the exam. When the boys in his class are playing up, he lets them get on with it and simply starts reading. Reading his own stuff, I mean. We've had to warn him a couple of times on that count."

"Has he ever had problems with young pupils? I'm just asking, you know. I'm not suggesting anything," added the Deputy-Inspector.

"Well" – the Director of Studies shrugged his shoulders – "I don't know if he has ever had that kind of problem, but I can tell you if Amadeu had ever tried it on with a girl student, he'd have stopped after getting a good slap in the face. I mean, I can't imagine any of our students has ever felt the least attraction for someone like Amadeu, and, on the other hand, Amadeu is no Adonis physically speaking. Besides, I think the snide jokes (to put it politely) the students would crack in such a situation would soon come to the attention of the teachers. I have no memory of any complaints of this nature."

"Thank you very much. That's all we needed to know."

"I'll give you my telephone number, Deputy-Inspector, in case you want to meet and continue this conversation," said the Director of Studies, giving her a card. "Or if you ever come here as a tourist and want a dining partner."

"Thank you, but I'm married." The Deputy-Inspector blushed a deep red.

"So am I, don't worry. Monogamy is so boring..."

The Deputy-Inspector made it clear she was angry, but deep down she felt gratified. That maths teacher wasn't to be sniffed at. There was something interesting about him, and he was handsome into the bargain. She knew she'd never see him again, but she hoped his less than subtle insinuations came to the attention of her very busy husband. Her Jaume was always much more passionate when he had a reason to be jealous.

"Heavens, Maria del Mar, that guy wanted to date you..." said Serra as they went to get into the car.

"You men are a bunch of rogues..." she smiled back at him. "Come on, Serra, time for lunch."

They went to a restaurant with a set menu. While they waited for their lunch to be served, the Deputy-Inspector told her colleague the Vic police had reported that an old man diagnosed with Alzheimer's had disappeared five months ago and was still missing. A nineteen-year-old girl who lived at home and wanted to be a model had also disappeared, but she'd taken a couple of suitcases and made off with her parents' savings, a couple of conservative reactionaries who reckoned the Liberal Democrats were on the extreme left and tried to avoid contact with immigrants lest they be de-Catalanized. The Deputy-Inspector was whispering, because she was aware the other diners were staring at her with their antennae on full alert.

"I don't think there can be any connection between these two disappearances and our suspect," she added, "but you never know. Maybe he turned them into sushi..."

Their first course was boiled cauliflower, followed by *butifarra* and beans. As they were on duty, they had to stick to mineral water. Deputy-Inspector Maria del Mar ordered ice cream for dessert and Serra, who was slightly sweeter-toothed, went for the home-made cake. Before they left the restaurant, while Serra was finishing the camomile infusion he had ordered to help his digestion, and was the object of the quizzical glances of the locals, the Deputy-Inspector went to the lavatory to change her Tampax.

"What about a little glass of something for the road, sir? On the house," asked the bar-owner.

"No thank you! I'm on duty," Serra answered, pleased by the suggestion.

"I guess you're investigating the case of that writer murdered in Barcelona?"

"Well... no... I mean, yes..."

"Amadeu didn't seem such a bad lad," the bar-owner continued casually. "Rather full of himself, perhaps, but I'd never have said he could do anything like that. Obviously, appearances can deceive, can't they?"

"Yes... I mean, no... Well... In fact, it's all rumours really," Serra was starting to sound nervous. "I mean we're not sure the other disappearances have anything to do with any crime or the suspect."

"That's right, the Valls' daughter. Good people... In other words, the police suspect that maybe..."

"No, not at all, all I said was..."

At that moment the Deputy-Inspector emerged from the lavatory and walked emphatically towards their table. The bar-owner knew he wouldn't extract any more information from the *mosso* with her around and decided to retreat to the bar. He'd realized the woman was in charge and that her colleague was very green.

"Well, Serra? How about it?"

"Right you are!" responded Serra, standing up, relieved because he was sure the Deputy-Inspector wouldn't have approved of that rather rash conversation he'd just been having with the bar-owner. "You see, Maria del Mar?" he began euphorically when they reached the door. "I didn't drop us in it this time. Nobody's realized we came to Vic to investigate whether Amadeu Cabestany is a cannibal!"

The silence that descended on the bar would have been sepulchral if the television hadn't been switched on. Every head turned and Deputy-Inspector Maria del Mar Alsina-Graells felt her back being pierced by the gaze from four dozen bulging eyes. Luckily, it was her spirits that sank to her feet and not the Tampax, although it was a close thing. The Deputy-Inspector automatically closed her eyes and began to pray, begging the earth to swallow her up or to go back in time. It couldn't be. Within hours Cabestany's cannibalism was the talk of the town.

15

The news of Amadeu Cabestany's alleged habits was splashed over the following day's front pages and began to stress everyone out. First, Amadeu's lawyer and his wife, who was already flat out on their sofa after downing potent tranquillizers, and, naturally, the prosecution, the judge responsible for the case and the police. The stress translated into a series of furious calls to the Director of the Model demanding he find out where the fuck – to quote verbatim – that macabre story had come from and how it had got out. The forensic declared there wasn't the slightest sign of any cannibalistic practices on Marina Dolç's corpse, and the fact that the population of Vic were adamant one of their ranks was a depraved cannibal had a reasonable enough explanation if one considered how an aspiring *mosso* had blurted out and kick-started the rumour, as more than a dozen eyewitnesses could confirm. Amadeu, who'd also glanced at the story in the paper before a disgruntled inmate took it and graphically indicated what he used the dailies for when going to the lavatory, thought the description of cannibal was a metaphor referring to his use of tradition and literary sources, which hardly made his day. It was fine to say he was inspired by his favourite authors but not that he devoured them like a cannibal, as the article suggested.

Everybody in the Model had seen Amadeu Cabestany's photo on the front pages and it had created a real fuss. The director had shut himself away in his office at dawn and had ordered his minions to open an investigation to find the source of a rumour that, judging by the judge's hysterical screams from the other end of the line, could cost him his career. Two hours later, his minions were unanimously agreed that all the evidence pointed to Paquito Expósito, a prisoner in the fifth gallery.

"Bring him to my office immediately," spat out the director.

The director was aware that all that mess was his fault, and was very worried. If he had bitten his tongue, rather than rushing to ring the judge in order to impress her... But that was ancient history and perhaps there was a perfectly reasonable explanation. Anyway, he ruminated while waiting for Paquito, perhaps the cannibal story was true and he might get out of this shit almost unharmed. It was too much to believe that that bunch of brainless fools had invented the whole thing, and he was hoping Paquito Expósito would explain himself and help clear up the mystery.

"Come in, Paquito, sit down, please," the director began, trying to be pleasant when the latter knocked on his door.

"Very sorry, Director," responded Paquito limply. "I didn't know what it was all about, except that I'd put my foot in it."

Paquito Expósito had been in the Model five years. He was around fifty but looked ten years older. All his teeth were decayed and he was a former heroin addict inside for drug trafficking and the illegal possession of firearms. He had one year to go until his release, if he was lucky and didn't land himself in it. The director knew he was playing with an advantage.

"Come on, Paquito, tell me where the fuck this story about Amadeu Cabestany being a cannibal came from. I've heard it was you who spread the rumour..."

"You mean Hannibal? The lad in the fifth?"

"Yes, he's hardly been inside a fortnight," the director continued.

"But I ain't spread nowt, Director, sir. I swear I ain't. I just told a mate what I'd read in the newspaper."

"Paquito, the newspaper didn't say Amadeu Cabestany was a cannibal." The director knew he had to be patient with Paquito.

"Oh, yes, it did, Director, sir! Maybe not like that, but that's what it said: that he'd bashed a woman to death with an apple. I read that. And the guy ate the apple."

"What do you mean, he ate the apple? Where did you get that from?"

"The photo," responded Paquito, as if it were self-evident. "You could see from the photo that he'd bitten a chunk out."

"But Paquito, it wasn't a real apple. It was a statue. A prize."

"Nah. How could he bite it if it woz a statue? Besides, excuse me, Director, sir but the prize woz wine."

"Wine? What do you mean, wine?" the director frowned.

"The paper said it plain enough: wine's the prize. And it must have been a good'un because it woz in capitals," Paquito wriggled his way out.

"This is beyond me."

Although the air-conditioning was blasting away, the director began to sweat. He now had an inkling it was all one massive misunderstanding that had snowballed and snowballed because no one had bothered to stop it in its tracks.

"Director, sir," the minion who was standing by the door interrupted his flow of thought, "perhaps Paquito is referring to the fact it was the sixth Golden Apple award, which was written in Roman letters and could be read as 'VI' in capitals." This minion was a marine biologist who had rashly returned from the States a couple of years ago, hadn't found a decent job anywhere and had ended up getting a post in a prison.

"You see? VI, I told you so." Paquito's self-image was immediately boosted. "The prize woz wine. You're Catalan, ain't you? You should know what 'VI' means!"

"My God, how idiotic!..." muttered the director. "But what about Cabestany eating brains? Don't tell me you read that in the newspaper too?"

"Oh, I don't know nowt about that," Paquito retorted. "I reckon that's Cigala. He read the paper as well."

"You mean Raimundo Pérez, in the fourth gallery," clarified the minion.

"I know who you mean..." The director was starting to lose his patience and noticed how his blood pressure was momentarily going crazy. "But Paquito, that's impossible because Cigala is illiterate."

"And so what? That ain't no reason to be ashamed. The psychologist told us that," responded Paquito, proud that his therapy had come in useful at last.

"I mean, Paquito, that he's illiterate, he can't read the papers," answered the director, appealing to his common sense.

"Oh, yes, he can! Everybody can read the papers, Mr Director. It's a duty. Or a right. Or the duty of a right..." Paquito responded, getting into a tangle. "A constitutional right. And what about Knocksie, Mr Director, he did him in. You know he did."

"Knocksie died of a heart attack, Paquito."

"Yeah, course he did, because he told him summat like in the film, and Knocksie copped it. That caused the attack. I saw that 'appen."

"The doctor said Knocksie's heart was in a bad state and he could have had a heart attack at any time. It was a coincidence," retorted the director, trying to get Paquito to follow the logic of his argument.

"Right, it woz also a coincidence they nobbled me in the airport with that suitcase and that pistol that supposedly didn't belong to yours truly and I ended up in jug, right? Well, coincidences don't exist, the lady psychologist told us that as well. I mean to say Hannibal is like the guy in the film. The two is queer sods," he declared. "Besides, they've got the same name."

"Paquito, films are one thing and life..."

"But it's all in the papers today, Mr Director!" protested Paquito, who was going from strength to strength.

"The papers" – the vein in the director's neck had swollen and was about to burst – "are full of it, you invented it and the story got out!"

"But if the papers say it's true, Mr Director..." insisted Paquito, now in a shrill voice.

He'd definitively blown it. A man with progressive ideas whose bedside reading was *Crimes and Punishment* by Cesare Beccaria, had given in to temptation and accused Amadeu Cabestany before the judge on the basis of a rumour, thus denying him his presumed innocence. All he could do was to try to turn the situation round.

"That's enough of this nonsense, Paquito. Amadeu Cabestany is no cannibal. He is suspected, I repeat, suspected for the moment of killing a woman and no more than that. So this had better be the story circulating around here. Got it, Paquito? Because I understand you've only got one year to go before you're out on conditional release, right? I wouldn't want that lengthened for any reason." The director had decided to change his strategy and have recourse to the tried and tested methods of old. "And I don't think you'd be very happy if in the year you've theoretically still got to spend with us your 'intimate time' was eight on a Monday morning, would you?"

"Fuck, no! That would be a bastard, Mr Director! My girlfriend can't do it at that time of day."

"Right, so you'll go straight from here and tell your colleagues it was all a joke, or a misunderstanding or whatever you want. But this rumour must stop. You got that, Paquito? The judge is very annoyed and quite right too."

"Whatever you say, Mr Director. I expect I can fix that. Course if you could give me extra 'intimate time', I'd go for it even better…" Paquito tried to negotiate.

"You do what I told you to and then we'll talk."

Paquito wrinkled his eyebrows – something he knew you were supposed to do when you were thinking. He was at a loss.

"All the same, is or ain't Hannibal a cannibal?" he asked, wanting to be clear.

"Look, Paquito, that's enough of that rubbish. Don't make me angry, because I'm at the end of my tether. Clear off and remember what you've got to do."

Paquito returned to the fifth gallery awash in a sea of doubt. He didn't know what to think. Nevertheless, he only had a year until his conditional release and wasn't going to risk losing that, so he decided to do what the director had ordered him to do: namely, to persuade his colleagues that their Hannibal, however much his name was the same, was no cannibal. However, Paquito continued to keep his distance from Amadeu Cabestany. As the psychologist giving him therapy used to say, better not tempt fate.

After Paquito left his office, the director picked his phone up to try to tell the judge it had all been one big misunderstanding, an unfortunate joke played by the inmates. He felt unable to reproduce his surreal conversation with Paquito Expósito and mumbled all kind of apologies. He then wrote a short press release saying it was all a rather dud joke that had unhappily prospered and that, consequently, the rumour concerning Amadeu Cabestany's peculiar culinary habits had no basis in fact. A few hours earlier, the papers had received another release from the *Mossos d'Esquadra*'s press unit. They regretted that a group of citizens of Vic had misinterpreted a comment made by an aspiring *mosso* as he left a restaurant. The following day, some papers – but only some – published a retraction, but lamentably by that stage, Vic was already a city besieged by vultures. Luckily for Amadeu and his family, the butchers and shopkeepers of Vic, gathered at an emergency meeting, agreed that publicity about the alleged cannibalistic tastes of one of their townsfolk might damage their sausage industry, so they organised an on-the-spot demonstration to scare off the press with a show of carving knives while a unit of *Mossos d'Esquadra* looked the other way. The journalists, mostly trainees on temporary contracts, decided not to wound local sensibilities and turned tail, mostly because someone had told them that pig farms and slaughterhouses are, as everybody knows, a perfect place to get rid of snoopers. The news item gradually cooled off and the papers ceased to mention it.

There was a degree of unease among the *mossos*. The Deputy-Inspector had to put up with being bawled at for an hour and a warning on her file, and the aspiring *mosso* Marc Serra received a kick in the balls delivered by a Deputy-Inspector who allowed him to enjoy the virtues of chastity for a while. It turned out the judge was bilingual, and that, if necessary, she could swear like a trooper in more than one language, while the director of the Model decided to take flight and take a few days' leave for private business and thus avoid having to give further explanations. Paquito Expósito came out of it rather well; he finally succeeded in getting an extra "intimate time" with the prostitute who'd recently been doubling as his girlfriend.

Unluckily, the rot had set in, as far as it impacted on the dusty carpets of the literary Parnassus where Amadeu Cabestany aspired to tread.

16

Ernest Fabià had been in Tarazona a little over a week and his morale had lifted noticeably. It wasn't geographical distance by itself which had helped put things into perspective, and not balloon recent events out of proportion. It was the fact that he was now living in the micro-cosmos of the Translators' House and its peculiar micro-universe of the picturesque city of Tarazona that made him feel as if he were infinitely more distant from the hustle and bustle of Barcelona than the four hundred kilometres actually separating him from his problems. Tarazona was a frontier city, close to the provinces of Soria, Navarre and La Rioja, and it was a challenge to get there by public transport. To begin with, as he felt no desire to sit behind the driving wheel again, Ernest was obliged to take the Talgo to Saragossa from Sants station. Then he had to get a much more rickety train that left him in the small station of Tudela in Navarre, and from there a local bus that finally dropped him in Tarazona. Because of the delays, which he was told were quite normal, whether a result of snow, rain, accidents or striking workers, he'd failed to make his connections and spent hours and hours waiting in each station. He'd left home at eight a.m. and had reached the Translators'

House just before eight p.m., as the sun was setting in a riot of blazing colour that took Ernest's breath away. The imbalance between geographical distance and his twelve-hour journey to Tarazona had plunged him into a state of mental confusion akin to jet lag. When he finally did arrive, he was floating in a dream, as if the strange but familiar world surrounding him wasn't entirely real. Nevertheless, Ernest didn't find the sensation entirely unpleasant. Remorse effectively began to fade into the background four hundred kilometres away from Barcelona, and the anguish consuming him also began to ebb, swept away by the warm wind blowing from the peaks of Moncayo.

If he'd caught a plane to New York, Moscow or Casablanca, it would have been a quicker journey. But now he was in Tarazona, a small city with historical buildings undermined by property speculation, that he'd only heard of because it was the seat of an offbeat institution created and led by translators. The House was full in June, mostly with foreigners, and English was the language most commonly heard. Outside in the street Spanish was the language used, a Spanish heavily impregnated with the local Aragonese accent, *mañico*, that lengthened the last syllable of every phrase as if in a *jota* lilt, and was characterized by the constant use of diminutives. Ernest was no longer plain Ernest but *Ernestico*, a *café* was now a *cafetico* and he was now a *mozico* rather than a *home.* On the other hand, Tarazonans were open, gutsy, fun-loving people, fond of Holy Week processions, red wine and honey cakes. They also loved sport, which they practised in two ways: running in front of small cows along the city's steep, narrow streets, and throwing tons of tomatoes at each other in the

Town Hall square the day of the local fiesta. Past local celebrities included such diverse figures as the variety singer Raquel Meyer, the comedy actor Paco Martínez Soria and the philosopher Gracián, who wasn't born in Tarazona, but who, luckily for the city, had died there. At the time he was buried in a common grave since nobody anticipated he'd become famous centuries later, and local archaeologists had for years been trying to find his bones, though their macabre objective remained unclear. Worthy descendants of their forbears, the present-day inhabitants of ancient Celt–Iberian Turiasso were stubborn, proud and suspicious, particularly of weekend tourists from the metropolis who came to peer at old stones and, naturally, the eccentric characters continually parading through the Translators' House.

Ernest was welcomed by the centre's director, a woman in her forties who was a crazy chain-smoker. She was also from Barcelona and spent days on the phone managing crises. She apologized for not meeting him with a car in Tudela, which was only twenty minutes away, but she didn't drive and her secretary was off sick with depression. Ernest had come to that back of beyond in flight from incipient depression brought on by a bad conscience, so this news floored him somewhat. Did the inhabitants of Tarazona have depressive tendencies? He said nothing, but something stirred inside him and he began to regret the journey he'd just endured.

As usual, the centre's director had organized a kind of welcome supper with the rest of the translators staying in the House, but she'd assumed that Ernest would arrive after lunch and have time to rest and acclimatize to his new environment. Instead Ernest barely had time to drop his rucksack, ring his wife, tell her he'd arrived safely and take a shower (a cold one at that, because the gas-oil tank was empty and they'd been waiting for a refill for days). They had a table reservation for nine, the director explained as she showed him to his room, but not because nine was the normal supper time in Tarazona: it simply happened that most translators resident came from countries where supper after seven o'clock was considered a sign of Latin excess they found hard to stomach. In Tarazona, and even more so in the summer, local customs were very different to those of Calvinist Europe, where most of the translators were from, and none of the half a dozen or so restaurants scattered throughout the city opened their doors before nine. If they wanted to dine out on the House, the translators had to accept a degree of hunger. At a quarter to nine on the dot, an out-of-sorts Ernest, five famished translators and the director, who seemed slightly off-key, left the House in single file en route to a tasty meal.

The House was currently home to a Finn who translated from Swedish, an Englishman who translated from German, a German woman who translated from Russian, a Norwegian woman who translated from French and a Catalan who was translating Marina Dolç into Spanish. As the centre had only five bedrooms and Ernest was the sixth resident, the German and Norwegian women, who'd met thanks to the European network of Translator Houses and were friends, were sharing a double room where they often played hosts to small parties. As for Adrià Ruiz, Marina Dolç's translator, he was slightly younger than Ernest and also lived in Barcelona, on the left side of the Eixample. Naturally they knew each other, but only by name.

Ernest spoke good English, so the translators agreed to use that language to converse with. The English translator, who looked the most eccentric of the bunch, half hippy, half lord, was the only one, apart from Adrià, who had a smattering of Spanish. He'd spent a number of summers on the Costa Brava, but his accent was so authentic that nobody understood him, especially when he spoke in his own language. On the other hand, the English the director babbled was as incomprehensible as her British colleague's. However, as she was the one in charge and didn't look as if she would suffer fools gladly, no one dared say a thing.

In the course of supper Ernest discovered, much to his relief, that the secretary's sick leave due to depression stemmed from the fact she wanted an increase in her salary, which implied she wasn't so much depressed as impoverished in her thinking. He was also informed the Prince of Asturias was to visit the city the following day to see the restoration work on the cathedral, and that was why Tarazona was bristling with over a hundred tall, brawny security police one could easily detect by their camouflage as tourists dressed up for a safari. Moreover, a translation congress was scheduled for the weekend and the director had an unresolved problem: there were more attendees registered than there was hotel capacity. June was marriage month in Tarazona and the city's hotels couldn't cope with the demand.

That first night they ate and drank, drank and ate, and, for the first time since his accident, Ernest found he could relax. He also got merry, though he wasn't the only one or the worst for wear. The Finn and the director seemed to be racing neck and neck to the bottom of a bottle of home-made *orujo,* as the Finn fell into a stupor in step with the grim poems he was reciting while the director's English improved spectacularly under the impact of the Galician liquor. The director won and left the restaurant in a dignified fashion, even though she was on her knees after vomiting in the lavatory.

Ernest got up around noon the next morning, his body hung-over but his spirits refreshed. He didn't remember much; the binge had seen off his nightmare and he felt cheerful. After eating a sandwich and drinking a Coke, he was about to start working when the director, who'd barely recovered from the night's excesses, summoned all the translators to her office and asked them to make themselves presentable as they had to go and shake the prince's hand in the town hall. Although she was a republican, that human chimney intended to make the most of the royal visit by securing a better base for the House. Like the rest of his colleagues, Ernest didn't dare say no, even though the only clothes in his rucksack were a pair of old jeans and some unironed shirts he'd grabbed straight from the clean-linen basket. As soon as he saw how the director and the English translator were dressed up, he realized he'd no reason to worry.

When the reception was over, after being put on display before the future monarch like monkeys at a fair, with their director acting as mistress of ceremonies and leaving the prince and local bigwigs quite speechless, the six translators decided to drink a few *vinicos* to swill out the bad taste from their mouths and, in the process, escape from the director, who was threatening to press-gang them into viewing a local painter's exhibition, no doubt with some dark ulterior motive. As on the previous night, they returned in the early hours, and not necessarily to the same bed. This wasn't the case with Ernest, who felt obliged to remain faithful to his wife now his remorse was beginning to fade and the serious economic problems that had forced him into petty crime seemed like ancient history.

On the following days, Ernest closeted himself in his bedroom to get on with his translation, and that made him feel happier. As he was working on an English novel, from time to time he went and consulted his British colleague over any doubts he had, or went to look at his emails. By night, even though Tarazona didn't get any cooler, Ernest went out on binges with the other translators. They drank, ate and argued heatedly about literature, writers and translation problems. Then they zigzagged euphorically back to the House early in the morning. Unlike Ernest, they all led fairly unconventional, offbeat lives and were really passionate about the writers they translated. Perhaps from the point of view of the locals, Ernest and Adrià were the least eccentric of the bunch, and that, together with the fact they both shared Catalan as their mother tongue and worshipped Kafka, meant they quickly became close friends.

Adrià had confessed to Ernest that he wasn't crazy about Marina Dolç and only translated her novels for the money. Ernest also sometimes had to translate novels that weren't very good, but, given the pittance they were paid, he was glad to do so because they were easier to translate. Unlike Ernest, Adrià wasn't married and had no children. He lived alone and spent his free time seducing young women and writing short stories and poems he never published.

Adrià had been at the Translators' House for a month. He'd gone there to translate *The Heart of the Labyrinth,* the novel Marina Dolç had published before being awarded the Golden Apple award. Adrià had almost finished the translation, and as soon as he had, he'd start on *A Shortcut to Paradise* at full pelt. Adrià was sick of Marina Dolç's novels, but they paid the rent on his tiny flat and didn't burn up any brain cells.

The death of his star author had happened when Adrià Ruiz was at the Translator's House. The nature of the crime was so shocking that journalists had come from Saragossa to interview him, but Adrià had only met Marina on a couple of occasions and he'd never even heard of Amadeu Cabestany. From the moment he saw the news on television, he started to buy a newspaper every day and read with interest the articles about Marina, as if being up to date on the murder was part of his work. He sometimes mentioned them to Ernest, who preferred not to read the press, particularly the Barcelona papers, as a precautionary measure. That Thursday, when Ernest was on his ninth day of convalescence at the Translators' House, it was Adrià who showed him the article reporting on the allegedly cannibalistic habits of the writer from Vic and the accompanying black-and-white photo. Ernest almost fainted.

He immediately recognized the man he had mugged when he left the Up & Down club, and his heart began to race. His first thought was that, quite unawares, he'd had an encounter with a dangerously disturbed murderer, but when he'd read the article, he realized the enormity of the situation. At the very moment when, according to the police, that madman had killed Marina Dolç, he, Ernest Fabià, was at the other end of Barcelona holding him up at toy-gun-point. Unless Amadeu Cabestany possessed the divine gift of ubiquity that allowed him to be simultaneously the victim of a theft and killer of a renowned writer, the police had got it wrong. He hadn't killed Marina Dolç. He couldn't have. Ernest Fabià had just discovered he was the witness to his innocence. A vital witness.

The fact the papers mentioned a possible serial killer involved in acts of cannibalism meant the pressure in his chest was slightly relieved. The crimes being hinted at were so horrific that, in reality, one extra was irrelevant. It was obvious that if he didn't corroborate the suspect's alibi, something he could only do by revealing his own guilt as a mugger, and they sentenced Amadeu for the murder of Marina Dolç, then the real killer would get off scot-free. Ernest didn't know what to do, and didn't dare ring his wife or ask his new friend for advice. He was stressed out the whole day, and excused himself that evening on the pretext that he had a bad headache. Ernest locked himself in his room and spent the evening alone, a prey to remorse, nicotine and alcohol.

The following day when the papers published a retraction, stating it had all been a misunderstanding on the part of the prison's inmates, Ernest's life-line was gone. Amadeu Cabestany was no longer a depraved monster accused of one more act of butchery because of Ernest's silence: he was a wretched writer unable to prove his alibi. Ernest now had to add to the remorse in his conscience a moral responsibility of an infinitely greater weight: the responsibility to save an innocent man from unjust punishment. That meant taking the bull by the horns and reaching an important decision, one way or the other.

But it wasn't easy, because there were other people at stake. Ernest had a responsibility to look after his family and a duty not to traumatize his children. It wasn't simply the punishment he might receive; that wouldn't be severe given his lack of a criminal record and that was what least worried him. No, what really was worrying him was what would happen when his seven-year-old son Jordi found out that his father was a common thief who didn't take him to school because he was locked up. What would his parents, wife or friends think of the crime he had committed? Who would believe that the pistol he had used to threaten Amadeu was indeed a toy? Who would ever trust him again and give him work? If he confessed, he'd not only sink himself but would push his whole family over the precipice, in the best tradition of Classical tragedy. But if he kept quiet and didn't go to the police, how would he ever look at himself in the mirror again? How would he stay sane knowing his hands were besmirched by that shameful silence?

At his wits' end, Ernest went up to his room and shut himself inside with a bottle of JB and two cigarette packets. He spent the whole day there but was unable to reach a decision. He was a physical wreck in a state of mental paralysis. At a quarter to eight someone knocked on his door and Ernest realized he'd dozed off. It was the director, who had organized an outing that evening to the monastery of Veruela to a concert of Baroque music. Initially, Ernest, who was tipsy, said he didn't feel at all well and would prefer to stay at the House. The director shrugged her shoulders, looked at the bottle of whisky and the ashtray full of butts and asked him to take care he didn't start a fire. Five minutes later, the

Norwegian translator appeared in his room, all made-up and scented, to tell him she also would prefer to stay back and not go to the concert. She'd bought a good bottle of wine and offered to make dinner for two.

Ernest knew that if he stayed in the House he'd have to fight off that woman, who was desirable and had been trying to get off with him for days. In his present disastrously low spirits, he wasn't at all sure he wouldn't end up succumbing to a wild night of sex, smoked salmon and alcohol. He spontaneously imagined her naked but for her knickers and took fright. This Nordic epiphany changed his mind and he prudently decided to go on the trip out. Although he wasn't a believer, he thought he might find an answer to his anguishing within the walls of that venerable monastery and, if he didn't, at least he wouldn't make it worse. If God existed, Ernest was prepared to give him an opportunity to prove it.

The monastery of Veruela is at the foot of Moncayo and fifteen kilometres from Tarazona, so they had to take taxis. The concert started at nine, and when they arrived the sun was beginning to set behind the mountain. It was cooler in Veruela than in Tarazona, but it was freezing cold inside the huge church where the concert was being held. Its impressive, twelfth-century walls kept rationality out, as well as the warming rays of the sun. It might be hot in hell, but the House of God, more than one must have reflected during that concert, was an icebox. Ernest started to sneeze after half an hour, and when he returned to Tarazona, at around eleven, he had a temperature and was shivering.

He spent the whole of Saturday delirious in bed, refusing to eat or let a doctor near him. Was that the signal he'd been searching for? And, if it was, how should he interpret it? What was the message the one on high was trying to send him with that untimely chill? Around noon the next morning, Ernest found the strength to go to the kitchen to brew up some coffee. While he was waiting for the coffee to percolate, he saw a newspaper opened at a half-page advertisement asking for citizens to collaborate in the search for a witness to support the alibi of the alleged murderer of Marina Dolç. It included the photograph the police had taken of Amadeu Cabestany and a mobile telephone number that, they insisted, wasn't a police number. Before he could have second thoughts, Ernest nervously copied the number onto a scrap of paper and, his stomach still empty, went up to his room to gather his things together. God, or whoever, had now certainly given him a sign that he could both decipher *and* contact on his mobile. Rucksack on back, he went off to the director's office. As it was Sunday and she wasn't there, he wrote her an apologetic note explaining he had had to curtail his stay at the Translators' House. He'd have liked to say goodbye to his other colleagues, especially Adrià, but nobody was around. Before leaving, while he was waiting for his taxi to come and take him to the station, Ernest decided to make a call.

"Mr Masdèu?" he piped. "You don't know who I am but we must talk. I'm the person who mugged Amadeu Cabestany the night Marina Dolç was murdered."

PART FOUR

17

On Friday the St John's Eve party on our roof terrace ended in a great splash, with the Rottweiler screaming and throwing eggs at our guests, furious because the *mossos* and Guàrdia Urbana were totally ignoring her calls and because the decibel-measuring gadget lay smashed in the middle of the street. The twins had the best time of it because after seeing off that gadget they went downstairs, cleared our fridge of eggs and tomatoes and repaid the Rottweiler in the same coin while the adults turned a blind eye. When the battle of the eggs began, Borja and Lola scarpered with the bottle of Cardhu, and the next morning, it was Montse and I who had to go up and clean the terrace. I spent the rest of Saturday playing with Arnau, and on Sunday we had lunch out. That evening, feeling totally lethargic, I accompanied Borja on a visit to Mariona Castany.

Although my brother's friend had only recently surfaced on the landscape of Catalan literature with memoirs that were already sold to a publisher, Borja was convinced Mariona could supply us with useful information about the deceased Marina Dolç, about whom we knew practically nothing apart from the fact she was a wealthy woman and a very successful author the critics agreed to hate. If we started from the hypothesis that Amadeu Cabestany wasn't her killer and the motive hadn't been theft, we could only refocus our investigation by ignoring forensic leads and concentrating on what kind of person the writer was, on her enemies, if she had any, and on finding out who would profit from her death. Her legacy was incredibly juicy, what with her properties, shares, cash and royalties, and the first thing we needed to know was who would stand to gain from her will. We hoped to obtain that information from Lluís Arquer, whom we'd arranged to see the following Tuesday on the Plaça Reial for an aperitif. In the meantime, Mariona had assured us she would try to find out any gossip we might find useful by consulting some of her writer friends. She had summoned us to her place for a drink at seven and seemed delighted to see us. She clearly liked to act as an aide to a classy detective like Borja.

Mariona was a slim, distinguished lady. Her white, wavy hair was gathered up in a bun. She was tanned and wore light make-up. If it weren't for her hands, which always betray whatever plastic surgery and botox struggle to conceal, nobody would have said she was over sixty. That afternoon she was wearing a sort of diaphanous red tunic and gold-coloured high-heeled sandals. I caught Borja's eye and discreetly touched my nose. Borja looked back at me. Message received.

As he is colour-blind – in fact, deeply colour-blind – this is the secret code we agreed as kids, from the age of seven, the moment Borja discovered he was unable to distinguish green from red: if the colour we are looking at is red, I discreetly scratch my nose, and if it's green, I put my hands in my pockets. Naturally it would be much simpler if my brother didn't insist on hiding this anomaly from all and sundry, but that's how he liked to play it. He didn't want anyone to find out he was colour-blind, particularly not Merche or Lola. It's beyond me, but he reckons it's a vulgar imperfection that doesn't marry with his desire to play the elegant and sophisticated man of the world.

Mariona sat us down on a sofa, where, according to her, Alfonso XII had also once sat, and immediately started on the matter in hand.

"My dear boys, that woman's past is a complete mystery," she informed us while pouring out three generous Cardhus. "I mean, no one knows where she comes from, though I have no doubt she's not from Sant Feliu," she announced proudly.

"What do you mean? Marina Dolç wasn't born in Sant Feliu de Codines?" asked Borja, taken aback after tasting that delicious liquid. "Sant Feliu is small enough for people to remember her and her family. Besides, I thought she lived there, and in a splendid mansion, at that."

"Yes, she did. And it's also true she told people she was born there. But that's not what the register says," she smiled slyly. "Take a look at this."

Mariona showed us a hazy photocopy of a birth certificate corresponding to one Maria Campana Llopis, born in Barcelona, in the Maternitat, 22 March 1954. Borja and I were all ears.

"For starters," Mariona went on, enjoying her dramatic coup, "she was fifty-two and not forty-nine. But that's nothing to worry about; we women like to play these little tricks," she remarked coquettishly. "However, as you could see, she wasn't born in Sant Feliu, but here in Barcelona."

"Perhaps she just happened to be born here, but her family was from Sant Feliu," I interjected. "You sure Sant Feliu has a hospital?"

"The real issue," Mariona interrupted, "is that nobody recalls her family in Sant Feliu. Marina certainly showered money on the town and the neighbours refuse to talk about her, so my sources tell me," she said enigmatically. "Last year, while Marina was in Italy, a student of something or other writing a thesis on her work visited the place and talked to the locals, hoping to find some skeletons, I expect. But she unearthed nothing." She shook her head. "Where the family lived, how she did at school or her father's line of work. Zilch."

"So where does her family live now? She must have a relative or two..."

"Ah, that's where you come in, my friends! *You* are the detectives. I have simply used my influence to secure a copy of her birth certificate and identify a couple of items of gossip. Not much, in sum."

"Go on then."

"She has an ex, but they were only married a couple of years, when she was very young. Apparently he teaches and they've barely had any contact since the divorce. Water under the bridge."

"But she must have other boyfriends," interjected Borja. "She was a good-looking woman and wealthy."

"You mean we wealthy women are more likely to have boyfriends than poor ones?" responded Mariona, fluttering her eyelashes and signalling she was offended.

"You know what I mean, my dear..."

"Well, as far as this neck of the woods goes, she seemingly had none. Which means that either she really didn't, or it wasn't a man... or was a married man," Mariona pontificated.

"In short, Marina Dolç wasn't born in Sant Feliu but lived in Sant Feliu and acted as if she had been born there. And, according to you, she may have had a girlfriend or a married man for a lover," my brother replied.

"Yes, in a nutshell," nodded Mariona.

Unlike those two, I'd never had the pleasure of meeting Marina, but I decided I'd stick in my oar as well: "I think you've both forgotten she had an Italian lover."

"True enough," agreed Borja. "Clàudia told me she had a palace in Tuscany and a lover there as well. An aristocrat."

"That's as may be, but no one has ever seen this famous aristocrat... But I gather the palace in Tuscany does exist and is magnificent. Evidently Marina is an art and antiques lover, particularly Greek and Roman works. Her private collection is one of the best in Italy. They say she spent a fortune on it. But obviously she had the wherewithal..."

"Well, she's hardly the first person to invent her own life-story," commented Borja, who knew all there was to know about such things. "It's very human. But I'm intrigued about the kind of life she led. She was very rich."

"She lived by herself and was childless. She travelled a lot, particularly abroad, promoting her own books, but she wasn't on the circuit here. The critics reckoned she was superficial and too commercial. They gave her horrific reviews!..." Mariona looked shocked. "One was especially vicious towards her books. I don't know if you have heard of him – Oriol Sureda. She has a very loyal readership now and that's why they envied her so."

"Sureda was there on the day of the prize. Do you remember, Mariona? He walked down to the bar with us," said Borja.

"Yes, that's true. I don't know what the hell he was doing at that party... he couldn't stand Marina!" our friend rasped indignantly. "I expect Sureda is a friend of Francesc, her publisher. Or perhaps Francesc was working on him to nip in the bud one of those reviews of his."

And then she added, "If anyone knows anything for sure, it will be Maite, her secretary. She worked for her for years and Marina always took her on her travels. But she's very discreet... A discreet and efficient woman. I'm thinking of contracting her to help me with my memoirs now she's out of work. She's agreed to see you tomorrow morning in Sant Feliu, as you requested."

"You're a jewel, Aunt Mariona," responded Borja.

My brother would sometimes address her like that, "Aunt Mariona", in honour of the friendship Mariona Castany and Borja's imaginary mother had enjoyed as young girls, a spin-off from my brother's fake aristocratic ancestry.

"So, Marina Dolç had a murky past," I said, returning to our subject.

"In fact, Marina Dolç had no past, Eduard. She was a nobody. I mean she didn't belong to any of our great families, or descend from writerly, artistic or patriotic stock. One would know if she did. None of her forebears has an entry in the *Catalan Who's Who?* let alone has a street named after them in Barcelona. She was an outsider," she said, jutting her chin out.

"But she *was* awarded the St George's Cross," I replied.

"And that must have cost her! It's the advantage of having a pile of money: you can buy everything, even respect."

"That didn't stop her bad reviews..." I insisted.

"That's true, Sureda never got off his high horse. But he was the only one. As a matter of fact, Marina's last two books were received much more positively by the critics thanks to the feminists, who read her as a kindred spirit."

"Mariona, you've turned into a real detective!" exclaimed Borja gallantly. "If we don't watch out, you'll be taking business away from us."

"I'm doing this for Clàudia, the poor dear. How could she bloody embroil herself with that twit Amadeu (if you'll excuse my French)..." she retorted, looking sorrowful.

"Sex and money, Mariona. It's what makes the world go round!" sighed Borja.

"Come on, there is such a thing as love..." I countered timidly.

Borja and Mariona smiled at each other and gave me condescending glances.

"Well, call it what you will," she conceded with a sigh. "I suppose Clàudia gets it from her family."

"Her mother, in her time, also fell for an adventurer, a private eye who moved in the underworld. She was married to a very wealthy industrialist and it caused a real stink, but they covered it up. Those were the days..." she said with a hint of nostalgia. "However, they do say that Clàudia takes after her father."

"They have the same eyes," I pointed out.

"Yes, but a different bank balance!" Mariona sighed. "Clàudia was an only girl and, despite all the fuss, she inherited the Agulló fortune. So you can see how she developed her love for literature! Though she takes her work seriously. Perhaps too much so. She's a fine woman."

"Listen, Mariona. What's happened to Marina Dolç's agent? Where is she? She must have one, I suppose?"

"Well, no, her publishing house acts as her agent, so I gather."

After pouring us another whisky, Mariona and my brother gossiped for a while about the high-society world in which they moved: the Liceo wasn't what it used to be, they'd caught someone cheating at bridge, the wife of a famous banker had had a heart attack at some dinner when she discovered she was wearing the same party dress as the bit on the side (to use Mariona's expression) of a left-wing politician. I did my best not to yawn and kept looking at my watch. Barça had kicked off a quarter of an hour ago and I was missing the match. Finally, Borja got up from the royal sofa and decided it was time to leave.

"Mariona, we'll leave you in peace. Thanks for the whisky… and titbits of information. By the way, you look just divine in red. Devilish but divine."

Mariona smiled, flattered. My brother knew how to soft-soap her.

"Oh, I almost forgot!" Mariona stopped us in our tracks. "Next Friday we shall be giving a small party in homage to Marina here, in my house. "I've been asked to " she added, unable to hide how delighted she was to host such an event. "I provide the house and the others will see to the catering. Her publisher will be there and a few writers and friends, the odd critic, journalist, the television people and a few politicians, of course. Clàudia will come too. Naturally you are both invited."

"We might find out something useful. Have you considered that if it's true Cabestany is innocent, Dolç's murderer might come as well?" asked Borja anxiously. "You'd better take care."

"Yes, that is the second thought I had. Don't worry, I shall tell Marcelo to keep a sharp eye out."

Marcelo is her butler, a brawny, courteous man who wasn't around that evening because Sunday was his day off. He's Argentine, is slightly (ever so slightly) limp-wristed and a very nice person. He's been working for Mariona for more than fifteen years and she holds him in high esteem. According to our information, he earns a fortune playing the part of a distinguished and deferential English butler.

"Out of curiosity," I dared to ask just before we left. "You said your second thought had been that the murderer might come to your party. What was your first?"

"A matter of etiquette, of course. I don't know what to wear. The world of writers is so peculiar..."

"Whatever you wear, you will look divine," chimed Borja, kissing her sensually on the hand, his eyes transfixed by the large diamond piece she wore as a ring.

"I know, I know," she said, as she opened the door and bid us farewell. "*Au revoir, mes beaux.* And don't give Maite too hard a time. I think she's very, very frightened."

18

The next morning was Monday morning, and as Merche's Audi was still in for repair, we had to take the bus to Sant Feliu de Codines. Luckily, it's only forty or so kilometres from Barcelona to the Vallès Oriental, and we arrived in less than hour, even though the bus made several stops. As we were early, we decided to go for a second breakfast. It was hot, and we chose a bar with a terrace surrounded by blackberry bushes that gave shade to the tables. We ordered coffee and pastries and also asked the waiter the way to Marina's house. We clearly weren't the first to do so. Faithful readers from all ends of Catalonia had come to poke their noses around on the excuse that they wanted to leave her some flowers. We also took the precaution of claiming we were fans, even though we carried no book as a talisman and brought no bouquet. The waiter gave us a long-suffering look and told us Marina Dolç's house was near a place by the name of La Font dels Àlbers. It took us ten minutes' brisk walk to get there.

Probably built in the nineteenth century, the house was flanked by an abandoned garden that created a gloomy atmosphere, as if its ivy veneer hid ancient, moss-covered statues that would turn into ghosts at night. It was a two-storey house with attics, and an old wrought-iron gate led from the road to the garden. A South American maid in a ritual grey uniform opened the gate. She ushered us in and said Marina Dolç's secretary would see us straight away. We followed her through the garden, silent and somewhat anxious. Maite Bastida was waiting in the entrance to the mansion, clutching a crumpled handkerchief.

She was a small, thin woman, who did indeed seem to be rather frightened. According to our information, she was thirty-seven and had been living in that house for five years. She wasn't ugly, but wasn't exactly pretty either. She was dressed smartly and comfortably, and her short, wavy hair was combed back. She wore glasses and her eyes looked tearful.

"Come in, please," she said, beckoning us into a sitting room furnished with antiques and bedecked with a selection of paintings from the Catalan landscape tradition. "Mrs Castany rang me and asked if I would see you. She said you were investigating the death of Mrs Marina..." Her eyes began to stream and she took a handkerchief from her pocket. "Excuse me, but I still haven't got over it."

"It's only natural. How long had you been living here with Marina Dolç? Was it five years?" I asked, kicking off our conversation. As Borja is sometimes rather shy, we thought it would be best for me to take the initiative.

"Yes, I'd been living here and working for her for five years."

"Though you're from Barcelona."

"Yes."

"I suppose you'll have to find somewhere else to live now," Borja said softly. "It's been a big blow to you as well."

"Are you sure you're not journalists?" she asked in a shrill voice. "Mrs Castany said you were detectives..."

"I'll be frank," confessed Borja. "Strictly speaking, we're not private detectives, but we *are* working on behalf of Amadeu Cabestany." Borja preferred to err on the safe side and avoid any misunderstanding. "He's the man accused of killing Marina Dolç, and, as you know, he is in prison. Though he is innocent."

"I see, and you want to find out who really killed Mrs Marina, isn't that so? That's what Mrs Castany said."

"Precisely. It's what we're trying to do. Unofficially, of course. That's why we'd like to ask you a few questions related to..."

"Would you like a drink?"

All of a sudden, Maite Bastida interrupted our conversation and rang a little bell. Three seconds later, the South American maid who'd let us in appeared.

"Yes, madam?"

"Guadalupe, would you be so kind as to bring us coffee and pastries? Thank you."

"Right away, madam," she said, disappearing.

Borja and I looked at each other askance. Something didn't quite square. Maite Bastida had behaved as if she were the mistress of the house and the maid acted as if that were the case. She wasn't arrogant, indeed was rather timid, but she did act as the lady of the house, not as a servant. According to our information, this Maite was a salaried employee. Super efficient, but merely a secretary at the end of the day. I remember I then jumped to the conclusion (Borja as well, I think) that they might have had something going on. This would explain Maite's behaviour and also why Marina Dolç's only known boyfriend was the mysterious Italian lover nobody had ever seen.

"I was saying," Borja tried to pick up the thread of the conversation, "that you won't be able to live in this house any more..."

"In fact, I will. Madame Marina bequeathed it to me." She paused, waiting for us to react. "Well," she sighed, "the truth will soon be out, so I'd better tell you now, as you've taken the trouble to come all this way. Perhaps you might be able to help." She took out a cigarette. "Do you mind if I smoke?"

"Not at all," replied Borja, hurrying to light up himself. I joined the party ten seconds later.

"Madame Dolç, Marina, is my aunt. My name isn't Maite Bastida, but Teresa Campana, but you can call me Maite. No one calls me Teresa now." And she added, after a pause: "I'm her brother's younger daughter. There are twelve years between my aunt and my father."

"Now this is a surprise!" Borja acknowledged, taken aback. "Her niece..."

"That's right."

"So why did everybody think you were her secretary?"

Maite Bastide – that's to say, Maite Campana – took a few seconds to answer. She seemed to be weighing her words carefully. I imagine she'd decided to make that confession before we arrived, a story that, as she herself had foreseen, would soon belong to the public domain. It's difficult to conceal that kind of situation when a murder is involved. However, as far as that particular detail was concerned, she'd obviously decided to wait until she'd seen us. She eyed us silently, thought it over and finally said: "My Aunt Marina once told me I should always trust Mrs Castany's judgement. They weren't exactly friends, but Auntie respected her. She said one could depend on her. Mrs Castany told me you were friends of hers."

"Indeed, she and my mother (may she rest in peace) both studied in a Swiss finishing school when they were young," Borja lied. "We do have a very special relationship with Mariona."

"And how do I know that if I let you into a secret it won't be all over the papers tomorrow?" she asked naively.

"Because, apart from being friends of Mariona, my partner and I are gentlemen," responded Borja suavely. "Besides, if your story isn't connected to your aunt's death and Amadeu Cabestany's innocence, you have nothing to worry about," Borja assured her. "I give you my word. Now, if what you are about to tell us *is* in any way related to the case..."

At that moment, the maid Guadalupe came into the room and interrupted our conversation. While she poured out the coffee, Marina Dolç's niece scrutinized my brother's face in search of guarantees. She'd realized who was boss. My brother returned her gaze and she nodded. Borja may have many defects, but normally when he gives his word he keeps it.

"Unfortunately, Mr Masdéu, we can choose many things in this life, but not our family," Maite continued once the maid had left. "The story I'm about to tell you will shock you, and I beg you not to let it go any further." She paused while we stared at her on tenterhooks. "Anyway, if you are right and that writer didn't do it, you ought to know about this. I'm doing this for her. For my aunt. In case it helps. As you are detectives..."

"Treat it like a professional secret. As if you were speaking to a priest," Borja reassured her.

Marina Dolç's niece tried to smile, breathed in and lit another cigarette.

"Auntie's parents, my grandparents, had her when they were getting on in years. They were always rather eccentric people, but, as they aged, their eccentricity got worse. They were both orphans, I don't know if that has anything to do with it. When Auntie was eight years old, her parents joined one of those satanic sects imported from America. I don't know what lured them in. Perhaps they were drugged, or were promised eternal youth... Nobody knows."

"Those sects are the pits," I ventured.

"At the age of eleven," Maite continued, "Auntie had to go and live with her parents in the United States. They forced her to. At the time, my father, who was Auntie's only brother, was twenty-three, and as he had reached his majority he was able to stay in Barcelona. Auntie, on the other hand, had to spend a number of years in the back of the beyond in the United States with a horde of fanatics and her crazy parents. She managed to escape one day, though I don't know the details. It was a subject she preferred not to mention."

Borja and I were stunned. We'd come to that house looking for some answers and what we'd just been told had made our hair stand on end. Was Maite or Teresa, or whatever the hell her name was, really Marina Dolç's niece or was she pulling our legs? And was the business of the satanic sect true or did that rather dowdy young woman also write novels in her spare time and had she got her wires crossed? As neither of us said anything, she decided to resume her revelations.

"Auntie managed to return to Barcelona when she was seventeen and went to live with her brother – that is, my father. I still hadn't been born, though my older sister had. At the time both my father and mother had turned very religious, possibly on the rebound from my grandparents' peculiarities. They spent entire days going to mass, praying and exorcizing their sins. It reminded Auntie too painfully of what she'd experienced in the United States and she could stand it for only a few months. She left a note saying that she was going abroad and disappeared. She spent a couple of years in Italy before finally coming back to Barcelona."

"I presume not very many people know about all this," my brother responded, deadpan. Maite nodded. "So tell me, were you forced to escape as well? Considering you acted as if you were her secretary."

"To an extent, but my case was different. My parents are very Catholic. Catholic and conservative. They pray to God rather than to Satan and practise chastity rather than sex..." She sighed. "There's obviously a branch of the family that has a real weakness for the life of the spirit!... I don't mean to offend you," she added suddenly, realizing she was holding forth though she hadn't the slightest idea what our beliefs were.

"No way; unfortunately, communication between the next world and us was suspended a long time ago. I assume Heaven isn't receiving our signals..." responded Borja, trying to be affable.

Maite smiled. She seemed more relaxed.

"I had to follow Auntie's example and make my escape. I was married to a husband who beat me and I had parents who said it was God's will and I should accept my lot. I didn't have any girlfriends outside the congregation, or anyone else I could have recourse to... So I thought of Auntie."

"In other words, you and her were on very good terms," I chimed in, trying to be nice.

Maite shook her head.

"Not at all. I discovered Marina Dolç was my Auntie quite by chance, one day when I was eavesdropping behind a door listening to my parents talk. They were both ashamed of my grandparents, who were now dead, and also of Auntie and her novels. They said they were pornographic and inspired by the Devil. That's why they never mentioned them or her at home."

She went quiet. She seemed tired. If her fantastic confession was true, it was an extraordinary story that could turn the case on its head. As far as we knew, Marina Dolç had never said a word about these things, in her novels or her interviews. It was as if she'd decided to shield herself behind a humdrum biography and build herself a new life, away from her dark, tortured past.

"It's a horrific story," I said, very moved. "How did you track down your Auntie?"

"According to her books, which I read on the sly, this is where she lived, and it turned out to be true. When I told her who I was and what was happening, she took me in immediately," she answered, wiping her tears away.

"And why did you decide to hide the fact that you were her niece?" asked Borja.

"Because I wanted a quiet life. I wanted my family and my ex-husband to disappear from my life and me from theirs," she said with apparent sincerity. "When I arrived in Sant Feliu, Auntie's secretary had just left and we decided I'd assume that role. I took charge of her diary, booked her hotel rooms, in a word, saw to the practical side of her life... I also accompanied her on her travels. I've seen a lot of the world in the last five years," she said sadly.

"You're a rich woman now," Borja interjected.

"I'm a lonely woman now, Mr Masdéu," she said, wiping another tear away. "I start shaking whenever I think my parents and my ex-husband will soon find out and come after me. Auntie would have known how to see them off, but I…"

She started to cry. I have to confess I felt sorry for her and that's why I decided to chance my arm. When we left Marina's mansion, my brother would probably be very annoyed, since her entangled story might be a string of lies, but for one reason or another, I believed her. That young woman was probably mad, or even a cold-blooded murderer. Or perhaps not. I had to make a choice and I did: I backed her.

"The fact is that we know someone who can help you," I suggested, looking at Borja out of the corner of my eye. "Someone who could perhaps spend a period of time protecting you."

"You mean a kind of bodyguard?"

"I mean someone who is used to protecting the goodies and fending off the baddies," I said, thinking of Lluís Arquer and his pipe.

My brother nodded silently.

"Well, I'll certainly think about it. I've got to think over such a lot of things, take so many decisions…"

Although the sky was beginning to cloud over, it was hotter and Maite went over to the window and shut it and then switched on the air-conditioning.

"Auntie preferred the garden to look on the wild side, though she didn't exactly go without," she said with a smile. "Fortunately I am also the beneficiary to the royalties on half of her books. If I weren't, I don't know how I'd be able to maintain this palace!" she sighed as she looked gloomily around the room. “I wouldn’t want to sell this house under any circumstance.”

Well, it was a welcoming house. I’d realized that the moment I’d stepped inside. It breathed peace as well as activity. It was evident no interior designer had got his claws into its fabric, because although slightly chaotic, it had a warm, strong character. It wasn’t one of those museum houses belonging to the rich people my brother liked to hobnob with, where you can’t find a speck of dust and everything seems sparkling new, even the antiques. Maybe there were ghosts, but they and the inhabitants had made their peace. You could tell.

“It was because of the sect that your Auntie let it be known that she was from Sant Feliu and changed her name...” said Borja, trying to fit all the pieces together.

“More or less right... Initially, she told me, it was to ensure her own parents and the people from the sect couldn’t track her down. I imagine she was also in flight from her brother and his religious obsessions. Later, when she became a famous writer with enough money to keep intruders at bay... I don’t know, I expect she preferred to forget her past and not have to enter into explanations about such a dreadful business. Especially as the grandparents died in a kind of collective ritual suicide in the United States. Like what happened in Guyana, but on a small scale.”

“And why did your auntie choose Sant Feliu?” asked Borja, returning to our interests.

“She apparently spent a summer here, when she was six, before the grandparents joined the sect. We always end up returning to places from our childhood, she used to say.”

"Not always..." I said. "Ever since our parents crashed on the Garraf coast when Borja and I were thirteen, neither of us has ever gone near Sitges."

"One last thing: do you know if your aunt had any enemies? If anyone had ever threatened her?"

"You mean apart from our family?" she said, smiling sadly. "No, not that I know of."

"And do you think it's possible someone from the family?... Possibly her ex-husband?..."

"Perhaps. But I think he lives abroad."

"Could it be someone from the sect? Someone wanting revenge?"

"I don't think so. What would be the point? These people are only interested in money, and Auntie had money, but it was always well tied up. Besides, why would they wait so long? The grandparents must have committed suicide twenty years ago..."

"No, it doesn't seem to make much sense..." I agreed. "On the other hand, they say your aunt had an aristocratic lover. Is that true or is that part of the biography she invented as well?"

"No, Roberto exists, but he's not an aristocrat, even though he looks like one. He's a very wealthy antiquarian who lives in Rome. He and Auntie were an item for twelve years. They loved each other a lot, but preferred not to live in each other's pockets." She shrugged her shoulders. "They spent long periods together in her palace in Tuscany, but liked to preserve their independence. He's a bachelor, and Auntie was divorced, as I expect you know. I found it hard to understand to begin with, but they both seemed happy. Roberto never came to Sant Feliu, and Auntie never went to Rome. Poor Roberto is beside himself with grief!"

"You said earlier that your aunt had bequeathed you this house and the royalties from half of her books. Where does the other half go? To Roberto?"

"Yes, he inherits the palace in Tuscany. He's rich enough to maintain it and I don't think he will sell it off."

"But what about the royalties on the other books? And the rest of her money and properties?" Borja had made some quick calculations. "It must be a tidy sum..."

"A small fortune. Auntie divided it up between different charity organizations working for children in the Third World. I know, because she insisted I accompany her when she went to draw up her will."

"Good heavens, how generous! She must have liked children a lot..."

"Not really. She couldn't stand them, in fact. She wanted to leave me everything but I persuaded her." And she added, as if by way of an excuse, "I don't need so much money."

"A curious point of view," rejoined my brother. "Just one last question. Why didn't you go to the Ritz with her? I understood you accompanied her everywhere."

"I caught one of those silly summer flu bugs. I was in bed with a temperature of thirty-eight and a half, and Auntie wouldn't let me go. I shall never forgive myself. If I'd been with her that night..."

"I expect you couldn't have done anything to help. Destiny..."

"Destiny is totally irrelevant." She shook her head. "Auntie didn't deserve that from anyone. Perhaps she wasn't the good writer she thought she was" – she attempted to smile – "but I can assure you she was a good person. If it's true that that writer is innocent, you must find the guilty party and put him behind bars." And she added, this time looking extremely serious, "I'm a very grateful person, as you shall see. I learned that from Auntie as well."

I suppose it is statistically very unlikely you will get parents who are so screwed up they join a satanic sect, but Marina Dolç had had that misfortune. She took to the grave the key to the mystery as to why the brainwashing didn't work on her, but at least she'd survived without feeling the need to write her memoirs or flaunt her personal drama in some television studio. Marina Dolç had built a life for herself beyond the tragedy of her childhood and had invented a biography that someone had inexplicably decided to cut short the night she'd received her most important prize ever. Yes, good and bad luck exist, and Marina Dolç tasted equal amounts of both.

We realized the sun had suddenly disappeared under thick, grey, storm-threatening clouds, and decided to leave. As we were saying goodbye, Borja reiterated to Maite that we would be extremely discreet but also warned her to be on the alert. It was on the cards that police or journalists would start digging the dirt and would uncover her aunt's murky past. Maite nodded silently and thanked us.

Big drops of rain began to fall as we left the house. To avoid arousing the curiosity of the locals and having to answer their questions, we decided to return to Barcelona immediately, since the local bus had just stopped in Sant Feliu. My brother and I were quiet and thoughtful on the journey. It wasn't as if we could talk about the case and the revelations of Marina Dolç's niece inside a packed bus, however loudly the Top 40 Hits were blaring away. On the other hand, if Lluís Arquer came up with the goods, we would soon know whether the business of the family and the inheritance were true. When we were on the outskirts of Barcelona, Borja broke our tacit vow of silence.

"Just imagine giving up all that cash for an NGO..." he said, unable to come to terms with such an idea.

"Well, that's what she said. Though she seemed sincere enough. Loads of money brings loads of headaches!"

"Right, Eduard, it's what Mother always used to say," Borja recalled.

"So it must be true."

Back in Barcelona, we decided to wait until we had the documentation Lluís Arquer had promised us before taking another step. Borja spent the Monday evening finishing Amadeu Cabestany's novel and I took Arnau to the cinema as promised to see a terrible computer-animated film. At nine, when I was cooking the spaghetti, my brother rang sounding desperate.

"Hell, I don't understand one word."

"What are you talking about?"

"This Cabestany guy's novel. I don't have a clue about what's going on... Though it's great for putting you to sleep."

"Tell me about it! I did my bit getting to the end of Marina's doorstop," I reminded him.

"And couldn't you?..."

"No. And goodbye, it's time for supper. See you tomorrow." And I hung up.

19

As agreed at our previous meeting, my brother and I were waiting for Lluís Arquer at one o'clock at the Ambos Mundos, drinking a beer, naturally. On this occasion we'd come with enough cash to cover the detective's fee and our drinks, and my brother had let me wear jeans. He was also dressed casually, though he looked much more stylish in his Ralph Lauren sweatshirt and Lloyd trousers. He'd arranged to meet Merche for lunch at half-past two in the Port Olímpic and was worried he might be late.

"So what *is* the state of play with Lola?" I asked in an act of solidarity with my sister-in-law.

"I'm seeing Lola tonight. Merche has a business dinner in Begur," he explained.

"You *are* busy..." I countered. I already knew because Lola had rung Montse that morning to ask her to go and help her buy a dress.

Although our table was in the shade, there was an oppressive heat in the Plaça Reial that made you drowsy. Lluís Arquer seemed to be taking it in his stride, since he was late. It was twenty past one when we spotted the detective approaching at a leisurely pace from the Ramblas, leaning on his stick and looking every inch a hoodlum. He was wearing the same white linen jacket, now possibly even more creased, the same straw hat and dark sunglasses. However, we noticed he was also carrying a folder under his arm.

"Have you got the cash?" he asked, not taking his glasses off and beckoning to the waiter.

"Have you got the paperwork?" asked Borja, looking at the folder.

Lluís smiled condescendingly and ordered a beer. He handed the folder over to my brother.

"I'm a professional. I told you I'd get it and here it is: a copy of the case file," he said smugly.

"Good heavens, what a lot of documentation..."

"I've given them a look over, in case you wanted my opinion." And he added magnanimously, "This is on the house."

Borja opened the folder and looked at the sheaf of papers. Lluís Arquer obviously had good contacts, because the file had everything: the autopsy report, the analysis of fingerprints found in the bedroom, a list of the clients staying at the hotel and the night staff, and another of the people who were drinking in the bar after dinner, the witness statements, the police's conclusions... We had our work cut out, so my brother went straight to the point.

"Well, then, Arquer, what do you make of it all?" he asked, impressed to be dealing with a real detective.

Lluís Arquer now slowly took off his glasses and hat and lit a cigarette. Like a star who knew what was expected, he took his time before he answered.

"I don't think this Cabestany did it," he said finally. "Killing someone isn't as easy as it seems. And even less so when you don't want to get caught. You need to be cold-blooded."

"And who told you Cabestany isn't?" I interjected, deciding to play devil's advocate. "Remember how disappointed he was when they didn't given him the prize."

Lluís Arquer looked at me if I were an insect not worth crushing underfoot and shrugged his shoulders.

"You only have to look at his face," he said. "I'm not denying the guy could kill someone. We all could in certain circumstances. But it's one thing to kill in a rage and quite another when you know what you're doing. They didn't find any fingerprints and that implies a degree of premeditation and guts. If this guy had killed her, he'd have thrown up on the spot. And no vomit was found in the room. Besides, who'd ever invent such a flimsy alibi? No." He shook his head. "It's obvious it wasn't him."

"So who do you reckon killed her?" Borja tried to provoke him into saying more.

"Do you think I've got magic powers or what?" Lluís Arquer grinned like an old cat. "Apart from the fact it's your case."

"You mean you've not the slightest clue." Borka stuck the knife in.

Lluís Arquer slouched back in his chair and extinguished his cigarette.

"Look, if what the hotel staff says is true, and between midnight and half-past two the only people who went in or out of the hotel were hotel guests and those invited to the party, it reduces the list of suspects from, say six million, to give a rough figure, to around… two hundred. I've checked the list and most of the customers were foreigners, well-off tourists on holiday and the odd executive passing through. Then there's the hotel staff on duty that night, around ten, if we include security, and the group of friends in the bar getting drunk gratis."

"You must be joking; the drink was not gratis," Borja assured him.

"Two hundred suspects are a lot of suspects," I noted, slightly downhearted.

"I think we can discount those staying at the hotel. Reservations are usually made two months in advance. The only exceptions were the victim, who made a reservation three weeks before, and the suspect." He coughed and gulped down some beer. "In Marina Dolç's case, it was her publisher who reserved the room, and in Amadeu Cabestany's, he was just very lucky, because he made his reservation that same day."

"What about the hotel staff?"

"I'd discount them straight away. Most are foreigners, people who are here to earn a living."

"But it could have been a robbery that went wrong? I mean that maybe the murderer was a thief who lost his nerve and left before he found anything. Maybe someone working at the hotel or a guest? They killed her, heard footsteps in the corridor and fled empty-handed," I suggested, perhaps over-hastily.

"It's a five-star hotel," he responded. "The corridor is carpeted, precisely in order to muffle the sound of the footsteps of guests who are prowling around at night. Have you never been to the Ritz?" It was obvious Lluís Arquer took us for a couple of amateurs. "Besides, according to the police, the victim opened the door and turned her back on her murderer. And the door to the minibar was open: that's important. Clearly she was going to serve some liquid refreshment."

"So she knew him," rejoined Borja.

"Or knew *her*," I pointed out.

"Elementary, my dear friend, but I don't think that deduction will get you your detective's card," Lluís Arquer responded sarcastically.

"So that reduces the list of suspects to the group of Marina's friends in the bar," my brother conjectured aloud.

"You've finally got there!" It was obvious he was the master and we were his apprentices. "We've gone from six million suspects to twenty or thirty in five minutes. Not bad, I'd say... Hey, lad, let's be having another round! And bring us some olives while you're at it!" he shouted to the waiter.

"And we can shorten this list," my brother continued, glancing at the file and studying the names of those invited to the party.

There were twenty names. They were the people drinking in the bar at around 2 a.m., when Marina Dolç announced she was going upstairs.

"It's odd the police haven't questioned you yet..." remarked the detective, looking at Borja. "There's a question mark by your name on the list and a note that says 'still to be interviewed'. But you're lucky: there are lots of witnesses who've stated you didn't leave the bar the whole night. And then you just disappeared."

"True enough... It's a long story..."

"A bit of skirt?"

My brother raised his eyebrows, smiled and shrugged his shoulders.

"I thought as much," added the detective. Though this time he'd got it wrong...

"Well," began Borja, prudently resuming the conversation, "we can discount Clàudia Agulló, Mariona Castany and myself. The dentist and his wife didn't move from the bar either, I was there talking to them... The Russian model didn't either (by the way, she had great legs). I suppose we can also discount Josefina Peña, who found the body and looks like a maiden aunt... And we ought to eliminate the town councillor and his wife," he added confidently.

"I'd like to know why you discount those two so readily," I stuck my oar in.

"Well," said Borja, as if he knew what he was talking about, "if that couple had wanted to take revenge on Marina or make her life difficult, they only had to invent some tax she'd not paid, or a bureaucratic oversight. The Town Hall is good at messing people's lives up. No, that couple was there to get in on the photo. Oh, and we should discount the publisher and his wife. Why the hell would they want to bump off their most successful author? It wouldn't make any sense."

"Perhaps Marina was having an affair with her publisher and his wife was jealous..." I suggested.

"Eduard, Marina Dolç paid for her minks and face-lifts. Nobody kills the goose that lays the golden eggs." Arquer nodded.

"Maybe not. There are still a good few suspects left," I pointed out.

"Ten or a dozen," Borja counted. "Not that many."

"Well, lads, I've done my bit. Now the ball's in your court," said Lluís Arquer, getting up.

The detective had more than earned his money and Borja quickly extracted an envelope from his pocket and handed it over.

"Seven hundred and twenty euros. What we settled for," said my brother.

The detective counted the money, smiled and put the envelope away. Before he left, I remembered our conversation with Marina Dolç's niece and decided to test him out.

"How would you fancy a short stay in the countryside to put some fresh air into your lungs? We know someone who..."

"Is this to do with Clàudia or what?" he cut me short. "I don't need any charity..." he said proudly.

"With Clàudia? I really don't know what you mean..." I said, acting as if I was surprised. "No, it's to do with a satanic sect, a very peculiar family and a husband who likes persecuting his ex," I said, hoping to intrigue him.

"Fucking hell! You two do pick them, don't you?"

Borja and I smiled. We'd just earned some brownie points.

"It turns out that Marina Dolç's secretary is really her niece and one of the heirs to her fortune," my brother explained. "It's a long and complicated story. She lives alone in a big house in Sant Feliu de Codines, and may require someone to protect her from her ex who's a psychopath and her rather lunatic family. Here's her number."

"A rich heir? Hmm..." He put the number in his pocket. "I could do with a change of air. It gets hotter and hotter here in the summer..."

"That's true enough. You do have a licence to carry arms, don't you?" I answered.

It was a foolish question, because he clearly didn't. Lluís Arquer belonged to another era, greyer but less bureaucratic, and he'd obviously decided not to adapt to modern times. He smiled, put his hat and sunglasses back on, and left as leisurely as he'd arrived, sauntering off into the crowd who were strolling on the Ramblas at that time of day with nothing better to do.

20

Montse was furious on Friday and didn't say a word to me during lunch. She had good reason. We'd bought tickets weeks ago to see some play or other at the Teatre Grec and I'd organized for Joana, my mother-in-law, to spend the night with Arnau. As the twins were almost fifteen, I'd arranged for them to stay over with some girlfriends, so we'd have the whole night to ourselves. But Borja had now agreed to spend that evening at Mariona Castany's fabulous mansion on Bonanova where she was planning a homage to Marina Dolç and we simply *had* to be there. We would no doubt meet some of the guests – perhaps even the murderer – who'd accompanied Marina on the night of the prize-giving, and it was a good opportunity to talk to everyone and see if we could uncover a lead the police hadn't spotted.

"You could at least have given me prior warning!" snorted Montse as she went into the kitchen. "Now I'll have to go with Lola!"

"But you always have a good time with Lola..." I remarked, trying to cheer her up.

"The one time that you and I were going out together by ourselves!..."

The fact is I'd have much preferred to go to the theatre with my wife than have to hobnob with a load of vain, embittered writers. But I'd committed myself with Borja, and, however annoying, work is work.

"I'm really sorry, darling. I know I've been very busy recently," I made my apologies. "We don't seem to be getting on the right track in the case of the writer at the Ritz."

"You don't say! Now you and Borja are into defending perverted criminals!" she shouted as I finished clearing the table.

This row had been dragging on for three days, from Wednesday when the newspapers published the item about the police suspecting that Amadeu Cabestany was both a serial killer and a depraved cannibal. Although the same papers had retracted the day after, it was a disturbing story. How come the rumour had started if it had no base in reality? Maybe someone among the powers-that-be was protecting Amadeu Cabestany, the prodigy of Catalan literature, and we weren't in the know? On the other hand, thanks to the police file Lluís Arquer had given us, Borja and I had lots to do. We'd been shut up in our office for nigh on three days minutely studying that heap of paper, page by page. As we didn't dare to go to a photocopying shop and ask them to copy the police file relating to a case that was still in the headlines, we'd had to share out the material and work on it in shifts. We spent Thursday evening comparing notes while having a drink at Harry's and the result of all our labour was most dispiriting: Borja and I were none the wiser.

Marina Dolç didn't seem to have any public enemies, apart from Amadeu Cabestany, and he had a more or less good alibi for that night. Her ex was being operated on for appendicitis at the Clinic, and Maite Campana (the police knew she was the victim's niece) had indeed been in bed with flu, as confirmed by Guadalupe and by the Sant Feliu de Codines doctor who visited her a few hours before the murder was committed. As for Marina Dolç's family (who the police had also investigated), her big brother and sister-in-law were on a pilgrimage to Rome to receive the Holy Father's blessing, whilst Maite's ex was in an Andalusian prison accused of physical abuse. Roberto, the famous Italian lover, a Mascarpone, was on a trip to Cairo buying antiques. The *mossos* had done a thorough job and had also investigated the guests and staff at the Ritz one by one: nobody seemed to have the slightest connection to Marina Dolç. So as things stood it looked as if Lluís Arquer was right, and if Cabestany was innocent – something Borja and I were beginning to doubt – the killer was to be found among the twenty people drinking in the bar on the night of the prize ceremony. The problem was that, apart from Amadeu Cabestany, none of the others seemed to have a single motive to drive them to bump off Marina Dolç, let alone to do it so melodramatically.

This time we'd agreed I would go and collect Borja at his place, naturally wearing my new suit, and from there we'd go to Mariona's. The homage was invitation only for a hundred or so and began at seven, though we wanted to get there early, and did so at three minutes to. Very few people had arrived. Journalists and television cameras were around, and drinks, though not canapés, were circulating. A small army of waiters stood to attention, ready to do their duty, and Mariona's butler, Marcelo, was supervising proceedings as efficiently as ever. He was a fine figure of a man, and his delicate manners contrasted with an athletic body that was midway between Johnny Weissmuller and Rock Hudson. Mariona had alerted him to our security worries and he'd promised to keep a beady eye out.

The modernist salon, where the event was being held, was dominated by a huge black-and-white photograph of Marina Dolç. It seemed very recent. I stared at her face – in particular, her eyes: they radiated an extraordinary serenity and bore the half lucid half bitter expression of people who've suffered a lot and refrained from speaking out. I thought how she wasn't at all like the extremely ingenuous heroines of her novels. No, Marina Dolç might have been many things in her life, but she'd surely never behaved like a fool. My brother, who'd known her personally, was in agreement.

Next to the portrait of the writer was a huge bunch of red roses and a copy of each of her books, as if it were a kind of altar. They'd also lit candles and a real pianist was playing pieces by Satie in a corner of the room where guests were now beginning to congregate. More people gradually came and the room filled up. Everyone greeted Mariona, whom they treated with deference but as a lifelong friend. Most people were acquainted and were dressed extremely fashionably. One lady had turned up in a long evening dress that jarred slightly and another was resplendent in high heels and baring her belly button above posh, trendily tight jeans. There was some variation among the men as well, but most wore a tie. That evening, Mariona wore white crêpe trousers and a pearl grey, Chinese dress coat embroidered with green-and-blue silk. I'm sure it was a unique garment and worth a fortune. Her hair was curly and flowing loose, and, as ever, she was only lightly made up. I didn't notice her shoes.

There were a hundred of us tightly packed in that space. Almost everyone had arrived by half-past seven and the waiters started bringing round the canapés that, as Mariona explained, were the creation of none other than Ferran Adrià. I had something of an upset tummy, I expect due to the heat, and was on a compulsory diet of boiled rice. I opted not to take any risks and stuck to the gin-and-tonic Marcelo had prepared for me, which they say is just the thing for an upset stomach. People were drinking, eating, smoking and conversing around us, and the volume of the chitchat was rising in intensity and tone. By eight o'clock you couldn't hear the piano at all, even though the pianist kept moving her fingers unabated. Borja, who had decided to eat and drink freely, pursued the waiters and their trays of canapés and just kept saying: "Out of this world, young man! Out of this world!"

We chatted to Clàudia, who initially seemed rather lacklustre, before sidling towards a little group of people whom Borja knew from the party at the Ritz. They were talking about Marina Dolç and we listened in. Borja told me who they were, and didn't pull his punches: Llibert Celoni, a writer who was fiftyish and swollen-headed; Agustí Planer, a ruthless critic who always raved about his friends; Ferran Fontserè, a poet about the same age as Amadeu Cabestany with a high opinion of himself; Amàlia Vidal, a feminist historian who doubled as a literary critic; and finally Eudald Suñol, a much younger writer of historical and adventure novels who was by far the best-selling author of the pack. They were arguing fiercely, and perhaps it was then that I realized something odd was afoot.

"Come off it, she was a shit author! I can't think why the hell we're celebrating her!..." I heard Llibert Celoni bawl.

"You're only attacking her because she was a woman!" retorted Amàlia Vidal. "And because you'd like to have her sales figures!"

"No, thank you very much. I would never want to prostitute myself to the rabble like she did."

"Well, fuck you, kid."

I couldn't believe my ears, and instinctively rubbed them. How was it possible that well-mannered, cultured people could use such language at a soirée of posthumous homage to Marina? However, I soon realized that was only the beginning.

"The problem today is that publishers publish lots of books but very little genuine literature." Ferran Fontserè was now holding forth. "Literature is now the preserve of us poets. The novel is dead."

"My sentiments entirely, but it all depends on the novel. The reviews of my last effort were first-rate..." Llibert Celoni said in self-defence.

"An unreadable brick!" erupted Eudald Suñol, turning a deep red. He was the only writer in that little huddle who really sold. "How do you expect people to read the shite you write?"

"Your books are the real shite! They're only good for wiping your arse on. It's you people who queer the pitch for us true writers!"

"And you're just one big mental wank!... Don't you ever read what you write? At least I'm not into abusing my readers..."

"Absolutely! You and your ilk refuse to take risks, you don't want to create a style, subvert… You write for the publishing industry and mass-produce literature as if you were processing hamburgers, you're not real writers."

"Hole in one!" waxed the poet as he gulped down the contents of his glass.

"*We*" – Llibert Celoni was waxing eloquent now – "are the heirs to the avant-garde and have turned literature into a lifestyle, not a *modus vivendi.*"

"Oh, you are *so* clever. But the avant-garde is a corpse that stinks to high heaven." Eudald Suñol put his hand over his nose. "You know, the problem with you folks is that you've no story to tell. That's why you write such *recherché* bullshit."

"'*We*', as you say, are moved to write about the important things in existence!" interjected the poet.

"You bet you are! The colour of your defecations is surely of universal transcendence."

"You're so thick you can't handle a metaphor!"

"Me and a million other readers!"

"I don't care a piss about your readers."

"Well, you should know, you're the piss-artist…"

I couldn't think what to do. The argument had clearly entered a critical stage and if one or other of the parties didn't back off they were heading for a punch-up. Borja was loitering suspiciously with Cláudia, seemingly oblivious. It struck me as very strange that nobody around seemed to be interested in the shouting match, now that insults were raining down from all sides. Upping the ante, Amàlia Vidal had decided to get in on the act.

"Marina was a woman and that's what's getting you lot hot under the collar."

"Look, darling, we're talking serious talk here. You women are all sugar and sweetness. What you write has the stench of hormones."

"Know what? That's something I can agree with," chortled Eudald Suñol, slapping him on the back.

"Well, in case you didn't know it, kid, you write with your cock," Amàlia spat back, appearing to be rather the worse for wear.

"And you can't wait for me to stick it between your thighs for a bit..."

"And wouldn't it be a very short bit..."

"We are the bold creators of literature, the explorers of virgin territories..." pontificated Llibert Celoni, deciding to ignore Amàlia. "We're not book-making machines."

"But you *are* a bunch of decadent ponces who think talent means being clever-clever."

"'Talent' being writing about conspiracies and magic potions, I suppose?" responded the poet sarcastically.

"At least we use our imaginations and get people reading."

"Reading rubbish. Soon nobody will know who the hell Shakespeare was."

"A chauvinist and an emotional bully!" shouted Amàlia, not knowing what to say to get them to take any notice of her.

"Shakespeare was also a popular author and wrote about historical subjects. And I seem to remember potions and ghosts make an appearance in his work," argued Eudald Suñol.

"You's gone barmy!"

"You are mad, speak properly, if you don't mind," responded Eudald.

"My God, have we sunk so low!..." groaned Agustí Planer, head in hands.

"We have lost this war..." Llibert Celoni seemed despondent. "This is the end... The end of literature..."

"Will *nobody* listen to me?" Nobody was taking any notice of Amàlia and she was furious. "I've had my cuntful of men!"

"Well, a pity you cut your bollocks off then."

To tell the truth, I can't say I've been to many literary soirées in my lifetime, but I'd always imagined them quite differently. You know, cultured, polite people conversing in measured tones, and, naturally enough, disagreeing courteously and never raising their voices. Everybody here was screaming insults. The scene around me was disconcerting, to put it mildly. I'd been so hooked by the row I'd been listening to that I'd failed to notice some ladies had stripped their blouses off and were displaying their bras, and most of the men, Borja included, were down to their underpants. There was a flurry of hairy legs under the piano and the pianist was no more to be seen. This posthumous homage was more like a triple-X adult movie, and even my brother seemed to have completely lost it.

"Oh, Eduard, my kid brother... See what makes the world go round!..." he shouted while trying to unzip Clàudia's dress.

"Shssh! Borja, what do you think you're saying? Or *doing* for that matter? You gone crazy or what?"

"Borja? What do you mean 'Borja'? I'm Josep... Josep Martínez, at your disposition, missie... She's a bit of all right, don't you think, Eduard?"

"Please, Borja, behave yourself."

"Oh my kid brother, the big..."

"Shut up!"

Luckily there was such pandemonium that nobody was paying him any attention, not even Clàudia, who didn't seem all there. Marina Dolç's publisher, also down to his underpants, was standing on the piano brandishing the microphone and trying to make a speech while his wife was attempting to snatch it from him, thinking to put his crotch to better uses. Joining in the fray, a half-naked woman, about my mother-in-law's age, threw herself upon me and tried to pull my trousers down. I managed to escape by a whisker.

Something was definitely amiss. Mariona was sitting in a corner of the room, eyes rolling, apparently in ecstasy. The floor around her was a sea of cast-off clothing and everyone was naked. Dancing like dervishes, if not copulating like crazy. Borja was busy groping a Clàudia much improved by her lack of garments and she was letting him get on with it. This homage to a prematurely deceased novelist had turned into an orgy.

I was scared and made my way as best I could to Marcelo, who seemed to be intact and contemplating the spectacle in a rage from another corner of the room.

"I told madam I didn't think stramonium canapés were a good idea. I did warn her, sir," he whispered in his Argentine lilt.

"What do you mean, stramonium canapés? What are you raving about, Marcelo?"

"It's one of Mr Adrià's concoctions, using a hallucinogen. I reckon he overdid the dosage. The menu says 'a hint of stramonium' but I think it was more like an overload..."

"Stramonium? Are you sure? I think that what's my grandmother called 'hell's fig tree' or 'angel's strumpet'..." Then I saw the light. "Good heavens, Marcelo! Stramonium is devil's weed, the plant witches used. These people have been poisoned!"

"That is clear enough, sir. But you don't seem affected..."

"I've got tummy problems, you know, so I kept clear of the canapés. We must do something, Marcelo! They've all gone completely mad!"

"I agree, sir. What do you suggest?"

"What do *you* suggest?" I responded timidly.

"You know, there aren't that many options. This is going to hit the headlines, *che*."

And that was when the free-for-all started. Llibert Celoni hit Eudald Suñol with a fist and things went from bad to worse. Eudald returned the blow and had the misfortune to strike Amàlia, who at the time was naked but for a black tanga that highlighted her cellulitis and spare tyres. Amàlia lashed out right and left, and very soon everyone stopped shafting the man or woman next to them (or both at once) and started pummelling the first person they laid their hands on. It was a battleground. Whatever item that could be flung – glasses, bottles, ashtrays – was hurled through the air. The pianist, who'd hidden behind the curtains to avoid being raped, had a bloody nose, and the waiters, who must have tasted a few canapés in the kitchen, had cheerfully joined in the debauchery. They were in the nude and busy throwing trays of food through the air like Greek athletes.

A brimfull glass of cava shattered on the Fortuny over the fireplace, at which point Marcelo decided enough was enough. He dragged Mariona into her bedroom, locked the door and rang the police. He asked me to accompany him and we both stood guard in front of the entrance to the mansion. As well as impatiently waiting for the security forces to arrive, we were ready to keep out the press, if necessary. As I saw Borja was still working on Clàudia and she didn't seem to be protesting, I let them be.

A dozen vans of *mossos* and an ambulance drove up in less than five minutes. An army of health-workers, carrying medicine chests, were now distributing atropine and sedatives at their discretion. I narrowly missed being injected, although I did accept a sedative because the recent spectacle had left me feeling groggy. Shortly after men in plain clothes, presumably secret police, arrived and took control of the house. Silently and systematically, they requisitioned film and photo cameras from journalists who were tripping with the guests, and discreetly took a few individuals away after they'd wrapped them in blankets. After a couple of hours, the effects of the stramonium began to wear off and the guests started to come round. They embarrassedly looked for their clothes and personal effects so they could leave. Fortunately only a dozen or so had to be taken to hospital, mostly with slight injuries.

When the *mossos* finally let us leave, it was almost 2 a.m. I took Borja home in a taxi, gave him another tranquillizer and put him to bed. He was in a poorly state and went to sleep immediately. I decided to return home, praying Montse wouldn't be waiting up for me. When I finally opened our front door, it was five o'clock and I felt like a rag.

Luckily Montse was snoring. The morning after, after grasping that the incidents on the previous evening hadn't been a nightmare, I decided not to say anything to my wife, for the moment. I wanted to speak to Borja first. I was convinced she wouldn't swallow the story about Ferran Adrià accidentally poisoning us with stramonium canapés, let alone about me not joining in the subsequent orgy, whether half- or whole-heartedly. When she told me she was going to get *ensaimades* for breakfast and that, en route, would buy the newspaper, I was expecting all hell to be let loose on the home front. It was impossible the débacle at Mariona's house wouldn't be headline news, but that was precisely what didn't happen. The papers inexplicably didn't devote a single line to that episode. They didn't publish anything on Sunday, or the day after. I'm not sure whether it was because too many well-known politicians and pillars of society were present or because Mariona is very wealthy and the tentacles of her influence stretch far. In any case, the night's events were silenced. Everyone agreed to say nothing and none of the guests mentioned that unfortunate soirée ever again, Mariona included. It had simply never happened.

I do know, however, that more than one person has never eaten a canapé again.

21

The first of July fell on a Saturday that year, and even though many people had gone on holiday the previous day as soon as they finished work, it was likely to be a difficult weekend on the road and a scrum at the airports. Barcelona was disgorging its inhabitants and restocking with packaged tourists, but we still had a long month ahead. If everything went well, Montse, the children, my mother-in-law and I would spend August in a flat in Roses that we'd committed to, but I couldn't see when we could start packing our bags. For his part, Borja had planned a week with Merche in Greece and was intending a second bite of the cherry in Menorca with Lola. He couldn't complain, although I thought it curious how we humans adapt to the most absurd situations. In all my brother's romantic intrigues, Merche, who lived with her head in the clouds, played the role of Borja's official wife, while Lola, who was inevitably aware of their relationship, had assumed the tragic role of mistress. From what Montse had told me (because my brother and I only talked about such things when it was absolutely unavoidable), Borja had assured Lola he was waiting for a propitious moment to break with Merche, when she wouldn't fall into deep depression. At least that was the classic cliché my brother trotted out to my sister-in-law, who in her secondary role as a clandestine lover was continually harassing Borja to get her the star role in the Broadway vaudeville they were staging.

An investigation can't be extended for ever; at least that was what Borja said. We were confident we would resolve the case, one way or the other, before the end of July: we would either find Marina Dolç's killer or the witness who would corroborate our client's alibi. Lunacy aside, Friday's soirée at Mariona's had been most instructive in terms of the bad blood existing between writers and we were starting to think the police were right and that Amadeu Cabestany was guilty. Besides, there was the cannibal business; although denied by police and the dailies, nobody could put it out of their mind. Even Clàudia was beginning to have her doubts, and that was a really bad sign.

After Friday's debauchery, Borja and I spent Saturday resting and recovering, but on Sunday Montse had parked the twins and Arnau at my mother-in-law's and, at Lola's insistence, we'd agreed to dine out as a foursome in the Barceloneta. It was strange because, if I thought about it, my brother and I had never before gone out for a night on the town with our girls. We'd hardly had the time when we were young, because Borja went abroad at the age of nineteen and, at the time, we were both young radicals more into politics than gastronomy. And we hardly ever went out with girls, I mean, properly, or at least as far as I was concerned. Twenty-five years on, my twin brother and I were now sitting in the Barceloneta with our respective partners, as if we'd been doing it all our lives, in animated conversation while we waited for our shellfish paella to be served on a terrace near the beach.

The surrounding cityscape had changed enormously over the last fifteen years and had little in common with my memories of going to the Sant Sebastià baths in the summer with my mother and having a ten-peseta lunch at one of the beach-cafés. All that had disappeared, together with the long line of shops and docks stretching down the coast that acted as an architectural barrier between the city and the sea. There was something fascinating about those huge, ugly buildings that only allowed glimpses of the sea that lurked behind those cheap brick-and-cement constructions, like an invisible, raucous giant protecting its secrets from our curious gaze. Now we had a Port Olímpic, a beach permanently packed with men in tangas and topless women and a promenade where people roller-bladed in summer clothes, listening to earphones, imagining they were in California. The city had reclaimed the sea, said architects and politicians, but amid so many designer shops, yachts and ridiculously dressed people, both sea and port had lost a good slice of their mystery.

While we drank our aperitifs and waited for lunch to arrive, I ranted against all the trashy modernity introduced by the Olympic Games which had destroyed that old neighbourhood of smugglers and fishermen. Borja, on the other hand, vehemently defended the need to adapt to modern times and abandon unproductive nostalgia, to the applause of Lola and her over-the-top designer earrings. Montse, who knows me well, realizes how sick I get whenever a traditional old shop is closed or rented out to make way for a fake tan centre or one of those pseudo-retro cafés with identical decors that are part of a chain. Perhaps it's because I'm getting old, but whenever the scenarios of my childhood alter, or, even worse, disappear, I feel increasingly despondent. And I know progress and change are part of life's rich pattern, and that no doubt the twins will feel the same nostalgia one day when they shut the McDonald's on the corner. My brother has other views, but I can tell you I will never forgive them for what they did to the Barceloneta.

"If everybody thought like you, Eduard, we'd still be living in caves..." was Borja's sarcastic comment.

"That's exactly where we're heading!" I answered, rising to his bait. "How do you think it's all going to end when there's no oil and the glaciers melt?" My wife, who was wearing a lilac, low-necked cotton dress, nodded in agreement.

"The world was also supposed to come to an end when the Pope died and look..." he joked.

I was about to return tit for tat when his mobile rang. Merche had gone yachting with her husband, but as she didn't suspect he was having an affair with Lola, it might very well be her. Lola scowled and Montse frowned at me, as if my partner's dalliances were in some way my fault. I tried to act dumb and Borja hesitated about whether to answer the call. Finally he did, and the expression on his face changed all of a sudden. He gestured to us all to shut up, which we did, and then extracted pen and paper from his pocket.

"I need to know what you look like. And what clothes you were wearing?..." I heard my brother say, as he wrinkled his eyebrows.

And then, "Listen though. You must tell me who you are. We must meet up," he continued solemnly.

Someone was in full flood at the other end of the line and Borja said little. He made only the occasional comment.

"No, no other witness has come forward... I don't know."

The call lasted four or five minutes. My brother simply listened. He finally said, "Wait a minute, no need to get in a stew. There'll always be time to go to the police... Look, give me time to think it over and call me back tonight... Yes, at about eight. Did you get that?"

That was the end of the conversation. Montse, Lola and I looked at him, intrigued, expecting him to tell us all. Either Borja was a very good actor or it was evident he'd not just been speaking to Merche.

"He's hung up. His number didn't show on the screen," he said nervously. And added, "Well I bloody never..."

"Well I bloody never what?" I asked, dying to know. Montse and Lola also seemed on the edge of their seats.

No, it wasn't Merche, but it could have been her husband; though, from what Borja had told me, her hubby wasn't at all worried about her and her bit on the side. They belonged to another world; the world of the wealthy, where appearances were what mattered. Nevertheless Borja didn't seem scared or stressed. Simply worried.

"The guy who just rang," he finally said, "is the man who mugged Amadeu Cabestany by the exit to the Up & Down club. It obviously pays to put ads in the newspapers."

"You're not kidding. But what if somebody's trying it on..."

"It's to do with the case you're investigating, isn't it?" interjected Lola. "Muggers and murderers... What an exciting life you two lead!"

"You don't know the half of it!" I exclaimed, thinking that none of this was at all amusing.

Our paella arrived that very moment and we waited for the waiter to serve us our helpings before resuming the conversation. It looked really good and we were hungry, but I'm sure we'd have all been happier if the waiter had brought it ten minutes later so Borja could have finished telling us the whole story. We ordered another bottle of white wine and Lola lit a cigarette.

"It might be a friend of Amadeu or Clàudia. Someone who wants to help him get out of the Model..." I said, worried.

Borja shook his head.

"I asked him what he was wearing. If you remember, Amadeu Cabestany gave the police a detailed description of the man who mugged him, and this information hasn't been published, precisely to avoid that kind of thing happening. According to Amadeu, the mugger was on the short side and wearing jeans, a white shirt, a dark, possibly brown blouson, a cloth cap that hid his hair and sunglasses. Oh, and according to Cabestany, he spoke in Catalan. The man who rang also spoke in Catalan and the description he gave of himself matches. It *was* him."

"If that's the case, it means Amadeu Cabestany is innocent."

"Yes, my boy! And I was beginning to think Clàudia was wrong in the head!"

"So case solved! We should inform the police."

"Yes, right, but there is one slight problem," answered a deadpan Borja.

"A problem? What problem?"

Montse and Lola looked at us admiringly and hung on our every word. Instead of talking about football or engaging in boring gossip about boring colleagues in the office, their men conversed quite naturally about crimes and murders like two professional detectives. Our lives might have lots of drawbacks, but you couldn't deny there were attractions, as that phone call had just shown. The wine was beginning to flow to Montse's head, because she kept refilling her glass, and Lola's hand had been lingering on Borja's thigh for some time.

"The man who rang – let's call him 'Mr X' – isn't a professional criminal," my brother asserted. "He rambled on about a car accident, a bank that was going to repossess his flat and that he couldn't get hold of the money he urgently needed so he'd decided to go to Up & Down and mug someone. He said he used a toy pistol."

"I expect all criminals tell a similar story..." I said, unconvinced.

"Yes, but he rang. We thought we'd get answers from the taxi drivers, or perhaps someone who went to the club that night, don't you remember? But it's the thief who rang, and it turns out he speaks in a very educated manner and doesn't swear. I mean he didn't say 'Hey, guy, I'm the guy who robbed that shit!' or 'Mate, what's in it for me if I sing?' He never even asked if there was any kind of financial reward. In fact, he sounded very nervous. Polite, cultured and nervous. What we have to ask is why."

"Why he speaks in an educated manner? Why he's polite?" I responded, taken aback.

"I mean" – Borja was beginning to lose his patience – "why he rang. I think he wanted to find out if any other witnesses had come forward. He told me he was ready to tell all to the police, but that if he did so his life would fall apart."

"You know, if he hasn't got a record, he'll only get a few months. The judges are lenient towards people who give themselves up."

"You said it. And what does that mean?" Borja was acting up for his audience, a Montse and a Lola who were all agog. "Mr X is someone who is not part of the crime scene, someone who has not involved a lawyer to do a deal with us, someone who has not tried to blackmail us. No, I reckon he's simply a guy down on his luck."

"So?"

"So we must make a move before his conscience drives him to the police."

"But, Borja, he's a criminal. He's committed a crime…" I objected.

"I don't know who it was who said that murderers don't exist, only people who commit murders, but I suppose the same can be said of thieves and muggers. Besides, Eduard, one swallow doesn't make a summer. We've all done something foolish in our time," he added magnanimously.

"Heavens, Borja, you never cease to surprise me," said Montse, impressed. "If your friends could hear you…"

In principle my brother is right-wing or, to be more precise, a member of an idealized aristocratic right characterized by its refinement and nobility of spirit, and which only exists, I fear, in his batty brain.

"Well, well... so it turns out you are a right-on fellow after all..." said Lola, pecking him on the cheek. We'd finished the paella and polished off two bottles of Viña Sol.

Before the situation degenerated any further, our waiter made a providential appearance, removed our plates and brought the dessert menu. As summer and a baring of bodies on the beach was at hand, Lola, Montse and Borja were on diets and went straight on to coffee and liqueurs, but I couldn't resist a generous helping of ice cream.

"So what now?" I asked.

"I don't know," Borja replied frankly.

"Boysh, me thinksh youves no opshun but to catch the moiderrer and forsh him to confesh..." slurred Lola.

"The problem is that it's not that easy, my love," my brother replied. "Let's just suppose Lluís Arquer is right and we can reduce the list of suspects to some fifteen or twenty people drinking in the bar. That's still a lot of people."

"We could make a list of possible motives," I suggested. "With a little bit of luck..."

"We could also consult the stars..." suggested Montse, who was beginning to sprawl over her chair.

Astrology, Tarot and I Ching are some of the complementary activities Montse's Alternative Centre puts on. I presumed she was joking.

"I know!" exclaimed an excited Lola, pouring out a drop more fire-water. "Yous should do a reconstrushion of the sheet... sheen of the crime, like Agatha Chrishtie in her novelsh."

"Dearie, that would be a great idea if we knew who the murderer was and if they hadn't buried her," I objected.

"Because there were only two people in the room where Marina Dolç was killed: the lady in question and whoever sent her over to the other side."

"Nooooguynooo!" laughed Lola. "I wash meaning the bar in the Ritsch. You musht find out where people were and who wash shatting with who… The moiderer musht have left the bar at shome shtage, right? You jush find the pershon who shlipped out. There were lotsh of witneshes. Eashy peashy."

"That's a great idea! I don't know why I didn't think of it!" shouted Borja enthusiastically. "You're brilliant, Lola!"

"And we'll unmask the murderer in front of the other guests, right? You've been reading too many novels." I couldn't think they were serious.

"Why not? It might work, Eduard," Borja's eyes were sparkling excitedly. "And if not, we can always have recourse to horoscopes and tarot cards."

Monste and Lola purred contentedly and looked on in agreement, delighted Borja wasn't as sceptical of alternative methods of knowledge as I am. A reconstruction of the events on the night would be right up the street of Elsa, the expert in matters esoteric at the Alternative Centre, who spends her time making astral charts for a load of strangers.

"We'll organize it for next Wednesday," decreed my brother, as happy as a sand-boy as he put the money to pay half the bill on the table. "We'll ask Mariona to help us." And he added, extremely confidently, "We'll catch them, Eduard, just you see if we don't."

I nodded and smiled sceptically. The road to hell is paved with good intentions.

22

That same day, at 8 p.m., Amadeu Cabestany's would-be mugger rang Borja again. We'd gone to my place to wait for our providential witness to call and, as the lift was out of order, we'd had to walk up the stairs, half in the dark: some bulbs had fused and there seemed to be no way to clarify whose responsibility it was to replace them. Borja kept moaning about the legwork and because he'd stepped on something slimy that was better left unidentified. While we were walking upstairs, we passed our neighbour on the second floor and Borja looked startled.

"My God!" he whispered. "The dubious characters that live on your staircase! Is he a junky, or what?"

"Don't be silly! That guy's a translator…" I rasped. "He's married to Carmen, that girl who came to our St John's Eve party with her two children. Have you forgotten? The poor guy! He had a very bad car accident months ago."

"He looked spaced out."

"Yes, he didn't look too good," I agreed as we headed for the dining room.

Merche and Lola had gone to pick up the children from the mother-in-law's and we'd decided to go straight home. It was a quarter to eight, and while we waited for Borja's phone to ring, I switched on the TV on the off chance they were showing a game. The phone rang a couple of minutes before the time agreed. It was him.

"A week," I heard Borja say. "We'll wait a week, as I'm about to put a plan into action. If we haven't bagged Marina Dolç's murderer in the next seven days, I'll ask you to go to the police myself (...). No, no, I'm confident it will go well, but if you don't see anything in the newspapers within a week, you'll have to tell the police," he warned.

My brother has this side to him. He can be hard-nosed when it comes to fleecing the rich, but can also show a paternalist vein when he gets the impulse to protect the weak, especially when they are in trouble with the law. According to Borja, and I thinks he's clear on this because he's suffered it in his own flesh, the law is one thing and justice quite another, and they don't always go hand in hand. I'm sure he's right, but, frankly, I'd have told that fellow he should go to the police immediately so they could release Amadeu, who was innocent after all. And, of course, I'd have let the *mossos* sort out who'd killed Marina Dolç and washed my hands of the whole business. But, it's obvious, I'm not Borja, I've not changed my name and don't have the nerve to act as if I were somebody else and play a double game with Merche and Lola.

Early next morning we went to our office to get the list of people drinking in the bar at the Ritz from the file Lluís Arquer had given us. We also rang Mariona, who, despite the deplorable scenes at her house on Friday night, was delighted at the idea of reconstructing the events of the night of the murder and volunteered to summon the suspects and organize everything. My brother then rang Clàudia and told her of our plan to catch the murderer and how we would need to spend a night at the Ritz to recce the location and prepare our soirée; she finally agreed to cover the extra expenses. She was a wealthy woman and it was hardly a great sacrifice.

"Are you sure we absolutely need to be at the Ritz on Tuesday?" I asked, surprised by his suggestion.

"Well, absolutely, absolutely, not really… But can you think of a better excuse to get a night gratis there?" my brother said with a smile.

"Frankly, Borja, I couldn't give a damn." I shrugged my shoulders. "I'd rather be at home with Montse. I don't suppose I can bring her along, can I?"

"No way."

"But if you only want to have a free night at the Ritz, why don't you go by yourself with Merche, for example? It gives me the —"

"Merche and her husband are no strangers to the Ritz. What's the matter with you? Aren't you curious to know what it feels like to be in the midst of luxury?"

"The truth is all those porters in hats and waiters in dinner jackets make me squirm," I defended myself.

"So start getting used to it."

Borja rang the Ritz. It was half-past twelve. He asked for the manager, whom Mariona, for her part, had already spoken to. The manager seemed curiously keen to cooperate, perhaps because Mariona, as well as being a very persuasive lady, is also one of the hotel's main shareholders. The reconstruction would be at nine next Wednesday evening. After persisting for a while, my brother succeeded in reserving for the Tuesday night the very rooms Marina Dolç and Amadeu Cabestany had occupied on the night of the prize. So it was official: the Martínez brothers were going to spend a night at the Ritz. I still didn't know what excuse I'd give Montse to justify such extravagance. I hoped she wouldn't be too angry and that, knowing her character, she didn't send me packing.

If Lluís Arquer and my brother were right, the murder suspects were simply the list of the twenty people who were in the bar when the novelist said goodnight and went upstairs to her room. We decided to review it while Borja filled me in on who was who.

"Well, here we have Mariona Castany," he said, consulting his notes, "and yours truly. By the way, Mariona is designated a writer, and I'm a financial adviser."

"There's a question mark next to you," I observed.

"Well, yes..." My brother decided to pass on that detail. "Let's see, then we have Amàlia Vidal, the feminist who was also at Mariona's... Carles Clavé, the writer who wrote an obituary for Marina Dolç... It's in the file."

"He was also at the homage at Mariona's, even though he never opened his mouth. They must be good friends."

"According to Mariona, they aren't. But it seems to be one of those things writers do," he commented. "There's also Josefina Peña, the woman who found Marina dead, and Oriol Sureda, one of her hardest-hitting critics. I remember him from the Ritz: a bald man, more sixties than fifties, smartly dressed and wearing thick black-framed spectacles."

"What a memory you've got!" I exclaimed.

"He looked evil and gave me bad vibrations. We've also got Llibert Celoni and Eudald Suñol, the two writers who had a punch-up at Mariona's."

“Here it says he’s ‘Eudald Suñol Clavé’. Is he related to Carles Clavé?” I asked out of curiosity.

“I’m sure. They’re all related in these circles,” my brother concurred. “Eudald is the one who got punched.”

“Yes, I remember. And this Ferran Fontserè was at the party as well, wasn’t he?” I said, reading the next name on the list.

“Yes, he was the poet, the younger guy. From what it says here, he works at the Ministry of Culture.”

“Well, we all have to earn a living. I don’t think poetry puts food on his table.”

“To continue: Francesc Viladecavalls, publisher and wife… Sebastià Setcases, the councillor at Barcelona Town Hall, and Anna Setcases, councillor at the Town Hall in Cornellà and wife of the aforementioned…”

“You didn’t notice, but he was the one in the red underpants. They matched his wife’s lingerie.” So my powers of recall weren’t that bad.

Borja grimaced and ignored my comment.

“Another famous writer, Carles Martín-Pinto, and his partner, Natasha Volivodka, who they say is an artist.”

“The one with the lovely legs, right?”

“The lovely legs you’ll see on Wednesday. We have Maia Mayol and Lluïsa Carbó, also writers. They don’t look very bright and nobody took any notice of them, but they stayed till the bitter end. Oh, and here we have Clàudia and that stuck-up critic Agustí Planer.”

“He really was a nasty piece of work,” I said, remembering the argument at Mariona’s.

“And finally, Albert Fonollosa, the dentist I spoke to, and his wife Pilar. They were friends of the publisher and didn’t budge from the bar the whole night.”

"What a crew!"

"It's what we have. If we exclude the people I'm sure didn't shift from their beverages the whole night – I mean, Mariona, Clàudia, the dentist and his wife, the Russian painter and myself – we're left with fourteen. Fourteen suspects."

"But do you think they'll all agree to come on Wednesday after what happened on Friday?"

"Eduard, nothing happened at Mariona's," responded Borja, suddenly turning solemn and adopting the tone of an offended gentleman. "Do please remember that."

"Don't worry. But I hope they don't serve canapés at the Ritz on Wednesday."

When I got home, I decided to tell Montse more or less the truth about what we were planning to do at the Ritz with the promise that I'd take her to spend a night there to celebrate our wedding anniversary. Meekly following my orders from Borja, I also asked her not to say anything to her sister. According to Borja, he needed to concentrate that night and didn't want Lola turning up and creating a diversion. Montse didn't really cotton on, but work is work though family may be family. However, she was annoyed and turned her back on me in bed while I cursed my brother's genes and bright ideas.

The next day I decided to help Montse with Arnau and, to smooth troubled waters, offered to go to the market. After lunch, I filled a bag with clean clothes, a toothbrush and shaver, and my brother picked me up at around seven. Borja had established himself in luxury at the Ritz at noon, but I had no wish to spend the whole day strolling around the hotel while he put on his millionaire act.

I was well acquainted with my brother's delusions of grandeur and understood his fascination for the Ritz. The Ritz is the oldest five-star hotel in Barcelona, and kings, politicians and artists eager for luxury and renown have slept between its sheets. In any case, I wasn't clear whether the fact that two commoners like Borja and I could have a night at the Ritz meant the establishment had become more democratic or was simply a symptom of its fall from grace.

"Hey, this is fantastic," Borja purred contentedly while I put my things in my room and he snooped around. Naturally, Borja had booked himself into Marina Dolç's room and Amadeu Cabestany's had fallen to me.

"Doesn't it make you feel uneasy to be in the room where Marina was killed?" I enquired.

"It's fine. They've changed the carpet."

"Well, to tell you the truth, I don't think it's very nice to be in Amadeu's room," I confessed, feeling rather scared to be in that luxurious bedroom.

"Marina's room is even more beautiful and top-flight..." Borja was now busy snooping around my bathroom.

"You know, Borja, I don't know whether I'll be able to sleep here."

"Come on, stop clowning!"

Borja showed me his room, which was in fact very similar to mine, and then we spent time planning the following day's encounter with the suspects. At nine thirty we went down for dinner, taking advantage of the fact that it was included in the room price, and then went for a drink in the bar where the guests had celebrated the prize. Some couples were there as well as four executive types in ties and suits drinking whisky and eating peanuts. The bar was reminiscent of an English gentlemen's club with leather armchairs and wood-panelled walls, and Borja was ecstatic and in his element. We drank a couple of Cardhus each and at around half-past eleven went up to our bedrooms. By that time the bar had emptied out; I imagine the tourists staying at the Ritz preferred the discotheques of the Port Olímpic or the traditional stroll along the Ramblas. Nonetheless, before I could go to my room, I had to time how long it took Borja to go up to, then come down from, Marina Dolç's room: exactly four minutes. If we added seven or eight to commit the murder, that meant the killer needed ten or twelve minutes to finish the job.

As I'd predicted, once in my room, I found it impossible to sleep. I showered and switched on the TV to try to distract myself and nod off, but it didn't help. I was wide awake and if I switched the light off and tried to get to sleep, I became even more restless. I rang Montse and talked to her, but she was watching a film with her sister and soon put the phone down on me. It's not that I believe in ghosts but it all made me very edgy. I don't like the dead, particularly when they leave a pool of blood behind. My mobile rang at 2 a.m.

"Hi, Eduard, how are you?"

"Borja? Is that you? What the hell's the matter?"

"Nothing really... I thought you might be finding it difficult to get to sleep."

"Well, you're right. I don't know what's up with me but I can't. What about yourself? Can't you sleep? I thought you'd be dreaming of the Windsors."

"I was worried about you. As I know you tend to be wimpish..."

"Wimpish? You're one to talk. I bet you can't sleep either. Seen Dolç's ghost yet?"

"Hey, stop being silly." He too seemed on edge.

"Good night then."

"If you like, I can come and sleep with you..." he suggested as if he'd be doing me a favour. "Tomorrow is our big day and I need you to be really wide awake, you know?"

"Mine's a double, Pep."

"Fine, they're king-size," he answered, making light of that fact. "Open your door, I'll be right with you."

So this was the big night Borja and I spent at the Ritz. Shit-scared and sharing a bed, like when we were kids. There was only one difference. My brother may be very refined and gentlemanly, but he snores like an elephant, something he didn't do as a kid. I finally got to sleep around four, but that night I didn't dream of Dalí, Cugat or any of those illustrious figures who had also lodged at the Ritz. I dreamed of our parents, who've never grown old although they died more than thirty years ago. Now, they look younger than us in the photos. I started to feel sad, thinking how we'd all become photos one day that someone would look at from time to time but then they'd be forgotten in a drawer, buried under a pile of ancient papers. I decided to get up, put myself under the shower and let it run and run. That's the problem if you try to dig up ghosts from the past. Sooner or later they put in an appearance.

23

Mariona had summoned everyone to the Ritz for 8 p.m., twenty people all told, and the hotel had agreed to shut the bar for an hour and ask the two waiters who had been on duty the night of the prize to stand behind the bar. The police had established two twenty-seven as the official time of death, and Borja intended to reconstruct what had happened between two o'clock, the time when Marina went to her room, and two forty, the time when Josefina discovered the corpse. As Marina had personally said goodnight to all the guests, we agreed the easiest thing would be to establish that moment as our point of departure.

Clàudia and Mariona arrived at seven thirty, the former full of expectation, and the latter simply intrigued. We went down to the bar to wait for the remaining guests to arrive, which they began to do at around seven forty-five. Everybody came, though some grumbled slightly. The suspects had abided by the instructions they'd received from Mariona in a disciplined way and, as a spur to memory, had donned the same clothes they were wearing on the night of the tragedy. Except for me, everyone was in their glad rags, even though they were hardly in a party mood.

The twenty individuals reacted in all manner of ways. Some were frightened and others were intrigued, but most seemed annoyed. I suppose they'd not dared say no to Mariona and were embarrassed by the spectacle they'd mounted on the day of the homage. I glanced at Josefina's dress and understood Borja's comments, although luckily he couldn't appreciate the dark lime green of the pattern that made it ghastlier still.

After everyone had arrived, Borja gave a little speech. He said he had proof that Amadeu Cabestany hadn't killed Marina Dolç and that *he knew* who the guilty party was. If he'd decided to bring them together that evening, it was because the murderer was one of that group of twenty and he wanted to give him or her the opportunity to confess. Those present looked at each other incredulously but nobody stepped forward.

"Very well, then," continued Borja rather nervously. "We shall proceed to reconstruct the events of that night. Before Marina started to go upstairs, I remember she waved goodbye and we all applauded her or said something to her. That was at about two. We should all now take up our places."

People started to form their small groups at the bar, silently and rather reluctantly. I stayed in a corner so as not to get in the way and stared at their faces. Borja had decided it would be a good idea to serve the same drinks so everyone felt the same as on the night and it gave the waiters something to do.

Mariona was in the corner by the stairs, as elegant as ever, and around her sat the publisher and his wife (looking like a crab apple), Llibert Celoni, Clàudia Agulló and Eudald Suñol, whom I think Clàudia had unsuccessfully tried to recruit to her agency. Except for

Mariona and Clàudia, who were drinking whisky, the rest of the group were on cava. At the next table were Borja, the dentist and his wife, who looked terrified, and didn't seem able to come to terms with what was happening. The dentist and Borja were drinking Cardhu and the wife was on tonic water. At another table, some distance away, were the councillor couple (who clearly weren't enjoying the event one bit), accompanied by Amàlia Vidal (who kept grimacing contemptuously in Borja's direction), Ferran Fontserè, the Russian painter with the lovely legs and Oriol Sureda, who had yet to open his mouth. Josefina was at the bar conversing with the two writers, Lluïsa Carbó and Maia Mayol. Carles Clavé and Agustí Planer were drinking gin-and-tonics at the other end of the bar, rather apart from the others.

"Let's see, Eudald," said Clàudia, addressing the writer sitting next to her. "You got up and walked to the bar, right?"

"Yes, I was sick of drinking cava and went to order a gin-and-tonic. Then I sat down with Carles and Agustí," he replied as he got up and changed places. "I had something I wanted to tell Carles," he added by way of justification.

"Then Agustí got up and I think he left the bar, didn't you, Agustí?" asked Carles Clavé. Agustí Planer and Eudald Suñol were daggers drawn and Agustí had decided enough was enough.

"Yes, I had to ring someone and there was too much of a racket in here. I went up to the lobby."

"And Oriol, you got up as well," added Amàlia drily.

"Yes, I went to the lavatory."

"Off you go then," she ordered him curtly.

Oriol Sureda obediently upped and exited through the door.

"I also had to go to the lavatory..." piped Lluïsa Carbó, timidly getting up from her chair.

"And we," said Josefina, referring to Maia Mayol and herself, who were at the bar, "took our glasses of cava and went to sit at the table next to Carles and Agustí. This young man," she said, referring to Eudald Suñol, "was already sitting there. I remember because he smoked all the time and the smoke was wafting our way."

"I'm so sorry," Eudald apologized.

"That's all right," said Josefina.

"Very good. So Agustí, Oriol and Lluïsa are now outside the bar," Borja recapped. "What happened next? Did anyone else leave?"

"I also had to go to the lavatory," the town councillor solemnly declared as he left the room.

"And then I saw the earring and picked it up," interjected Josefina, acting as if she was in fact picking something up from the floor. "I told Maia it was Marina's and decided to take it to her right away. Marina suffers from insomnia, especially when she's very tired... I went up the stairs to the lobby and took the lift."

There were two ways to reach the bedrooms from that bar in the basement. One was to go up the stairs and take the lift in the lobby, like Josefina. The other was to go straight up from that floor via the lifts by the toilets.

"And what time was that?" Borja asked. The suspects glanced at each other uneasily.

"I don't know. I didn't look at my watch."

"I don't know if it's of any help," volunteered one of the waiters, "but when that gentleman came back from the lavatory" – he was referring to Oriol Sureda – "he asked me what the time was. It was twenty past two. I remember that clearly because he told me his watch battery had run out."

"So I must have found the earring later on, because when I went up to Marina's room, that man" – she meant Oriol Sureda – "was at the bar. I noticed because he was finding it hard to sit up straight on his stool."

"Good, so we have another point of reference: twenty past two," concluded Borja. "Would Mr Sureda be so good as to take up his position. Marina was still alive at this stage, because we know her watch stopped at twenty-seven minutes past two precisely."

"So that must have been when I left!" said Josefina.

"But when Oriol Sureda came back, I'd been here for some time," protested Lluïsa Carbó, who was still outside. "I was talking to Francesc."

"That's true," confirmed the publisher.

"Oriol sat with us," said Mariona, "didn't he, Francesc?"

"Yes," confirmed the publisher. "We were talking about how ruinous it is to publish Catalan authors."

"Marina was hardly ruinous… That's why you gave her the prize, right?" interjected Llibert Celoni.

"She was an exception."

"Not now, if you don't mind," said Clàudia. "We're not here to debate the state of Catalan literature."

"I'm so sorry," Llibert Celoni apologized.

"Can I come in?" asked the town councillor. "I wasn't in the lavatory that long!"

"In fact, this gentleman was back in the bar when that gentleman asked me what the time was," said the waiter, pointing to the councillor.

"Very good," sighed Borja. "Come in then. So, if I've got this right, between two o'clock and the time when

Josefina came back to tell us Marina was dead, only four people left the bar… Lluïsa Carbó, Oriol Sureda, Agustí Planer and the town councillor. Marina was murdered at exactly two twenty-seven, but apparently by two twenty everybody was back in the bar except for you," he stated, referring to Agustí Planer.

"That's true. But the receptionist will confirm I was on the phone in the lobby all that time. And also there's the record of calls made on my mobile. I'd rather keep quiet about who I was talking to… ha, ha, ha."

"Agustí, we know all about your little affair with that journalist…" laughed the publisher.

Agustí Planer turned bright red and scowled at him.

"I found Josefina in the lobby and as she seemed like she was about to faint, I accompanied her downstairs," he acknowledged coldly.

"Yes, he was on the phone. He took me by the arm," confirmed Josefina. "I was feeling very queasy."

Everyone went quiet, waiting for a revelation that never materialized. Some people started looking at their watches. Borja's time had run out.

"So which of us is the murderer?" Clàudia finally asked, addressing my brother.

Borja didn't respond. He was smoking and seemed to be concentrating. The reconstruction hadn't gone as well as he'd hoped.

"Well, I don't know how you see it," said the councillor, who now looked genuinely angry, "but this means it wasn't any of us. As Mr Holmes, or Poirot, or whoever the fuck he thinks he is getting us to perform in this pantomime can see," he shouted at Borja, "when Marina was supposedly being murdered, we were all in the bar except for Agustí. And, according to Agustí, it's easy to prove his alibi because there's a witness who will swear that is where he was. Is this or is this not the situation?"

Everyone nodded. The councillor, a wily old coot when it came to asserting power and authority, had now taken control. Borja had gone as red as a tomato and still hadn't said a word. He didn't know what to say. He'd failed. Failed disastrously. A total cock-up.

"It's a pity, but I'm sure the police are right and it was Amadeu," sighed the publisher.

"Poor lad, he must have been blinded by envy," added Agustí Planer.

"He didn't seem such a bad guy..." interjected Maia Mayol.

"Though he was rather peculiar..." said the publisher's wife.

"So you think he is a cannibal as well?"

"How long do you think he'll go down for?"

Borja's pride was shattered and nobody was taking any notice of him. I'd have liked to have helped, but the truth was I didn't know what to say either. We'd gone down a blind alley, and if the murderer was indeed among that group of twenty suspects, he'd left us with egg on our faces. All we could do now was let them go off thinking it had been a wretched waste of time. It was almost nine and people were starting to look at their watches again. It was time for dinner.

"Very good, time we were going," said the councillor. "Come on, Anna."

"I must go as well," said Lluisa.

"And so must we. We've left our children with a baby-sitter," announced the dentist.

"I'm off as well."

"And so am I."

"OK, *au revoir* everyone."

"Shall we go for a bite to eat?"

"We look a picture dressed like this..."

"I'll give you a lift home, if you like..."

"I'll just change in the lavatory, I'm supposed to be going to see a film."

Borja was livid. It was the first big failure in his imaginary career as a detective and he couldn't believe it. Things hadn't at all turned out as he'd hoped and he was now in despair. He'd thought a reconstruction of the events on the night would betray Marina Dolç's killer, like in a novel. Unfortunately, things aren't so easy in real life, or perhaps the guilty party wasn't in fact part of that motley crew now beginning to exit the bar. No doubt the *mossos* had reached the same conclusion after questioning all the witnesses one by one, and that's why they'd opted not to do the *in situ* reconstruction we'd just mounted. My brother wasn't accustomed to not getting his way and didn't know how to handle the fiasco. He stood tight-lipped at one end of the bar.

Everyone left, except for Mariona and Clàudia. The bar at the Ritz started to fill up with hotel guests, and Mariona, who seemed disappointed, suggested we leave. Clàudia was angry and finally exploded.

"Now everyone is more convinced than ever that Amadeu is guilty and it's all *your* fault! Thanks a bunch!" she rasped furiously.

"Something went wrong..." I admitted.

"Clàudia, darling, don't you think Amadeu might have?... I mean you don't know him that..." suggested Mariona after patting her affectionately on the back.

"It wasn't Amadeu Cabestany," my brother said finally with a grimace. "I can prove he didn't do it."

"How? What proof have you got?" interjected Clàudia. "You mean you weren't lying, that you do know who the murderer is? So why didn't you say so, rather than making us waste our time." Clàudia was getting more and more hysterical. "I insist you tell us now..."

"Now..." Borja got up, looking out of sorts, but, in the phlegmatic tone he'd been rehearsing for some time, he added, "Now I need time to think."

24

Borja disentangled himself rather rudely from Clàudia and Mariona and he and I immediately headed up to Harry's to brainstorm. I had never seen him looking so downcast in the last three years. In principle, Lola's idea should have worked, but in practice it hadn't. This failure could only mean one thing: both Borja and Lluís Arquer had got it wrong and Marina Dolç's murderer wasn't one of the group they'd assembled at the Ritz.

"I don't understand," said Borja despondently. "I don't understand what went wrong."

"Don't keep chewing it over. I expect we were too quick to discount the hotel guests and staff... It might even have been somebody who came to the dinner and then hid somewhere, rather than go home, and waited for the right moment to go up to Marina's room. Or a passing psychopath," I added half-heartedly. "God knows."

"According to the police, after half-past one the receptionist saw nobody leave or come in. He was only away from his desk for a couple of minutes, and that was earlier, at around one, supposedly when Amadeu left the Ritz. That's why he never saw him leave. Besides" – he shook his head – "Marina Dolç wouldn't have let a complete stranger into her room or gone to get him a drink."

"Perhaps he was a handsome stranger," I suggested.

"Yes, and one of these days they'll make me a Sir. Do me a favour!"

I didn't know the title of Sir played a role in my brother's fantasies, but it seemed a bad sign that he was making fun of himself. I couldn't think how to cheer him up, and bit my tongue. I'd sworn I wouldn't come out with an "I told you so", but I must say I'd never been convinced by that brilliant idea spawned in an alcoholic post-lunch haze in the Barceloneta.

"What went wrong, Eduard? What went wrong?" he asked.

"I expect we relied too much on Lluís Arquer and assumed…"

"Of course, Lluís Arquer!" My brother gave a start in his chair. "Why didn't I think of that before?"

Without more ado, he took his black notebook from his pocket and dialled a number. He was looking uneasy again.

"Arquer? It's Borja Masdéu. I know it's late but we must see you. (…) Yes, today. It's urgent. (…) No, preferably today (…) OK. We'll be there in half an hour."

"Borja, how in the hell can Lluís Arquer help? You don't suspect that he…"

"Let's be on our way," he said, jumping to his feet. "I've agreed to met him in the Plaça Reial, at the Pipa Club. It would be better not to keep him waiting."

"The Plaça Reial? At this time of night? It's gone eleven!"

"Eduard," retorted my brother, a glint in his eyes and a hint of hope in his voice, "if anyone can help us understand what went wrong tonight, it's Lluís Arquer. The more I think about it, the more I'm convinced the murderer pulled the wool over our eyes."

"But Lluís Arquer..."

"I know he's on the crude side as well as being a show-off," my brother agreed, "but he has the advantage that he's looking at it from the outside and is strong on intuition. He was spot on when he told us that Amadeu Cabestany was innocent."

"True enough."

I sighed. That old detective had really impressed my brother. I couldn't see how he could help us, since, apart from Clàudia, Lluís Arquer knew none of the individuals involved in this business, but I know only too well that you can't reason with Borja when he's fixated on something.

"I'll ring Montse and tell her I'll be late home!" I exclaimed in a tone of deep resignation.

The Pipa Club is a bar with plenty of character on the first floor of one of those cloistered buildings around the Plaça Reial. There was no illuminated sign outside, and we had to ring a bell and go up the only staircase. It wasn't a clandestine dive but it seemed that way. In fact, it was a distinguished, old building that didn't have any large open spaces because it had maintained the original room layout. As its name indicated, it was a pipe-smokers' club, but you didn't have to be a smoker or a member to get in. The decor was deliberately English, with predictable homages to Sherlock Holmes and his pipe, and jazz music playing in the background. When we arrived, Lluís Arquer was already sitting at a table holding a glass of whisky.

"What the fuck *is* going on?" he asked, showing his annoyance at being dragged out of bed at that time of night. Nonetheless, it was evident that he was flattered someone might require his services so urgently. He was a bird of the night and must mostly have been grounded of late.

My brother cut straight to the quick and briefly explained the situation. He told him about the call from the mugger that corroborated Amadeu Cabestany's alibi, the reconstruction we'd tried to enact at the Ritz and the ensuing shambles. Lluís Arquer listened attentively and silently.

"I thought you might be able to help us understand what went on," he concluded. "I'm sure you are right and that the murderer was one of the guests at the party," and he added, "naturally we will pay you for your time."

"You can be sure of that," the detective came back at him. "For the moment, let's just order another round."

While the waiter was serving our three Four Roses, Lluís Arquer remained quiet, as if deep in thought.

"We've missed something, Arquer," said Borja dejectedly. "We went wrong somewhere."

"So," the detective recapitulated, concentrating hard, "on the one hand, we know that only one person was out of the bar when the novelist was killed. But the guy has a witness who corroborates that he was on the phone in the lobby the whole time."

"Exactly right."

"And, on the other, three people went out for a leak between two and two twenty as well as that fellow on the phone. Four all told, right?"

"Absolutely: Agustí Planer, who was in the lobby, Oriol Sureda, Lluïsa Carbó and the councillor," agreed Borja. "Josefina left the bar after two twenty, according to the waiter's calculations, and by that time everyone was back in the bar. I mean, everyone except for Agustí was in the lobby when Marina was murdered. No doubts whatsoever on that front."

"Hmm..."

Lluís Arquer retreated back into silence, deep in thought. He kept smoking and knocking back the whisky, but said nothing. Borja looked at him, half expectantly, half anxiously, and kept shifting in his chair. Until he could stand it no longer and interrupted him...

"Arquer..." Borja began.

"Shut up, for fuck's sake!" he snapped. "I'm thinking!"

Borja obeyed, and for a good few minutes Lluís Arquer smoked, drank and thought while my brother and I glanced at each other, at a loss. We didn't say anything either. I was beginning to feel sleepy and was afraid the two whiskies the detective had knocked back would send him to sleep right there.

"There can be only one explanation," he finally declared. "Marina Dolç didn't die at twenty-seven minutes past two."

"But the police..."

"The police," he thundered in his gravelly voice, "established a very exact time for the crime basing themselves on the fact that Marina Dolç's watch stopped. They took it that the victim smashed it herself when she fell to the floor and that it broke, signalling the exact time she was brained."

"Well, that does seem reasonable enough," I added.

"But in fact," continued Lluís Arquer, ignoring my interruption, "if you'd read the forensic's report you'd have seen that he wasn't so precise. That would be impossible." He drained his glass and ordered another.

"When the forensic examined the body, it was still warm. According to the report" – it was true Borja and I had skimmed over it because we'd found it rather upsetting – "pale patches had started to appear on her neck, and that happens, if my memory isn't failing me, twenty minutes after death, sometimes slightly later. In fact, the forensic examined the body at 3 a.m., and, according to his report, death occurred between two o'clock and twenty to three, the time we know the body was found. This twenty-seven minutes past two is a deduction made by *mossos* who no doubt have a university training…"

The man had a really staggering memory for detail, even after he'd downed a couple of whiskies. It was also obvious to us that he'd studied the file seriously. There are pensioners who devote themselves to playing dominoes or watching others toil, and then there was Lluís Arquer, who had studied in depth a report that mean nothing to him really.

"This indicates that it could have been her friend who found the body," deduced Borja.

"Her or any of the quartet who left the bar! Ten or fifteen minutes would have been enough for the killer to go to her room, do her in and come back down."

"Yes, my partner timed it," Borja explained. "Twelve minutes at most. But seven or eight would have been enough."

"There's something else too," added Lluís Arquer. "The victim was still dressed and wearing her jewels. She had only removed her shoes. This means she was killed immediately after she entered her bedroom. So, we can discount the woman who found the corpse, who left the bar after two twenty."

"Josefina? Why? I don't see that all…" I interjected.

Lluís Arquer sprawled back in his chair and smiled. He was undoubtedly kingpin and relishing his moment of glory.

"The victim had been in her room twenty minutes," he said. "According to the police, she didn't receive or make any calls, in other words she wasn't at all busy with anything. You'd expect her to have stripped off or at least to have taken her jewels off. Then she'd have realized she'd lost an earring and gone downstairs to look for it."

"Four suspects remain," Borja reminded him. "Lluïsa, Oriol Sureda, Agustí Planer and the councillor."

Lluís Arquer smiled and continued his breakdown of what had happened.

"As these suspects were out of the bar between two and two twenty, this means the killer didn't turn the watch back, but forwarded it to give himself an alibi. We have two points of reference: the moment Marina left the bar and the moment one of the waiters looked at his watch when a guest asked him for the time. Don't you think it slightly suspicious the guy's battery runs out precisely that night so that, most opportunely, he was forced to ask a waiter what the time was?" asked Lluís Arquer, arching his eyebrows. His breath was like a dragon's about to burst into flame. "In fact, he's the only one with a good alibi."

"The bastard!" erupted Borja. "He killed Marina, turned her watch forward and made us think he was at the bar."

"Yes, a bastard and a half," agreed Lluís Arquer. "What the fuck was the guy's name?"

"Sureda. Oriol Sureda," replied my brother. "He's the critic who liked to rubbish Marina Dolç's novels. A strange character."

"But what could his motive have been?" I asked. "OK, he had it in for her as a writer, but they didn't have any kind of relationship, be it good or bad."

Lluís Arquer shrugged his shoulders. That wasn't his concern.

"I'll leave you to work out the whys and wherefores," he said as he got up. "You know, I think I've done what was expected of me. I'm off to get some shut-eye."

"Thanks, Arquer. You solved the case. I don't know how to thank you..." My brother was being very emotional.

"No need to send a Christmas hamper. An envelope will do me fine."

"We don't have any cash on us at the moment, but we'll get you a cheque soon enough," my brother assured him. "You won't have cause to complain."

"Forget the cheque, that's fodder for the taxman! Bring me banknotes. And before Saturday. Didn't I tell you? I'm going to spend summer in Sant Feliu de Codines. I'm sure it will be much cooler there..."

25

Early next morning, we rang Clàudia Agulló and told her of our big discovery. Our deductions were faultless, she agreed, but there was a slight problem: we didn't have any evidence. No DNA or fingerprints of Oriol Sureda had been found in Marina Dolç's bedroom, and without a confession or any incriminating material proof we were going nowhere fast. We had no choice but to speak to the *mossos* and tell them of our theory. Perhaps if the police searched Oriol Sureda's flat, they'd find evidence or the critic would take fright and confess to all.

We were going straight to the police station and that stressed my brother out. He was aware his identity game wasn't a good introduction. It was very odd the police hadn't made any moves to question him, a witness who'd mysteriously disappeared from the scene of the crime the moment they showed up. We hoped, rather ingenuously, that it was a simple oversight.

"The Borja Masdéu business is only an alias, like an artistic pseudonym," Borja muttered nervously as we headed towards the Gran Via. "It's no crime."

"I suppose you're right..." I tried to gee him up though I was quite lukewarm about our prospects.

We stood in front of the police station on the Gran Via, on the corner with Rocafort, and, before going in, Borja and I took a deep breath. We told the *mosso* in the entrance that we wanted to speak to one of the policemen leading the investigation of the Marina Dolç case, but he said that was totally out of the question and asked us whether we really thought it worked like in the TV series. Borja persisted and threatened that we wouldn't move until we'd spoken to someone in charge, and the cop finally relented and picked up the phone. He spoke to someone, gave us a withering look and told us to wait. After telling the person on the phone who we were and making us wait more than an hour, he finally announced that Inspector Jaume Badia would see us in person. Borja and I glanced at each other, presuming that this was not good news.

He was a tall, pale, thin man in his forties, and we'd never have identified him as a policeman if we saw him in the street. His hair wasn't white but completely grey, and he wore rimless spectacles. A severe fellow in plain clothes, though you couldn't say he was frightening, as frightening as police are supposed to be, nevertheless he was intimidating. His beady blue eyes had an icy stare that made me swallow. I began to think we hadn't made the right decision.

"Inspector Badia, we're very grateful you've agreed to see us," Borja began after shaking his hand.

"Please do be seated, Messrs Martínez. Or would you rather I also called you Mr Masdéu?" he purred at my brother. His manner was polite but distant.

Borja wasn't expecting that blow and turned bright red. He was also struck dumb. The two men looked each other up and down for a few seconds, as if they were about to pull out pistols and fight a duel. Inspector Badia's gaze was really icy and not a muscle flexed on his face. He didn't seem angry or agitated, but simply looked at my brother like a bold chess player trying to guess his opponent's next move. It was Borja's turn and he finally reacted.

"We're here to help throw light on the murder of Marina Dolç," he said with surprising sang-froid as he accepted the Inspector's invitation to sit down. "Is my name that important?"

"That depends," the Inspector replied in that same soft tone. "What do *you* think?"

"I think that if you had believed my name is important and I'd infringed the law in some way, you would have arrested me by now," he replied very intelligently.

"I suppose, Mr Masdéu and Mr Martínez, that some day the taxman will scare the pants off you." The Inspector acted as if he was about to smile but it came to nothing. "We're too busy here for the moment. Tell me what I can do for you."

"In fact," my brother boasted, "we're the ones who can do something for you. We know who killed Marina Dolç."

"Oh, so that's it, is it? You're on the late side, because we know too. Indeed, Mr Masdéu, we not only know who it is, but we have him locked up in the Model. Or don't you read the newspapers?"

"You are wrong. It wasn't Amadeu Cabestany. If you have five minutes, we'll tell you why," my brother retaliated.

"Five minutes sounds about right," said the Inspector with a hint of a smile. I felt he was playing with us.

Borja took a breath and told him succinctly that we were working for Clàudia Agulló, that we'd reconstructed the events at the Ritz the previous day and had drawn a few conclusions. He told him the theory developed by Lluís Arquer (without mentioning his name), and how we'd reached the conclusion that Oriol Sureda was guilty. Borja said nothing about the call from the mugger. I suppose he was keeping that card up his sleeve as a last resort.

"Yes," replied the Inspector, "we are aware you are working for Clàudia Agulló. And that you were also a decisive factor in wrapping up the Lídia Font murder case," the Inspector continued unperturbed. "The truth is, Mr Masdéu, that we know lots about you both after your involvement in that case. Right down to the colour of your underpants."

Borja turned red again and swallowed. I saw myself handcuffed and on my way to the Carrer Entença and my legs went all wobbly. Fortunately the Inspector didn't seem at all interested in me and only spoke to Borja.

"The colour of my underpants," retorted Borja, recovering from that cheap jibe, "is irrelevant. We can discuss that later, if you so wish, but what I just told you is that we have discovered who killed Marina Dolç."

Inspector Badia smiled, clasped his hands above the table and rested his chin on them. He was like a teacher about to give a student his end-of-term mark.

"I might agree that everything you've just told me is eminently reasonable. Indeed ingenious and reasonable. But you have no evidence. Not a shred."

"That's why we are here."

"And besides" – the Inspector wasn't at all amused by that interruption – "your point of departure is that

Amadeu Cabestany is innocent. We start from the opposite hypothesis."

"Yes, a hypothesis that is simply based on the statements from a number of witnesses who say Amadeu Cabestany was incensed by the fact he'd not won the prize."

"That and the fact he threatened her in front of everyone," the Inspector reminded us.

Borja hesitated for a few moments. He'd no choice but to produce the ace from his sleeve.

"Do you think any of that would change if I told you we have a witness who can corroborate Amadeu Cabestany's alibi?"

"A witness?" Now the Inspector did seem interested.

"We have the man who mugged Amadeu Cabestany at around 2 a.m.," Borja purred, waiting for the Inspector to react.

"The mugger? You know the mugger?" the Inspector blurted out. This time he did seem to be taking us seriously. "Mr Masdéu, you are a constant source of surprises."

"We don't exactly know him, but I've spoken to him by phone," my brother continued. "As it would appear you know everything, I suppose you will be aware that Amadeu's agent, Clàudia Agulló, put some ads in the daily papers to try to track down a witness who'd seen Amadeu that night."

"I seem to recall that the contact mobile number was in the name of one Josep Martínez Estivill," he corroborated sarcastically. "We decided it wasn't necessary to ask the judge's permission to tap your phone."

"So he phoned me. The other day. The mugger phoned me. But I don't know what his name is or how to find him."

"It could have been anyone," the Inspector replied, shrugging his shoulders. "And if the only evidence you have is that a stranger you can't locate telephoned you and told you he was the person who perpetrated the robbery..."

"He told me what he was wearing on the night and his statement matches the one Cabestany made to the police."

Inspector Badia looked serious. He and Borja were level pegging.

"I'd rather not know how you got access to the police reports. Using a pseudonym is no crime but spying on police activities could cost you dear, Mr Masdéu."

"He isn't a professional criminal," my brother continued, ignoring that subtle threat. "That's why he phoned. He was in dire straits, he needed money and he had the bright idea of going to Up & Down to mug someone. He says he used a toy pistol. He thought Amadeu Cabestany was a wealthy man."

"I can see you are on the same wavelength," observed the Inspector ironically. "Mr Masdéu also wants to live north of the Diagonal."

"The individual in question is ready to give himself up if he has no other option, but the fact is I really feel for him. I assured him I would find Marina Dolç's murderer and he wouldn't have to go to the police," said my brother as if that was a perfectly reasonable thing to say.

Inspector Badia peered at Borja as an entomologist might scrutinize a rare species of beetle and said nothing. It was obvious my brother had aroused his curiosity although he still hadn't managed to classify him. I don't think he was disgusted by him but I'm equally sure he didn't really warm to him. He was simply a representative of a species the Inspector was unaccustomed to seeing.

"So why do you do all this, Mr Masdéu?" he finally asked. "Why do you take pity on a petty criminal? Solidarity amongst thieves?"

"Because he was a poor man." My brother didn't hesitate over his reply. "If he gives himself up, his life will be thrown into turmoil. And he *is* prepared to do that. But if the police arrest the real murderer of Marina Dolç..."

"And, to follow your drift, Mr Masdéu, what are you suggesting we do?" Our five minutes were long past.

"Search Oriol Sureda's home. You've said yourself that my explanation is entirely reasonable."

The Inspector hesitated for a second.

"If we accept that Amadeu Cabestany is innocent, and if we accept that Marina Dolç's watch didn't break when she fell to the ground, and if we consider that Mr Sureda's watch battery hadn't run out... Too many *ifs*. The judge won't countenance it."

"So then you'll fuck up that poor guy's life but you'll still have to release Amadeu Cabestany and Marina Dolç's killer will go scot-free," Borja challenged him.

"You'd better change your tone," the Inspector interrupted him drily. "Don't forget you're talking to an inspector of the *Mossos d'Esquadra*."

My brother can be rash. It's one thing to pull Mariona's leg, who I'm sure is happy for him to do that, but quite another to take on an arrogant, cold fish of a policeman. Just in case, I was saying nothing, just in case, and praying their exchange would soon be at an end.

"So why *do* you do all this, Mr Masdéu?" he asked again. "After all, Clàudia Agulló contracted you to prove Amadeu Cabestany's innocence. If it's true you have found a witness to back up his alibi, you two have done your job. From what you tell me, you don't know this man. Why all the deviousness? Why risk coming to see me? What do *you* hope to get out of this?"

Borja adopted his offended gentleman's stance and stared the Inspector in the eye.

"Nothing. Nothing at all. This is a question of principles."

"Oh, principles, is it? I get you, Mr Borja Masdéu Canals Sáez de Astorga," he said, consulting the papers in a brown folder on his desk. "So it's all down to a question of principles..."

"No." My brother was almost solemn. "You understand nothing. There are things in life that are important and things that aren't. If we," he said, referring to me and him, "give the impression we have a company that in fact we do not have in an office that isn't what it appears to be, and if we earn a few euros on the side following the wife of a top executive who goes to the gym too often, or find out what a politician's adolescent daughter gets up to after class, that's not important. You must think we deceive people and defraud the state, but all my brother and I are trying to do is to try to survive. You know perfectly well that the top executive or politician who contracts us defrauds and deceives much more than we ever do, and certainly does much worse things" – the Inspector smiled – "Well" – Borja was on fire again – "if a poor man takes a wrong turning at a difficult moment in his life and we try to ensure he doesn't spend the rest of his life paying for it, *that* is really important. Why do I do this, Inspector? Because I know life isn't easy. Life is only easy for the rich."

He said nothing for a few seconds. I'd been stunned by the way my brother had harangued the Inspector, who was obviously taken aback. I'd never heard him speak like that, and most surprising of all, my brother seemed to be totally genuine. It wasn't Borja speaking, but Pep, that same Pep who went to political meetings at the age of eighteen and ran in front of the fascist police. The same Pep who went abroad in flight from the dreary, routine life our uncle and aunt had planned out for him.

"Very well, Mr Masdéu." The Inspector had turned serious now. "It goes like this: today is yours, tomorrow is mine."

"I'm not sure I understand you."

"I will secure a search warrant on Oriol Sureda's place and, in exchange, you'll return the favour some day."

I looked at them both and pinched myself to check I wasn't dreaming. I couldn't believe my ears. The Inspector and Borja were doing a deal.

"And do I have to kiss your ring?" asked Borja with a grin, without sounding impertinent. He'd got all that off his chest and now seemed more relaxed.

The Inspector smiled again and ignored his comment.

"Let's simply agree that I'm doing Mr Borja Masdéu a favour and that Mr Borja Masdéu will be happy to cooperate with us one day when we're in need of a ruined high-society heir. What do you think?"

"It seems eminently reasonable to me," replied my brother.

"Let's get to the point then," he said, picking the phone up. "I've always had my doubts about Amadeu Cabestany. He doesn't look like a murderer. But it's also very likely we won't find anything suspicious in Oriol Sureda's flat and that he won't confess. It's even possible it wasn't him."

"In that case" – Borja's tone was much less strident now – "I'll ask you to do all you can to help the witness who will come forward and oblige you to release Amadeu Cabestany from prison."

Inspector Badia nodded. A man of his word seemed to be lurking behind that vinegary countenance. He said goodbye to us as icily as he'd welcomed us and added he would give orders to allow us to be unofficially present during the search. He warned us not to say or do anything, unless the *mossos* themselves asked us to. He must have thought we were so involved in the case we might even be of use.

The next day, at 8 a.m. exactly, a detachment of *mossos* rang the bell to Oriol Sureda's flat, flourishing a search warrant, and, as nobody answered, the *mossos* opted to force the door open. Music was playing, which we later discovered was an aria from *Madame Butterfly*. It was the only sound to be heard. Borja and I nervously followed the *mossos* who were leading the way.

It was then we saw him. Oriol Sureda was in his pyjamas, crouching in a corner of the dining room, looking at us but seeing nothing. His face wore several days' stubble and he'd peed himself, judging by the stench in the room. The *mossos* stared at him, asked him a few questions, and, seeing he didn't respond, called an ambulance. They then searched the flat. It was a large flat, no doubt a family inheritance, and there were books everywhere. Initially nothing caught the *mossos*' attention, except for a locked room they decided to enter by force. This room was also full of books, shelved in double or triple rows, but the titles were very different to the ones in the rest of the house. That secret chamber contained the worst literature from the twentieth century, a surprising collection of the worst kind of best-seller that would give any cultured individual heart tremors. They were in the strictest alphabetical order, and Marina Dolç's works occupied pride of place on a single shelf. There were various editions of each of her books and many of the translated versions.

We shuddered and stumbled out of that room. The ambulance took twenty minutes to come and the nurses removed Oriol Sureda, who simply stared silently into the void, a look of terror on his face. We had now completed our assignment and once more we'd been successful, but it wasn't as if we could feel happy. Few things in life are more disturbing than the terrified gaze of a defenceless lunatic.

PART FIVE

26

Amadeu felt as if he was floating in a dream during the first days of his release. Initially he was annoyed by the injustice he had suffered at the hands of the *mossos* and furious at the rumour about his alleged cannibal appetites, but his anger soon gave way to a feeling of gratitude and pleasure when he realized how his fortunes had changed. The day they let him go, seconds after Oriol Sureda had bleated a kind of confession, he wasn't just greeted by his wife and family when he left the Model, but by the Under-Secretaries for Justice and Culture, and more than twenty journalists scrummaging for a photo and an interview. Amadeu had suddenly gone from being a blood-curdling killer to become a victim of the system, and that lent him a half heroic, half tragic halo that everyone agreed suited him to a T. A leading publisher had offered him a tempting contract to write a book about his jail experiences, and a film director had taken out a film option and wanted him to write the screenplay. To be sure, he'd been deeply saddened by Knocksie's death, but it had shown the huge power poetry can wield. That inmate had been so moved by his rhymes that he'd suffered a heart attack.

In the end, it seemed his miserable time in prison had been worthwhile. But it was only an illusion, a false impression that evaporated as soon as Amadeu returned to his city. Yes, things were different in Vic. Instead of giving him the hero's welcome he was expecting, they treated him standoffishly, like a criminal who'd escaped the tentacles of justice by dint of devious ploys. The folk of Vic hadn't really come to terms with his alleged cannibalism and, to be on the safe side, they preferred to act like the inmates of the Model and simply avoid him. There was a widespread feeling of paranoia over the city that Amadeu couldn't handle. The good folk of Vic were afraid of Amadeu Cabestany the teacher and writer.

In September, classes resumed at Amadeu's secondary school and the teachers eyed him with more reticence than usual and avoided him in the staffroom. Most suspiciously, the pupils behaved politely and obediently in his classes, which was the envy of the other teachers. His friends began not to return his calls and, in that bleak atmosphere, his wife relapsed into deep depression. His daughters had no friends and there was tension at home. Even the parish priest, a lifelong acquaintance, suggested one day that, as God was everywhere, it might be better for him to live elsewhere for a while.

To complicate matters further, the daughter of the councillor for culture in the Vic Town Hall was one of Amadeu's pupils, and her father had been on tenterhooks since the restart of classes. What if, for some reason he wasn't privy to, someone had decided to cover up that nasty business? What if her teacher was still a cannibal and was eyeing up his daughter's tender flesh? Being a politician, the councillor knew only too well how the world of politics worked: driven by favours, cover-ups and stabs in the back, naturally.

The afternoon their daughter came home a couple of hours late, he and his wife were unimaginably distressed. The fact that Llum – yes, Light *was* the girl's name – was sixteen years old didn't lead them to think she might be smooching with her boyfriend in the park or dancing at a disco with her friends. The next morning, the councillor decided to begin the process of distancing his daughter from Amadeu, and made an early call to the councillor for culture. She was a rather unpleasant woman, but, fortunately, belonged to his party and they'd known each other from their university days.

"Dolors, we've got to do something about this Amadeu Cabestany. He shouldn't be allowed to stay in Vic."

"What do you mean?" asked the councillor, sounding surprised.

"It's because of all that kerfuffle, you know… It won't have a happy ending. Someone will lose it and we'll have a tragedy on our hands." He remembered how he himself had just cleaned his father's gun and gone out of his way to buy bullets.

"So what the hell do you expect us to do? He didn't kill Marina Dolç and the rumours about his cannibalism were down to a stupid misunderstanding… Besides, he's a civil servant. We can't throw him out of the school just like that."

"That's up to you. You can't say you weren't warned."

The councillor hung up. She was worried. They'd already made one hell of mess of that whole affair. Of course, there might be a solution, she pondered. The plan to open up a cultural centre in Lapland had been paralysed for months because they couldn't find anyone who wanted to go. One of the priorities of her mandate was to establish contact with minority cultures, but Lapland was a long way away from the Costa Brava, freezing cold, and no candidates had come forward. Amadeu Cabestany was really the best solution available, and she could always give it a patriotic slant and offer him the position of director of centre on an executive director's salary. Amadeu would have to learn the two variants of the Sami language and give Catalan lessons to a handful of Laplanders, but the post would give him ample time to write his novels and they'd find him a publisher. The councillor could include in the package the award of the St George's Cross and the Blue Ribbon of Catalan Literature in fifteen or twenty years' time when all this scandal had blown over, if not before. It was bait the despondent Amadeu in hostile Vic couldn't fail to nibble.

Amadeu and his family soon reached a decision. His wife was slightly reluctant to begin with, but agreed to pack their cases as soon as she saw the salary they were offering her husband and that accommodation and the children's schooling were also thrown in. Perhaps Amadeu was right and they needed a radical change of air, even if it was the icy blasts of Lapland. It was also a way to isolate her husband from that woman who acted as his agent and was still running after him. If they didn't like it there, Clara Cabestany ruminated, working up her enthusiasm, they could always contemplate a return to Catalonia.

By November, he, his wife and daughter were installed in Jukkasjarvi, in Swedish Lapland. It was certainly freezing and they had lots of free time. After a few weeks of wallowing in the mythical whiteness of those hills and mountains that had turned their back on time and history, Amadeu Cabestany decided to give up writing novels and concentrate on poetry, which he'd always felt comfortable writing. The incident with Knocksie had been decisive in this respect. He would write a verse saga and tell the world of the tribulations of his small country and the exodus of its sons to the boundaries of the polar circle. It would be translated into every language, including the two variants of Sami, and finally he and his name would scale glorious heights on their way to immortality.

If his country sent him to fly the flag in distant lands, thought Amadeu, he should feel proud and grasp the nettle. He would make the supreme sacrifice and learn a language that had four hundred words for reindeer and, in exchange, Laplanders would learn Catalan and that corner of the planet would protect the language of his ancestors from pollution by foreign tongues. They would also strive to prevent the pinkish white of the Arctic snow from blurring their Mediterranean identity, so the heritage of Wilfred the Hairy permeating their DNA didn't vanish in that deserted back of beyond. The Virgin of Monserrat, the Catalan flag and a Barça poster they'd been given when they'd departed now dominated like The Last Supper the dining room of the log cabin where they now lived, forever reminding the Cabestanys of the need to keep the flame of their origins flickering in the distant lands of Saint Nicholas.

27

"What are you doing, Dad?"

"Shush, Jordi, let your father be. He's writing a novel."

"What's a novel, Dad?"

"A novel," replied Ernest Fabià, looking up from the notebook where he was jotting, "is a story for adults."

"Do you adults like stories then, Dad?"

"Yes, of course."

"And does your novel have any dragons and princesses?"

"Something of the sort."

"And a secret room?"

"OK. So you want a secret room?"

"And a witch? Will there be a witch?"

"OK, I'll include a witch…"

"One that's very frightening, right? With lots of warts."

"Yes, sir: a horrible witch… And we'll give her a wart on the nose. What do you reckon?"

An astonished Carmen had been tenderly admiring her husband for some time. She'd been right to send him off to the Translators' House for a few days, even though she'd never got a clear idea about what really happened in that small Aragonese city. In fact, to begin with, when Ernest came back to Barcelona slightly early, he was quite ill. According to him, he'd got a cold and the dry climate of Tarazona hadn't suited him. The fact was he'd come back in a frail state and Carmen hadn't known what to do. Ernest complained his back hurt and used that excuse to justify his bad temper and low spirits.

However, Ernest's mood had changed a couple of weeks ago. He seemed enthused by the idea of writing a novel and was working on it non-stop. His computer was on fire. Had he had a fling with a translator in Tarazona? Was that why he'd come back early, his wife wondered. Perhaps he was burying himself in work because he felt guilty? After analysing his behaviour, Carmen concluded he'd not been philandering: he hadn't given her flowers or been unusually affectionate. He was the same as normal, like he was before his accident, or even better. This new Ernest reminded Carmen of the Ernest she'd known ten years ago in the fiestas of Gràcia, when they were a couple of innocents without a care in the world. She fell in love with him straight away; he took slightly longer.

Carmen impulsively approached him from behind and kissed him on the shoulder. Ernest had finished the draft of the first chapter that afternoon and had given it to his wife. Carmen was waiting for the kids to finish their snack and go and watch TV before starting on her reading. As it was Saturday and hot, she'd take them to the park later on and they'd leave Ernest in peace to get on with his writing. That evening they were expecting friends to come to dinner and had decided to order pizzas. There was no need to tidy the house and Carmen preferred reading to cooking.

Things were also going well for Carmen and she was happy. One morning, when Ernest was in Tarazona, she bumped into Montse, her neighbour, on the staircase and confessed how much she hated her work and how she regretted seeing so little of her children. A couple of days later Montse offered her a free massage and a job as secretary at the Alternative Centre for Holistic Well-being. Although they all worked overtime, Montse told her, they were short-staffed. The partner who saw to the accounts had got a new boyfriend and had decided to call it a day. And although the state of the Centre's finances didn't warrant it, they needed someone to look after the paperwork and act as a receptionist. Montse couldn't cope by herself. For the moment, they couldn't pay more than she was earning at the lawyers' office, but she'd be working two minutes from home and in a much more pleasant atmosphere. The place was certainly trendy: Montse and her partners sold short sessions of personal care at a cheap rate, using tarot, group therapies or yoga, and their female customers always left feeling good and smelling sweet. Carmen didn't personally believe in all their outlandish activities, but she was soon infected by the positive vibes and recommended the place enthusiastically to all her friends.

The kids had finished their snack. It was half-past five. Ernest was shut away in his study taking notes, lost to the world. As he had to translate books written by other people to earn his bread, he could only devote weekends and the odd moment in the evening to his own novel. He didn't know how long it would take him to finish, but when he had, it would be a weight off his mind and he'd sleep soundly once more. For the moment, he was saving behind Carmen's back in order to get the two grand together to repay Amadeu Cabestany and send him a letter of apology. That would close a stressful chapter in his life that, conversely, had served to show the stuff he was made of.

The kids announced they wanted to watch cartoons on the TV and, for once, Carmen hadn't said no. After putting the dishes in the sink, she picked up the first chapter of the novel and disappeared into the kitchen. She made herself a pot of the jasmine tea she'd been specially recommended at the Centre, sat down and started to read: "After his wife had left to take the children to school, Pau Gelabert sat down in his pyjamas at the formica kitchen table where they had eaten breakfast and decided to analyse the situation with a cool head."

28

We were into the second half of July, and as there was nothing urgent that morning demanding my attention, I had got up late. Besides it was a Monday, a day that always invites inaction, and nobody was at home. Before dropping in at the Alternative Centre to prepare the afternoon's anti-smoking therapy session, Montse had taken Arnau to summer school while I cleaned the kitchen and tidied the house. The girls were away at camp and wouldn't be back until Wednesday, and peace reigned in our flat. It was horribly hot in Barcelona and everyone was talking about the terrible toll wrought by climate change, but in a couple of weeks we'd all jump in the car and be off to spend August in Roses. The twins had insisted we go there because they have friends there and even though Roses in the summer is not exactly a paradise of tranquillity and is also very hot, the prospect of fleeing Barcelona and parking our bums near a beach made the oppressive heat seem a little less so. Although I was still sweating, I felt in high spirits and was getting ready to have breakfast when the phone rang.

"Eduard." It was Borja, and he seemed rather excited. "Have you still got that copy of Marina Dolç's novel you read?"

"I suppose I must have if Montse hasn't thrown it in the rubbish bin," I replied, wondering what he was leading up to. "Don't tell me you want to read it! It's really bad..."

"Bring it to the office," he replied drily. "Make sure you don't forget. I'll expect you at twelve." And then he hung up.

I was intrigued by my brother's laconic call, but, as Borja sometimes does that kind of thing, I took it philosophically. It was still only half-past ten, so I had time enough to enjoy a leisurely breakfast and shower. Once I was dressed, cleaned and combed, I searched for the novel, which was in the dining room, half hidden on a shelf, on top of a book of short stories. I put it in a bag and ran to catch the bus that would take me to the office. I was there by a quarter to twelve. So was Borja.

Thanks to the rather steep fees we'd charged after solving that case, which Clàudia had settled to the last nought without the least protest, my brother had decided to buy an expensive, powerful electric fan we were now trying out for the first time. Although we were about to shut up shop and go on holiday, we still thought we'd get our money's worth from that gadget this year given that summer extends into October. Of course, we had an air-conditioning contraption in the office, but it didn't work, like the radiators. It was yet another decorative detail, like the fake mahogany doors that supposedly led to our offices, which only hid a stretch of wall. I was all sweaty, and I greeted my brother and let the breeze from the fan blow away the sweat dripping down my cheeks, then handed him the bag and asked why he'd suddenly spawned an interest in Marina Dolç's manuscript. My brother smiled and winked. Some crazy idea was buzzing around his head.

Borja anxiously grabbed the bag and, the moment he took the manuscript out, the pages began to fly from his hands and flutter around the office. I'd forgotten to tie them up with the rubber band for trussing chickens, which I'd mislaid God knows where. The powerful fan did the rest, and in a few seconds the office was full of typed pages zooming in every direction. Borja was upset and clicked his tongue.

"Fuck! What a disaster!"

"It's one hell of a fan."

"We'd better collect them up," he said, switching it off. "I said I'd be there at one."

"At one? To do *what* exactly?"

"To take the novel to the publishers. Apparently the other copies have disappeared. They've been thrown away or lost. This copy," he went on, referring to the pile of pages scattered over the floor, "is the only one left. The secretary at the publishers forgot to make a photocopy when she sent it to Clàudia for you to read. This is the original manuscript, in fact."

"You can't be serious! The members of the jury all had their own copy…"

"They've thrown them away. It's what you're supposed to do."

"I don't believe it."

"The novel was typed, so there's no diskette or anything," he continued as he collected up the pages.

"But now we have a slight problem, my lad," I warned. "These pages aren't numbered."

Borja stopped picking up pages and looked at me aghast. He'd turned pallid.

"Fuck me…" he mumbled as he checked there wasn't a numbered page anywhere. "How the hell will we?…"

"Perhaps her niece in Sant Feliu has a copy," I suggested.

Borja shook his head.

"No, I've asked her. Maite looked for a copy but she couldn't find one anywhere. Obviously her aunt never bothered to make copies... So this" – there was a look of despair in his eyes – "is the only existing copy of what is reputed to be Marina Dolç's masterpiece."

"So we're well and truly in it!"

We surveyed the scene. Five hundred unnumbered pages littered the room. Luckily the window was shut. There was no way we could fix this.

"You'd better phone and tell them what's happened. Perhaps with a little patience..."

My brother shook his head.

"The problem is the publishers are prepared to pay a reward to get their hands on this manuscript because they are desperate. Just imagine, a novel that's cost them a hundred thousand euros and they don't have a copy! They've offered me three thousand euros if I take it today." He paused to ponder. "But if we take a pile of pages without any order to them..."

"I don't see a solution."

Borja looked at me in that way I've grown to dislike. I swallowed. I knew he'd just had an idea. Another crazy idea.

"You've read it." He was testing the waters.

"Yes, but it's twelve o'clock, and an hour's no time. Forget it. Perhaps we could do it over a week, patiently... But I think even that would be tight."

"I'll ring them and say I'll be there at four, after lunch. I don't want to upset them."

"Don't you ever listen to me?" I insisted. "I told you in three hours I'll only have made a start!"

He smiled. His eyes were shining like when he was a young kid and up to no good.

"You just watch."

Borja picked up a pile of pages and started to order them following a very curious method: the last lines of one page simply had to mesh – more or less – with the first of another, irrespective of any meaning. The fact the novel was a kind of monologue and not divided into chapters made it even more difficult to find the original order, but Borja simply got on with the job.

"'He passionately caressed... the trumpet she gave her nephew for Christmas?' Borja, it doesn't match up," I remarked, not needing to exercise much critical insight. "And what about this? 'She felt a searing pain... on the sleeve of the blue dress sewn by a Parisian seamstress?'"

"No, that sounds fine. Don't be silly!"

I shrugged my shoulders. As I knew my protests would serve no purpose, I let him get on with it. In the end, we had half an hour to spare.

"But no way is this the novel that Marina Dolç wrote!" I exclaimed. "Everybody will see that."

"I'm not so sure. Her publisher said he'd only skimmed over it, and I expect the jury members did the same. Besides, you heard the things the critics were saying at Mariona's, the mental fog they live in... Let me do what a man has to do."

"I'm not sure... It's supposed to be Marina Dolç's posthumous magnum opus... I don't think it's ethical," I declared as we left the office.

"Bah, I'm sure the publishers will sort it out when they get round to editing it," he responded knowingly as he bagged the pages. "Let's stop soul-searching and go get the three thousand euros. After all, it is only a novel."

29

The Spectator, Wednesday 20 September 2006

REVIEWS

OFF THE BEATEN TRACK

Novel

A Shortcut to Paradise
Maria Campana (Marina Dolç)
The Golden Apple Fiction Prize
The Chameleon Press
Barcelona 2006

Agustí Planer

When a writer we are accustomed to see selling astonishing seven-digit numbers of her industrially packaged novels to a mainly non-reading public surprises us with a work that must surely enter the literary canon alongside the great masters, this is a rare, if not unique, event. This is indubitably the case with *A Shortcut to Paradise*, the posthumous novel by Maria

Campana, that many predict will turn the literary world topsy-turvy and occupy a place of honour in the annals of Catalan letters.

The first thing the reader must ask himself when confronted by this difficult and dense novel is how is it possible that the author of conventional novels of such scant literary merit like *The Rage of the Goddesses* and *Milk Chocolate*, to mention only a couple, can be the same person who penned the bold and lucid reflections we discern in *A Shortcut to Paradise*. The answer doesn't come easily. Maria Campana, better known as Marina Dolç, made her debut on the Catalan literary scene in 1993 and none of her previous novels anticipated the explosion of technique and will to experiment we discern in *A Shortcut to Paradise*. We don't know how long she took to write it or even when she started, and her tragic death will possibly leave unanswered most of the questions academics will ask from now on. Nonetheless, it is to be hoped that this splendid novel will initiate a more attentive and subtle reading of her entire oeuvre, that may perhaps reveal aspects latent in her previous works that a superficial glance – or one informed by prejudice – unfortunately skipped over.

Beneath the seemingly commercial title of this novel one detects the throbbing beat of one of the crucial works of twentieth-century human thought: *Off The Beaten Track* (*Holzwege*) by Martin Heidegger, that subtly provides us with the key to its interpretation. Maria Campana's at once dazzling and opaque prose is a forest full of paths, leading nowhere in particular, that the writer wanders in an attempt to vanquish the anguish (*Angst*) generated by the consciousness of death. This journey, as the philosopher from Heidelberg wrote, is a necessary step in order to attain self-transcendence and leave behind the trivia of existence, the fall (*Verfallen*), in order to open our selves up to a "state of resolution" (*Entschlossenheit*) that climaxes when fear in the face of death felt by the novel's main character – the countess of Catalan stock Lucrècia Berluschina de Castelgandolfo – transmutes into freedom in the face of death. The countess is Everyman, individuals with trivial lives heading towards an understanding of our being (*Seinsverständnis*) that ineluctably compels us to formulate *the* ontic question in relation to the nature of existence. Step by step, along the forest paths that Maria Campana treads with a prose that is at once poetic and disturbing, the novelist reminds us that that which is man's, what Heidegger denominates as "being there" (*Dasein*), is not the mere fact of existing, but, as the philosopher suggests, the ontic possibility of being. We are in this world only as project (*Entwurf*) and are – and this is the great lesson one draws from the novel – what we come to be.

Maria Campana, in her last novel, decided to eschew easy success and crude complicity with her readership and accepted the challenge of taking risks and placed her writing at the service of the quest for aesthetic endeavour with an evidently stylistic intent, a risk that few authors dare to run in this day and age. *A Shortcut to Paradise,* like all great novels, contains more poetry than prose, and that is not happenstance. Prose explains and analyses; poetry condenses and interrogates. All great literary figures have been great poets or have finally sought refuge in the stunning lyricism of verse to speak to us about the tragic awareness of our mortality. It is always affirmed that Catalonia is a land of poets, and the case of Maria Campana only confirms this truism once again. Between Parmenides's opaque *Poem* and the disturbing prose of *A Shortcut to Paradise* there is the poetic, hope-filled thread that Theseus trails to avoid losing his way in the labyrinth of nauseous existence, the same thread traced by all the great works of Western literature, irrespective of literary genre. With the timeless wisdom of an Ariadne, Maria Campana accompanies us on these tortuous short cuts, *off the beaten track*, and confronts us with the irresolvable paradoxes of our human condition. The closing sentences of her novel sum up this epistemological and stylistic challenge and focus the reader on *the* transcendental ontic reflection: "When she bid farewell to her lover, the countess asked herself who she was, a swarm of insects and butterflies flying in every direction. Spring was definitively sprung, and the warm air wafting through the window made her drowsy and sank her into a state of intense melancholy. She decided to pour out a glass of champagne and, quite unawares, fell asleep and dreamed of a forest."

Epilogue

When Oriol Sureda got up that morning at exactly eight o'clock, nervous but in an excellent mood, he decided he would go to the barbers for a trim. He was expecting an extremely important visitor that afternoon and wanted to look smart. He'd hardly closed his eyes the whole night, but had got up strangely infused with energy and couldn't stop smiling. He felt as if he'd become reconciled with the world, he was hungry and ate breakfast without grumbling about the blandness of the biscuits or the watery nature of the decaffeinated coffee he was condemned to drink for the rest of his life. After breakfast, he took a shower and dressed while humming the Toast from the *Traviata*, in the same good mood he'd got up in and ignoring the jokes and gross insults from the other inmates.

It was sunny outside, but the morning still retained the cool air of the first days of spring. When he opened the window, Oriol thought he caught a lungful of the scent of freshly mown lawn. He looked through the bars and saw how the lilies and roses had flowered in the night and changed the wintry visage of that grey landscape that was beginning to seem too familiar. The trees were covered in small leaves gently rustling in the breeze, and even the lawn seemed carpeted by minuscule daisies that contrasted with the exuberant bushes of red roses growing along the walls. He stood there endlessly contemplating that landscape out of a pastoral ballad until the auxiliary was forced to move him away from the window and lead him into the recreation room; he decided to ask the nurse's permission to cut a few roses with the idea of offering them to his guest that afternoon.

"What roses?" asked the nurse, looking out at the concrete yard Oriol was observing in ecstasy from one of the security windows in the television room. "There aren't any flowers here. And certainly not any roses, they've got thorns and you could hurt yourself..."

Oriol didn't flinch but kept gazing at that garden which only existed in his head and which, in some way, resembled the bucolic landscape from Van Eyck's polyptych he had personally admired some time ago in Ghent cathedral. Oriol had always been struck by the strange atmosphere of peace emanating from the central panel of that retable, the solemn, ritualistic silence suffusing that tumultuous scene. A silence broken only by the slow drip of blood condemned to flow eternally from the wound of the Mystic Lamb, proudly standing up on the altar... Now, as he observed that garden stretching out beyond the bars, which he alone could see, Oriol wondered whether to make a bouquet of white lilies or a more daring item of red roses. He finally decided on roses, which he felt were more appropriate. He knew the countess liked them and they were also his favourite flower, though he couldn't remember when such a preference dated from.

While the other inmates watched television in the recreation room, irritated one another or simply sat there doing nothing, sedated by their respective medications, Oriol informed the nurse of his ideas concerning the trim his hair needed. He also spoke to her excitedly of the other preparations he'd been pondering in connection with the visitor he was expecting that afternoon. He was disappointed when the nurse told him (albeit very nicely) that he wouldn't be seeing a barber for a couple of weeks and that she couldn't go out and buy him a bottle of his favourite eau de Cologne because bottles and alcohol, even if in the form of eau de Cologne, were banned from the ward. Nor could she get him a tie. As he should already know, there was no need of ties or belts in that place. And however passionately Oriol tried to tell her that a visit from Countess Lucrècia Berluschina de Castelgandolfo merited a little relaxing of the strict rules reigning over that institution, the nurse was equally pleasant and inflexible and soon after returned with a small plastic glass of tap water and a red pill that Orol didn't recall being part of his usual intake. He didn't offer any resistance and meekly swallowed it, smiling all the time, though the sewery tang of that tepid water was nothing like the refined taste of the Perrier water he'd drunk for years. Even his disappointment at the nurse's lack of understanding couldn't spoil Oriol's day. In a few hours, he would be taking tea in the garden in the company of his beloved countess, conversing with an elegant, refined and seductive society lady. He'd sprinkle a little water over his hair and comb it back, he decided resignedly. He trusted that the velvety roses he was intending to give her would at least be the scented variety.

"Sureda is acting oddly today," the head nurse informed the doctor, who was absorbed in trying to get his computer to work. "We gave him the usual, just in case."

"We have a meeting of the control committee today. And the councillor's visiting this afternoon… Moreover, three or four staff are away, as you know," the doctor replied, his eyes glued to the screen. "It's not the best of days… Do you think he'll try to commit suicide again?"

"I don't know. In fact, he seems positively elated. He said somebody or other is paying a visit this afternoon. Let's hope he doesn't start the others off!…" the nurse added quite negatively.

But Oriol Sureda was at peace. Serenely at peace. It was true he sometimes had all manner of strange thoughts that would torment him and cause him to suffer one of those violent attacks that could only be subdued by medication administered intravenously. But that wasn't the case today. The thoughts that sometimes besieged him came in the form of hazy, disturbing memories that plunged him into a mood of deep despondency. Over the last eight months, the time he had spent in that institution, the disorder provoked by those memories had led him to attempt suicide on a couple of occasions. Evidently he had failed. He was tormented by images of a misspent life, split into two Oriols, that his brain strove to forget. Every now and then, however, thanks to the zeal of his psychologists and their therapies, those images struggled with renewed vigour to find a place in his consciousness and suddenly surfaced amid painful flashes of lucidity. Oriol rebelled and tried desperately to keep them in the shadows of his mind, locked and bolted in a corner of his brain, where they couldn't hurt him. At moments like that, when his memory hurled out fragments from his previous life, Oriol screamed out loud, impotent and deeply wounded. He recalled the jibes, the contempt, the lies and pettiness with which he had always treated others and that had caused him to lead a solitary life, without friends, without affection. For years Oriol had striven to erect a wall of arrogance and indifference around himself that one of the two Oriol Suredas cohabiting inside his head had finally demolished.

Everything was different now. He no longer lived alone, or wrote those savage, acid reviews or was forced to read those boring books he hated. Within those walls everyone was full of concern for him, whether he slept well, was hungry, whether he was happy or distressed. Oriol felt that the staff of Can Brians even treated him affectionately, as if they disregarded the savage crime that had led to him being admitted into that psychiatric institution that was a wing of the prison. Oriol couldn't remember the murder they accused him of, but there were lots of things he no longer remembered. Not that he tried very hard. He didn't want to go backwards; he didn't want to go back to being that Oriol Sureda he had come to hate. At last he could allow himself to be vulnerable, at last he could cry, sing, shout and give vent to everything he was feeling, and he was never alone. He could spend a while rereading the novels of Marina Dolç, without having to hide away, he could converse with her characters, even agree a time to take tea with them. As he'd been so insistent, the doctor had agreed to let him keep the manuscript of Marina Dolç's last novel, the one that had won the prize, and out of all the characters created by that writer who the other Oriol had cursed so often, the countess had been his favourite for months. Countess Lucrècia Berluschina de Castelgandolfo, so sensual, agreeable and understanding, was unlike any of the women who had rejected him in the course of his life.

The inmates went out into the yard to exercise in the mid-morning and he amused himself cutting imaginary roses in the non-existent garden all around. After a lunch of frozen greens and two pieces of breaded meat with chips, he went back to his room. He cleaned his teeth, sprinkled a little water over the little hair he had left and combed it. While his colleagues took a siesta or masturbated leisurely, staring at the ceiling, he sat down next to the window and waited for the countess, with that imaginary bouquet of roses on his lap. He was impatient but in no hurry. If he had too much of anything, it was time. Time that extended or shortened according to the medication they gave him or his unpredictable changes of mood.

The countess arrived three hours later, at around five, fortunately just as the doors were reopened to allow the inmates to take more exercise in the yard. She was cheerful and charming, adored his roses and regaled him with anecdotes about her last journey to Paris and the fiestas she organized at her residency in Rome. She invited him to accompany her on her next trip to Provence (this would be in the autumn) and he was delighted to accept because he had no other commitments in the autumn. They spent a good couple of hours together, chatting and sipping tea, like two old friends who haven't seen each other for ages. They spoke of future projects, laughed and swapped secrets, both cocooned in the same complicated dream in that corner of the world contrived from remnants of fiction. When one of the nurses said it was turning cold and he should go inside, Oriol and the countess said their goodbyes, nostalgia already striking in their hearts, with a polite kiss on the cheek, and she promised to come back to see him soon, when one of the auxiliaries took his arm and led him inside. Oriol was upset at being led away like that, but didn't resist. He was too happy and didn't want to dispel that twilight magic with a row or a protest he knew would be in vain. Perhaps he might have a bad day tomorrow, as the nurse had predicted, perhaps those memories he so struggled to forget would come back to haunt him in a few hours, but that afternoon, while he was taking tea in the garden with the countess, bathed in the fragrance from the roses and the melancholy light of that spring crepuscule, Oriol had understood the meaning of an uncomfortable word that had always been a stumbling block in his vocabulary. A word that had tiptoed through his life, that he had read thousands of times in thousands of books but had never been able to pronounce without it snagging on the road or path that had to carry it from his brain to his lips. Now that word flooded over him like the mellow light, like the strong scent from those roses he remembered smelling early one morning blended with the stench of death. Night had descended over his mind as well, and he wasn't clamouring for the light.

Inside, in the dining room, the other inmates were growing impatient as the insipid smell of dinner wafted from the kitchen and the auxiliaries struggled to keep order and make their voices heard in the middle of that tumult of curses and obscenities. Oriol said nothing. Sitting on his chair, he smiled a docile, vacuous smile and silently savoured the taste of that brave new word he had just vanquished. Within those white walls that isolated him from his darkest demons, a prisoner of the drugs he was obliged to take to fend off the nightmares and darkness that often accompany clairvoyance, for the first time in his life, Oriol Sureda was happy.

AUTHOR'S NOTE

The author of this novel had no desire to parody, describe or recreate any real-life situation or person. All the characters that appear are her inventions and any similarity with reality that might strike the reader is simply a coincidence.